THE GOOD
THE BAD AND
THE MURDEROUS

Sid Chance Mystery No. 2

Chester D. Campbell

Copyright © 2011 by Chester D. Campbell

This book is a work of fiction. All names,
characters, places, and incidents are products
of the author's imagination or are used fictitiously.
Any resemblance to actual events or locales or persons,
living or dead, is entirely coincidental.

10 9 8 7 6 5 4 3 2 1

Cover design by Doug Bell

Printed in the United States of America

Library of Congress Control Number: 2011913520
ISBN 978-0-9846044-4-9

Night Shadows Press, LLC
8987 E. Tanque Verde #309-135
Tucson, AZ 85749-9399

Also by Chester D. Campbell

Greg McKenzie Mysteries:

A Sporting Murder (5)
The Marathon Murders (4)
Deadly Illusions (3)
Designed to Kill (2)
Secret of the Scroll (1)

Sid Chance Mysteries:

The Surest Poison (1)

For all the great men and women who carry the
badge of the Metropolitan Nashville Police
Department. They risk their necks day and night
to keep us safe. We owe them more than we can
ever repay. The occasional rogue bad cop should
not sully their reputation in any way.

Notes & Acknowledgments

Cops play a prominent role in this book as they did in the first Sid Chance story. The Miss Demeanor and Five Felons Poker Club includes a homicide detective and a patrol sergeant, along with my PI's and two others from related professions. As in real life, there are bad cops, too. I recently had the privilege of attending the Metropolitan Nashville Citizen Police Academy and am happy to say I've never encountered a nicer bunch of people than the officers I mingled with. We got a taste of what they face very day on the job, and much of it isn't pretty.

The character Djuan Burden is a composite of youthful killers who appeared in a series of newspaper articles about problems associated with trying juvenile murderers in criminal court as adults.

Among the people who provided help in putting this book together were Field Training Officer Ken Alexandrow, Michelle Crowder (who directed the Citizen Police Academy), various other officers who provided details not knowing their answers would appear in a book, Judge Hamilton Gayden, and Dan Weikal, administrator in the Davidson County Sheriff's Office, which runs the Metro jail. Any procedures that don't ring true are my goofs, not theirs.

Thanks as always to early critiques by my colleagues in the Quill & Dagger Writers Guild, and a special thanks for the editing skills of Beth Terrell, now known as Jaden Terrell since moving up in the publishing ranks.

Of course, none of this would have been possible without the perseverance of my wife, Sarah, who worked tirelessly to keep the home front together while I indulged in my fictional fantasies.

1

H E WAS A YOUNG man, dark as the back side of the moon, dreadlock tentacles crawling down his shoulders, brooding eyes filled with questions. Djuan Burden hesitated just inside the small medical equipment store in Nashville's Green Hills section. It resembled the aftermath of a spring storm, shelves bare as though swept by the wind, scattered trash on the carpet. A stack of boxes tumbled in the doorway to the back room. An acrid odor added to the confusion. Splayed on a small desk at one side lay a few papers and yellow No. 2 pencils piled as if for a pick-up-sticks game. Were they moving out? He approached the desk, where someone sat facing the other direction, his head barely visible above the back of an executive chair.

Djuan tossed the document he'd brought onto the desk. "Sir," he said in a deep but subdued voice, "we have a problem."

The man said nothing. Didn't move.

Djuan was about to speak in a more strident tone when he realized the smell he had first noticed was gunpowder, a once-familiar odor he had not experienced in years. He edged around the desk until a lifeless face came into view. A bullet hole in the forehead glared back at him like a vacuous third eye.

Face flushed with panic, Burden broke into a run for the door. He darted a frantic glance toward the street as he dashed from the building, headed for the old Ford with the bruised front fender. Blinded momentarily by the afternoon sun, he groped for the door handle, crammed himself into the small sedan. The tires screeched as he swirled around, corrected, and veered toward the street. Too fast, he realized, as it attracted the attention of a tall man in a dark business suit who glared at him from the sidewalk. Though he had been driving only a short time, the skill had come naturally to him. Now his driving instinct held but one message—get the hell out of here!

Traffic along Hillsboro Pike slowed his progress, although it hardly rivaled the impending home-bound rush hour. He ducked his head as a police car passed, traveling in the opposite direction. The specter of that cold, dark prison cell still haunted his befuddled mind.

THE FOLLOWING MORNING the phone rang on Sid Chance's old-fashioned roll top desk, a battered piece of family history he'd inherited from his grandfather, a crusty old Nashville cop. He turned to the window, where a glowing spring morning showered sunlight over a precision rank of buttercups that marched alongside the parking lot.

Sid checked the caller ID, lifted the phone, and said, "Morning, Jaz. What's up?"

"Trouble is what's up. Are you ready to take on the Metro Nashville Police Department?"

She'd had major problems with the media lately over a claim that she had made racial slurs about one of her company's employees. Sid asked, "Are the cops after you, too?"

"This isn't about me, Sid. I'm sure you read the story where Djuan Burden got arrested for murder again." This was not the successful business executive Jasmine LeMieux voice but that of passionate crusader Wonder Woman.

"I did," he said, unsure what this might be leading to. "Out of prison only six months, and he's right back to his old tricks.

Shot a store owner named Omar Valdez, as best I recall."

"Your memory is prodigious."

"Memory, the warder of the brain."

"Where did that come from?"

"Macbeth."

She sighed. "Okay, Mr. Shakespeare. This situation is dramatic enough. Burden's granny doesn't think he shot that man, and Marie agrees with her."

"Marie?"

Sid stroked his short black beard in wonder. What brought this on? Marie Wallace was Jaz's live-in housekeeper, a long-time family retainer who had been her nanny when she was a child. In earlier times she had served as a welcome buffer between Jaz and her autocratic mother.

"Burden's grandmother, Rachel Ransom, is an old friend of Marie's," Jaz said. "She explained the situation and asked Marie what to do."

"From what I read, she'd better hire the best criminal defense lawyer in town."

"She can't afford it."

"So what's Option Number Two?"

"I called Arnie Bailey. Bailey, Riddle and Smith has a couple of sharp young lawyers who're interested in trying their hand in Criminal Court. Arnie said they would take the case pro bono."

Sid carried the phone over to the coffee pot near the window and refilled his cup. "I'll bet the DA won't have a pair of neophytes sitting at the prosecution table."

"True. So Arnie's boys will need some expert professional help." Her voice had turned softer, with the persuasive touch he knew so well.

"Do I detect Messrs. Pro and Bono headed my way?" Sid asked.

"No. Mrs. Ransom can afford your fee, and I'll volunteer my help."

Jaz's first priority was her position as Chairman of the big travel center chain called Welcome Home Stores. She had inherited a majority interest, but she wasn't concerned with its day-to-day operations. That allowed her time to work occasionally as an associate with Sidney Chance Investigations, something she had done since Sid's involvement in a troublesome toxic chemical pollution case a few months back.

"Have you talked to Bart about Djuan Burden?" he asked.

"Bart's no help. He arrested the boy for murder back when Djuan was twelve years old, but this shooting took place out Hillsboro Pike. That's West Precinct territory."

Bart Masterson, one of their fellow players in the Miss Demeanor and Five Felons Poker Club, was a homicide detective in the East Precinct. That took him out of play in this case, but from what Sid had read in the newspaper, this was a situation where a little help on the inside could be crucial.

Sid took a moment to consider the role of Marie Wallace. He respected her as a strong, discerning woman. He recalled how she had seen through her grandson's attempts to cover up a disturbing incident from his past that provided a significant clue in the pollution case. But she hadn't faced the kind of people he'd dealt with in a nearly thirty-year career as a National Park Service ranger and a small town police chief.

"I'm not sure Marie has it right this time," he said.

"Why don't you reserve judgment until you've talked with Djuan's grandmother?"

"Look, Jaz, I'm still a rookie at this private investigator business. This sounds like a pretty iffy way to further my reputation as a PI."

"If he's innocent, you'll prove it, Sid."

He started to push a little harder but shook his head in

resignation, acknowledging further argument at this stage would prove useless. She had worked persuasion to a fine art. "Okay. Let's get with Mrs. Ransom and see where it stands, but I'm not promising anything. Have you had time to dig up some background on Burden?"

"Nothing good. He's been behind bars since he was in the sixth grade. Now he's twenty-five. I have news reports on the trial. I'll fax it to you."

A LITTLE LATER, Sid sat in his office near RiverGate Mall in suburban Madison, digesting the file on the child murderer. The boy's father had deserted the family long before the night Djuan fatally shot a man more than twice his age. His young mother possessed a lengthy rap sheet, spending much of her time in and out of court on drug charges. She struggled to provide food for the table. As the oldest child, Djuan felt it his responsibility to help keep clothes on the backs of his younger siblings. He did it by taking to the streets in the projects where they lived, slinking about in the darkness, stealing and selling drugs. One night at the tender age of twelve, he sold four dime bags of pot to a young man who complained of poor quality and threatened to seize the boy's drug supply. During the argument that followed, the youngster pulled out a pistol and shot him. A kid standing nearby saw what happened. They arrested Djuan the next day. The judge sentenced him to fifteen years in prison after a guilty plea.

Sid found it all too familiar. During his ten years as police chief in Lewisville, a small town southwest of Nashville, he had witnessed the inevitable destruction of young lives from poverty and drugs. It affected communities of every size. He had never seen a case where the killer was so young, though. The conventional wisdom said prisons served as breeding grounds for future violence.

Was that the real story behind Djuan Burden?

I hated to dash her expectations, but statistics said Djuan Burden was guilty as hell.

2

NOT FAR PAST I-440, which served as the western demarcation line for "downtown" Nashville, Sid turned off Charlotte Avenue, looking for Rachel Ransom's address. When he found it, the small white frame residence with a postage stamp front yard seemed to have been squeezed between a pair of tired-looking houses twice as tall, sliced into apartments. Sid parked on the narrow street behind an older model blue Ford with a dented front fender. Newly green leaves sprouted from a scattering of maple trees along the sidewalk. The piquant smell of hickory smoke from a nearby barbecue joint wafted past on a gentle morning breeze. Jaz already stood on the sidewalk by the time Sid skirted the front of his car. He usually opened the door for her, though he'd learned it sometimes impinged on her sense of independence.

They presented quite a contrast as they walked toward the narrow but tidy front porch, a big man with ruffled black hair and beard to match, both highlighted by sprinkles of silver, and a shorter blonde woman. At six-six, Sid stood better than a head taller than Jaz. He was broad-shouldered with a modest waist for his height. She had a shapely body that remained well-toned years after she'd left the professional boxing ring. In her mid-forties, she had a winning smile that turned heads wherever she went.

"You must be Mr. Chance and Miss LeMieux," said the

stocky woman in a long, dark blue dress who answered the door.

They both nodded, and Sid followed Jaz in shaking the outstretched hand. Rachel Ransom had the wrinkled exterior of a woman long familiar with hard work and the sad brown eyes of one who had seen more than her share of trouble.

"We're sorry about what happened to your grandson," Sid said as an icebreaker. "Was he living with you?"

Mrs. Ransom ushered them inside. "Yes, he came here when he got out of prison. He's a good boy at heart." A tone of sadness tinged her voice. "I hate to admit it, but my daughter was mostly responsible for the trouble he got himself into."

Sid noted the colorful throws with tasseled ends that covered a sofa and two chairs in the small but neat living room. "You have a nice place here," he said.

"Thank you. It's not much, but it's mine."

Mrs. Ransom made her way hesitantly to a silent TV and switched off the picture. Almost certain the midnight black of her hair was something other than natural, Sid looked to the worry lines that creased her face to help judge her age at somewhere in the seventies. Photos of a few smiling teens and a couple, no doubt the Ransoms at an earlier age, sat atop the television set.

After they were seated, Sid leaned forward, elbows on his knees. "Why did you say your daughter was responsible for what happened to Djuan?"

"We didn't raise that girl to be the way she turned out, God rest her soul." The elderly woman struggled to keep her composure. "Darlene got really rebellious as a teenager, married right out of high school. The boy told her he was goin' to be a pro football player. Well, the only thing he knew about pro football was how to gamble on it."

"You were living in Nashville then?"

"When she got married?"

Sid nodded.

"We were. Her dad and me moved to California not long after that. George worked in construction, and there was plenty going on out there. If I'd been around during those years, I might've been able to change things. That no-good husband of hers ran out on Darlene as soon as the twins were born."

"So you weren't here when Djuan got into trouble," Jaz said.

"No. George got hurt and we moved back to Nashville about the time of Djuan's trial. I didn't know the boy had been running wild at night, hanging out with a gang of young hoodlums."

"Before I decide whether I can be of help to you, Mrs. Ransom, I'd like some background on Djuan. We need to go over everything you can tell us about what happened at that store."

"I'll be happy to tell you whatever I know."

Jaz ran a slender hand through her hair. "Why are you so sure your grandson didn't commit this murder?"

Mrs. Ransom's eyes narrowed; her voice softened. "He told me he didn't do it, and I believe him. He vowed to change his life when he got out of prison."

Sid took a deep breath. He'd hoped to hear something a little more convincing. He cut his eyes toward Jaz, and she pursued the subject a little further.

"There must be more to it than that," Jaz said, keeping her voice low-key. "Marie said you were quite certain of his innocence."

"He went to that place in Green Hills because of me," Mrs. Ransom said. "Since he hasn't been able to find a job, the boy's tried to help me all he could. I have problems with blood pressure and diabetes, and I get lots of papers from Medicare.

I never paid attention to any of that stuff. Long as they pay their share of my bills, I'm fine. But when Djuan picked up one that just came, he said something didn't look right."

"Did they claim you owed money?" Sid asked when she paused.

"Nothing like that. Matter of fact, it looked like they paid too much. It showed I had gotten stuff like one of these wheel chairs that runs around on a battery."

"A power chair?" Jaz asked.

"I guess that's what they call it. They said I had one that cost several thousand dollars. I never heard of such. I can walk as good as Marie Wallace. Djuan said Medicare paid a lot of money to this place out on Hillsboro Pike, but the paper showed I still owed hundreds of dollars on it."

"And that's why he went out to the store?"

"Yes'm. He took that paper out there to find out what was going on."

"The newspaper story said the police found a document with his fingerprints on it."

"That was it. He told me he dropped it on the desk before he realized there was something wrong with the man."

"Did Djuan come back here as soon as he left the store?" Sid asked.

She nodded. "I've never seen the boy so scared. He was all bent out of shape."

"What did he say?"

"At first he wouldn't tell me anything. Just said it was nothing. He was tired and wanted to go to his room. But when I kept after him, he finally gave up and told me what had happened."

Jaz nodded. "The newspaper said he claimed he'd found the man dead at his desk."

Rachel Ransom's brows knitted; her voice turned brittle.

"He didn't just *claim* he'd found a dead man. He found one."

"I'm sorry." Jaz gave a contrite twist to her face. "That was the newspaper's choice of words. I didn't intend to sound like he wasn't being truthful."

Sid leaned back on the sofa. "What, exactly, did Djuan say happened when he got there?"

She bowed her head, the agony of her thoughts hanging like a shadow across her face. She spoke slowly. "He walked in and saw they was moving stuff out of that place. After he dropped the Medicare paper on the desk, he went around to where he could see the man's face and realized the fellow had been shot."

"And he panicked," Sid said.

"Yes, sir. He thought about calling the police, but he knew they'd never believe he didn't shoot the man. And he was right."

Sid pulled his pen and a small note pad from his pocket and started writing. "Did you talk to the detective who came to arrest Djuan?"

"There was two of them, but the big one did all the talking. The short one—he had a little mustache like Clark Gable—just sat there staring at me like I was some kind of insect."

The Gable mustache comment convinced Sid he had been right about judging her age. "What did you tell the detective?"

"I told him about the Medicare form, that the boy had gone out there to check on it for me. Djuan didn't know that dead man from Adam's off ox."

Sid squelched a smile. He hadn't heard that expression since his grandmother used it when he was a boy. "What did the detective say?"

"He was a big man, nearly as tall as you. He gave me a snarly look and said, 'You're his granny, right? And you want to keep him out of jail.' That policeman claimed Djuan argued with the man and did like he did when he was twelve. That's a lie, Mr. Chance. Djuan is determined to make something of himself now."

Despite his doubts, Sid reacted with an investigator's mindset. He turned to Jaz. "We need to find out who owns that building and get permission to take a look. Hopefully the scene hasn't been too badly disturbed."

"Already checked," she said. "It's handled by a real estate firm we do business with at Welcome Home Stores. Metro said they would release it as a crime scene this morning. The agency says it will take awhile to get someone out there to clean it up."

"They probably didn't know Prime Medical was skipping out."

"That's right. The rental agent said he was completely in the dark. The tenant had paid through the end of the month."

Sid turned back to Rachel Ransom. Despite the sympathy he felt for her, he still had issues. "The newspaper story said they found a weapon."

"They searched my house and turned up an old gun my husband bought years ago. I don't know if he ever shot it. I know he hadn't in recent years. He just kept it for protection."

"Did you have it hidden?" Jaz asked.

"Not really. But it was in the bottom of a cedar chest in my bedroom. I use the chest mostly for storage. I had old sheets and tablecloths in there. I'd forgotten all about the gun. They messed up everything looking for it."

Sid tapped the pen on his pad. "Would Djuan have known where it was?"

"No, sir, I'm sure about that. It wasn't in a place where he'd've been looking for anything."

"Could he have gone in there after he got home from the medical supply store?"

Mrs. Ransom shook her head vigorously. "The boy went straight to his room when he got here. When he came out, we sat in the kitchen talking until the police arrived."

"Did you tell that to the detectives?"

"I sure did."

"Do you know what caliber the gun was?" Sid asked.

"The policeman said it was a twenty-two."

"Let's hope the murder weapon wasn't a twenty-two," Jaz said.

Rachel Ransom looked from Jaz to Sid, arms hugging herself as if it were cold, though the room felt warm. She spoke in a pleading voice. "You've got to help him, Mr. Chance. Please. The boy has suffered enough."

Sid spoke softly. It wouldn't be easy. "We'll do what we can."

3

WHEN THEY WERE back in the car, Sid looked at Jaz. "I'm sorry, but if the forensics folks determine that gun fired the fatal shot, it's sayonara for me."

"As it should be. But I agree with Marie. I have a feeling the young man didn't do it, and I don't want to see him railroaded."

During her multi-faceted career, Jaz had served a few years as a Metro Nashville policewoman. Sid valued her opinion, but he weighed it against studies that showed juveniles tried as adults were likely to re-offend sooner and more often than those tried in juvenile court. The odds were not on Djuan Burden's side.

Sid started the car and backed away from the blue Ford. "Call Bart and see if we can meet him somewhere. I'm not getting the same vibes you are."

She pulled out her smartphone with all the latest techno gimmicks and got Homicide Detective Bart Masterson on the line. He agreed to meet them at a fast food place in the Inglewood suburb.

Fifteen minutes later, they walked into the restaurant to find the tall, lanky detective lounging in a back booth with a cup of black coffee. Sid stopped at the counter to get himself a cup, plus a cappuccino for Jaz. She had switched to the French vanilla-flavored concoction after burning out on coffee as a cop.

"Hi, guys," Bart said, twitching the inverted V of the black mustache that made him resemble the Masterson of Wild West fame. "Do we have a poker game Thursday night? Unless something happens, as it likely will, I'll be there."

"We'll meet at Sid's office," Jaz said. "I've talked to the others."

The others in the Miss Demeanor and Five Felons Poker Club were Patrol Sgt. Wick Stanley, retired crime reporter Jack Post, who had dreamed up the colorful name for the group, and former Criminal Court Judge Gabriel Thackston. Each of the six members had current or former connections to law enforcement and met when the spirit moved them for a lively session with the cards.

Bart gave her a wary eye. "Is this little rendezvous about the Djuan Burden case?"

Sid set the cappuccino in front of Jaz and slid into the booth beside her. "Yeah, the Omar Valdez homicide. Who's working it?"

"The aptly named Victor Grimm," Bart said. "You probably don't know him. He got passed over for sergeant a couple of years ago. Carries a chip the size of a concrete block."

"Sounds like just the kind of guy who'd love to talk to us about proving his suspect's innocence," Sid said.

"When his mind gets set on the way it is, you'd have an easier time driving a team of mules up a steep hill than getting Grimm to change." Bart tilted his head and frowned. "You don't really believe that kid is innocent."

It didn't have the sound of a question.

"His granny thinks he is," Jaz said, "and she makes a pretty good case for it."

"Your man Grimm found a gun at Burden's grandmother's house," Sid said. "We need to know if they tested it, and what they found."

"Good luck. He wouldn't give me the sweat off his brow," Bart said. "If you get anything out of the Grimm Reaper, I'll see you get the Sherlock Holmes Award."

"No quid pro quo?"

"Hell, Sid, I wouldn't owe that creep something on a bet."

"What about the TBI lab?" Jaz asked. "Don't you have a buddy over there?"

Since Metro's crime lab was still a work in progress, they used the Tennessee Bureau of Investigation's state of the art facility. The TBI firearms section could ferret out most anything you needed to know about a gun and its ammunition. Sid had dealt with the state lab while police chief in Lewisville, but his contact had moved on following staff cuts.

Bart shrugged. "I'll see what I can find out. I think you've taken on a lost cause, though. Burden never showed any remorse for what he did to that guy years ago. I doubt that he underwent some kind of character metamorphosis during his time in prison."

"Don't be so judgmental," Jaz said. "I've known lots of people who changed their actions as well as their thinking over time."

"How many were killers?"

Jaz kept her silence.

Bart looked across at Sid. "How do you propose to get this boy off the hook?"

It was a question Sid had been pondering, a question for which he could see but one answer. "With your Detective Grimm unwilling to pursue the case any further, it leaves us only one choice. We'll have to find the real killer."

"And where do you plan to start looking?"

Sid turned to Jaz. "Do you remember if the newspaper story said anything about what was in the document they found with Djuan's fingerprints on it?"

She shook her head. "I'm fairly sure it didn't. What are you thinking?"

"Mrs. Ransom said Medicare had paid the medical supply company in Green Hills for a power chair she didn't get. That sounds like Medicare fraud, particularly with the store closing like this. Where criminals are involved, murder is always a possible outcome."

Bart looked across at Jaz and smiled. "Wonder what the newspapers would say if they knew you were trying to prove that black boy innocent?"

"Just goes to show that stuff they've been writing about her is bullshit," Sid said.

Jaz lowered her cappuccino cup. "It was a put-up job to cause my company problems. One of our major competitors has been paying people to pull all kinds of tricks. They sent teenagers to try and buy beer, then made claims about improper handling of lottery tickets."

Bart twisted his face in a grimace. "If this is their doings, it's making a mess for you. I saw where they're getting the NAACP into it."

"That woman flat lied," Jaz said. "I'd never use that kind of language on anybody. Marie is furious about it. Our company attorneys are looking into it. They hope to find evidence she was paid off."

Before he could reply, Bart's phone rang. He answered it, grunted an acknowledgment, and switched off. "Sorry, gotta go. Lieutenant's got some crappy idea for me to pursue. If you come up with anything you want to bat around, give me a shout."

After he had left, Jaz fiddled with the half-filled cup in front of her. "Medicare fraud is the FBI's bailiwick. We need to talk to Mrs. Ransom again, get her to request another copy of that EOB Detective Grimm found at the scene."

"If she's right about what happened," Sid said, "Grimm chose the answer that took the least amount of detective work. I doubt if he gave a thought to the Medicare angle. He hasn't likely mentioned anything to the FBI."

"He wouldn't want to bring in the feds, for sure."

Sid glanced at his watch. "Call your real estate friends and see if somebody can meet us at that store in Green Hills. I'll get hold of the lawyers at Arnie Bailey's office and try to arrange a meeting after lunch."

Jaz looked around at him, eyes twinkling. "And what classy restaurant are you taking me to for lunch?"

Sid turned his head toward the counter. "They have great hamburgers here. We can probably find one just like it on Hillsboro Pike. I'll even pop for the cheese. Maybe an apple turnover for dessert."

She looked at him with narrowed eyes. "You really know how to treat a girl, Mr. Chance."

He grinned. "I'm an equal opportunity employer. You get to eat the same stuff I do."

He knew she was accustomed to eating in executive dining rooms and fancy private clubs, but it hadn't always been that way. She had lived frugally during the years of exile after incurring the wrath of her aristocratic mother.

"Since we won't be too far from my house," Jaz said in a mocking voice, "I'd thought about telling Marie to fix us one of her delights for lunch. But if that's your attitude, we'll just dine on burgers."

Sid drained his coffee cup and shrugged. "Okay, I surrender. Take me to Marie and I'll give you a rain check for a classy restaurant."

Marie Wallace's dishes rivaled those of a gourmet chef. She had started out cooking at a small restaurant early in life. She parlayed that into a talent for preparing delightful dinners when Jaques LeMieux entertained lavishly as he built Welcome Home Stores into a formidable enterprise.

Jaz pulled her phone from her handbag with a sneaky smile. "I knew playing the Marie card would get you."

She made arrangements for them to check out the former medical supply store while Sid used his cell phone to schedule a meeting with the legal team for two o'clock. They headed out to his car and drove across town to the Green Hills area, a more upscale part of the city. It included a major shopping mall filled with classy shops and lots of strip centers with familiar brand names.

The morning had warmed rapidly. Sid doffed his lightweight jacket after parking in front of the single-story building that also housed a small clothing store and a florist shop. "Prime Medical Equipment" was lettered on one window. A CLOSED placard hung on the door. Sid opened the console, pulled out a couple of pairs of latex gloves, gave one to Jaz and shoved the other into his pocket.

He saw someone through the window as they approached the building.

A young woman in a tan business suit opened the door, her face shadowed by a brooding look. "Miss LeMieux?" she asked Jaz.

"Right. You must be from Apple Realty. Thanks for coming over."

"There was still crime scene tape across the door when I passed by earlier this morning, but it was gone when I got here a little while ago. Made me wonder if I should let you in, but the boss said the police gave us permission to occupy the building again."

"Sorry if I caused any problem," Jaz said. She nodded at Sid. "This is Private Investigator Sid Chance. We'll be looking around a bit to figure out what happened. If you have someplace you need to go, you could check back with us in about an hour. Here's my cell number."

The woman took her card, stared at it a moment, then looked up. "You sure this is okay with the police?"

Jaz smiled. "I'm sure."

The woman still looked uncomfortable. "All right. I'll give you a call."

"Good move," Sid said after she'd left. "We don't need her standing around looking over our shoulders."

They crossed to the desk, which showed the residue of the search for fingerprints.

"I don't see any blood on the chair," Sid said. "It could mean the bullet didn't exit the skull. If that's the case, the medical examiner should have recovered it, giving the possibility of a match to the gun. We really need some info from the TBI lab."

Jaz stared at the chair. "Let's hope Bart can get it."

Everything from empty soft drink cans to discarded brochures advertising a popular brand of power chair lay scattered about the floor. "You take this area, and I'll start in the back room," Sid said. "Check every piece of paper you can find for any information about Prime Medical Equipment and its owners."

Jaz began with the cluttered desk, while Sid turned to the door leading to the rear of the building. A stack of boxes lay overturned in the doorway. The top one had spilled an assortment of small items including wheels for walkers. Checking the other boxes, he realized they were dummies used for display, bearing pictures of equipment outside but empty inside. The room beyond contained only a table and a couple of chairs, a coffee maker with an inch or two of black liquid in the carafe, a telephone, a small TV set, and a pair of letter-size boxes under the table. There was a rear exit, out of sight of the front entrance and most of the front room. Checking around and finding nothing else of interest, he stooped to examine the small boxes.

They had been taped shut. He pulled on his gloves, took out his pocketknife and slit the tape on one of the boxes. Inside he found an unopened package of brochures for durable medical equipment, a few folded posters, and, oddly, an American flag. He unsealed the second box. It contained a few large manila envelopes fastened with metal clasps. Holding the top envelope carefully so as not to disturb any latent prints, he spread the clip and pushed the flap open.

Slipping out a sheaf of papers, he read down a list on the top sheet. It contained names, addresses, dates of birth, Social Security and Medicare numbers. As he realized the impact of what he'd found, he turned to call out to Jaz but stopped when he heard someone come in the front door.

"What the hell are you doing?" a loud male voice demanded.

Sid quickly slid the papers back into the envelope, dropped it into the box, and placed the first box on top of it. He hurried out to the front, where he saw Jaz facing a large sandy-haired man in an ill-fitting gray suit.

The man looked around at Sid. "Who the hell are you two, and what's going on here?"

He stared through icy blue eyes that gave him the look of an overgrown bully. From Bart Masterson's description, Sid had a pretty good idea who they were dealing with. "We have the owner's permission to be here," Sid said as he stripped off the gloves. It wasn't quite true, but close enough. "Who are you?"

"Metro Detective Victor Grimm." He shoved his coat open to display the badge clipped at his belt.

Sid took out his ID. "Private Investigator Sidney Chance. This is my associate, Jasmine LeMieux."

Grimm scowled. "I've heard of you, and I know all about the lady and her reputation. You must be working for those Bailey-Riddle lawyers that won't let Burden talk anymore."

Sid said nothing.

"You know that boy's guilty as sin," Grimm said.

Sid cocked his head, eyebrows raised. "And you're prepared to prove it?"

"Damn right. With his record, it won't take much."

"What did the ballistics test show?" Jaz asked.

The detective's fat lip curled upward. "It'll show just what I expect it to show, that Djuan Burden fired his granddaddy's old Saturday night special and killed Omar Valdez."

They didn't have the results yet, Sid translated. "You find his prints on the gun?"

"We're not releasing any information," Grimm said with a toss of his head. "The case is still under investigation." He shifted his gaze about the store. "So what are you two gumshoes looking for, poking around with your rubber gloves? A source told me some private eye was messing around here."

No doubt the real estate woman, Sid thought. A relative or a neighbor. He perched on the edge of the desk and let a thin smile play across his lips. "We wanted to make sure your crime scene guys didn't leave any interesting tidbits behind."

"If they did, I guarantee you it won't get Djuan Burden out of that murder charge. A citizen saw him run out of here, jump in a car, and race off. The witness called nine-one-one and gave us the tag number that was registered to Burden's grandma. We found him and the gun there."

"Did you get a confession out of him?" Jaz asked as she stripped off her surgical gloves and dropped them in the chair where Valdez had been shot.

"Hell, he came out a hardened criminal. They don't give up easy. But we got him by the balls."

Grimm's pompous attitude was wearing thin on Sid. It bordered on déjà vu, a replay of what he had experienced in dealing with his old Lewisville nemesis, Sheriff Zachary. The sheriff had charged him with taking a bribe from a drug dealer, which was ultimately exposed as a frame-up, though it effectively ended his career as police chief. He shared some of the detective's reservations about Burden, but Grimm hadn't said anything that would refute Rachel Ransom's account.

The overweight detective gave a derisive twist to his lips. "If you two want to stay on the good side of the law, you'd best stop tinkering with a Metro homicide case and go back to chasing scumbag husbands."

Sid straightened to his full height, which gave him a few inches on Grimm, though he could hardly compete with the other man's bulk. He took a step toward the officer, which left them barely a yard apart, and gave him a cold stare.

"I spent ten years on the right side of the law as chief of police in Lewisville," he said. "And I'm well acquainted with my rights as a private investigator."

When Sid shifted his weight, Grimm bristled. "I don't give a shit if you were a small town cop or Director of the FBI, Chance. You take one more step and you'll find yourself in handcuffs."

Jaz stepped up beside Sid. "I suggest you be a bit more civilized about this, Detective." She spoke in a cool but calm voice. "Since you released this store as a crime scene and there's a closed sign on the door, you have no right to barge in here without a search warrant. You say you know me. You must know I can have a team of lawyers on your back quicker than you can call code five thousand."

The Metro Police code for officer in serious danger.

Grimm stood frozen like a statue of Buddha, if the venerable icon had been about to burst a blood vessel. After a few quick breaths, he blurted, "Don't think you've heard the last of this."

And stormed out.

4

JAZ LOOKED AROUND at Sid and took a deep breath. "I guess I took care of any potential cooperation from the West Precinct."

"I don't think there was ever any potential," Sid said. "The less I see of that meatball, the happier I'll be. Don't worry about it." He turned toward the back room. "Come in here and look at what I found."

He pulled the gloves on again, opened the box, slipped the papers from the manila envelope, and showed them to her.

Her lively blue eyes widened. "This doesn't leave much doubt, does it? Some of the names are checked off. I wonder if Rachel Ransom is in here?"

"Most likely. We need to get this to the FBI."

He called a contact he'd made in the local office while working an earlier case and told Jaz someone would be out shortly. She thought about sitting in the executive chair to wait but, realizing what had happened there, changed her mind and perched on the edge of the desk. During the wait, they studied the papers she had found, which provided meager information on the firm. One item was an overdue utility bill. Since he was abandoning the place, Valdez no doubt had little interest in such trivia.

Sid questioned her on how the racial slur matter currently in the news had affected her.

"It's been aggravating," she said, giving a casual shrug and a slight roll of her head, "but it hasn't caused any real problems." It was an understatement, and she realized he probably knew it.

He gave her a somber look. "Don't hesitate if there's anything I can do to help."

The door opened and a muscular young man with intense brown eyes walked in. He showed Bureau credentials that identified him as Special Agent Baron Eggers. Sid introduced Jaz and himself and explained that they had been retained to help a young man believed to be falsely accused of murder. He opened the manila envelope and told how he had found the papers.

Agent Eggers accepted the sheet of names and looked down the list. "Metro didn't see this?"

Sid gave his head a confirming shake. "They were only searching for evidence relating to the murder. They already had a description and a suspect."

"You'll probably find Djuan Burden's grandmother's name in there," Jaz said. "She got a Medicare EOB saying this outfit had supplied her an expensive power chair, which she didn't need and never received."

Eggers' gaze swept the area. "Looks like they'd made their killing and were folding their tent. Medicare's doing a better job with the new regulations, but some of these fly-by-nighters still slip through the cracks. Know anything about Prime Medical Equipment?"

Jaz had scooted off the desk. "I found this letter that identifies it as a corporation."

"They don't get as much scrutiny as an individual owner. Was it local?"

"Listed this address and Omar Valdez as president, Elena Ortiz as secretary-treasurer."

"Ortiz lived with him, didn't she?" Sid asked.

"According to the news story, she identified the body. It wasn't clear if they were married or not."

"We need to look into whether this shooting was personal with him," Sid said, "or business related. It looks a lot like a professional hit. The killer could have used a suppressor."

"Wasn't there just one shot fired?" Eggers asked. "A good hit man uses at least two to make sure the job is done right."

"Maybe this one wasn't a seasoned professional," Jaz said. "Or else he had great confidence."

"Well, good luck with it." Eggers shrugged. "We've got enough on our plate. We leave the homicides to Metro unless it involves a federal crime."

"What if it turns out to be involved with the Medicare fraud?"

"Doesn't appear that way." He tilted his head and studied Jaz for a moment. "You look awfully familiar. Have you been in the news lately?"

Sid looked askance. "She's in the news frequently, but lately it's been about a spurious charge of racial slurring. Jaz is chairman of Welcome Home Stores."

Eggers eyes glowed in recognition. "I'm sorry. I remember now. And you're the guy who was involved in that pollution case in Cheatham County."

"That's me."

"Let's keep in touch. I'd be interested in anything you turn up about Mr. Valdez or Miz Ortiz and Prime Medical Equipment."

"Be happy to," Sid said. "With your resources, I'd be surprised if we found anything you didn't."

"I don't like to pass up any possibilities," Eggers said.

"Know what you mean. We'd also like to hear of anything you might come across involving Valdez's murder. Anything that indicates Djuan Burden didn't do it."

"Fair enough."

THE TOWERING OAKS and maples that led up the curving driveway from the gate were leafing out, but not enough to mar the impressive view of the two-story French colonial mansion before they reached the crest of the hill. The property was located on Franklin Road not far from the county line. Sid parked in a patterned brick area, and they walked toward the wide veranda that spread across the front of the house and down one side. John Wallace met them at the front door."

"Marie wants you to come back to the kitchen, Miss Jasmine," he said, giving a nod of recognition to Sid. A man of few words, he was large and stocky with muscles that bulged beneath a shirt as white as his short hair. Well-laundered blue jeans extended below the shirt.

Jaz turned to Sid. "Go on in my office and I'll check with Marie."

Sid entered the bookshelf-lined room Jaques LeMieux had called his hiding place and took a chair beside Jaz's cluttered desk. He glanced at the two computer monitors, one with a colorful eighteen-wheeler bouncing about the screen. The other showed a log-in box. He picked up a copy of the morning newspaper and checked the other page one stories. He'd already devoured everything about the Djuan Burden case. The main headline chronicled the latest shenanigans of the state legislature, now in session.

"I've already read that malarkey," Jaz said as she came through the door. "There's nothing worth reading."

"I see they're still arguing about where you can carry a weapon."

"A lot of truckers carry them, so we permit it in our stores. Looks like you can take a gun just about anywhere you want, except in government buildings."

"The bad guys will take them anywhere, legal or not."

"True."

Sid waved at the computer screens. "You going to check out Prime Medical?"

She took her seat behind the desk. "Marie's bringing our lunch in here. We're having a fruit salad and strawberry muffins."

"With coffee?"

"For you."

Sid pulled his chair closer to the big screen monitor. "Go for it. We don't have long before it'll be time to head for Arnie's office."

She had just opened the Prime Medical Equipment website when Marie walked in, pushing a small cart laden with trays bearing bowls of chopped fresh fruit topped with scoops of orange sherbet. She had coffee for Sid and hot tea for Jaz.

"You're a doll, Marie," Sid said. "It looks delicious."

She gave him a cherubic smile. "And you're a flatterer."

"No flattery intended. Just the facts, ma'am."

"And thank you for helping my friend, Rachel."

"Okay, you two," Jaz said. "Let's get busy with this investigation. Thank you, Marie."

Sid started on his salad and looked up at the screen as Jaz scrolled down the page. "The website looks legitimate enough," he said.

"Enough to fool the casual observer." She clicked on some links. "A lot of the pages are blank...'Under construction.' Just enough official-looking stuff to sound real. I suspect it was copied mostly from somebody else's site."

"What does it say about the company background?"

"Established a year ago by veteran medical supplier Omar Valdez. Nothing about how he got the title 'veteran.'"

"Try him on Google."

The Google results page showed a long list of men named Omar Valdez. One was a Canadian boxer, another an actor, a third called "Mr. Cucumber" on his Facebook page. The only entry for Nashville's Omar Valdez was a link to the newspaper story about his murder. A telephone search gave his address at an apartment on Granny White Pike

"I'll delve into him more thoroughly on one of your high-powered search engines when I get back from Bailey, Riddle and Smith," Jaz said. "Let's see if the corporation is legitimate."

She did a check at the Secretary of State's site and found Prime Medical Equipment, Inc. listed as chartered earlier in the year.

"The Apple Realty people said they had been in the building less than six months," she said.

"From what I've learned on the subject, these scammers only set up shop for a few months. As soon as they collect a nice sum from Medicare, they fold their tents and move on before the investigators get wind of them. Change the name, find a new location. Like Agent Eggers said, if it's a corporation, I don't think they get as much scrutiny." Sid checked his watch. "We'd better finish up here and head downtown."

BAILEY, RIDDLE AND Smith's offices occupied a suite on the twentieth floor of a downtown high rise. Sid and Jaz were escorted to the walnut conference room where he had first met Arnie Bailey back in October. The lawyer hired him then to track down a defunct firm responsible for a massive chemical spill, his first major case as a PI. A wall of windows looked out on a block of smaller buildings and the Victorian warehouse district that had been transformed into Nashville's lively tourist mecca known as "The District." Across the Cumberland River rose the concrete mass of LP Field, where blue-and-white-clad

Tennessee Titans football fans swarmed like colorful bees around an oval-shaped hive on fall Sundays, plus a couple of week nights.

Arnie Bailey came through the door, a short, chubby figure with an elfin grin. Two younger men followed, one tall and thin, the other more in line with the senior partner's physique.

"I hope you guys haven't put in too much time on this," Arnie said, sounding apologetic.

Sid gave him a critical look. "What does that mean?"

"The boys had a little chat with Djuan Burden at the Metro Jail and looked over what the DA has on him. They think his best course is a plea bargain."

5

Aftergetting over the initial shock, Sid stared at the lawyer. "With all due respect, counselor, I think we need to sit down and have our own little chat. It sounds like our opinions are a hundred and eighty degrees apart."

"I agree," Jaz said. "I doubt that your client would go along with it. I'm certain his grandmother wouldn't."

Arnie looked around at his young colleagues. "I think we'd better talk, fellas."

He introduced the tall lawyer, who reminded Sid of Jimmy Stewart in *It's a Wonderful Life*, as Brainerd Hersholt. The smaller man was Hardy Vandenberg. As Sid learned, Hersholt's movie actor look wasn't far off course. A Yale Law School graduate, he was a descendant of famed movie actor Jean Hersholt, who was honored annually by the Hersholt Humanitarian Award given at the Oscar ceremonies. A graduate of Duke Law School, Vandenberg was the son of an old friend of Arnie Bailey.

After they took seats at the table, Vandenberg spoke up. He was an intense young man, outspoken in his beliefs. "The DA is ready to go after Burden on this one. If he can tie that gun from granny's house to the murder, he's going to opt for the death penalty."

"This doesn't sound like a capital case to me," Sid said.

"A shot through the forehead at close range is pretty damning for a guy already convicted of one murder."

"They can't bring up that conviction in the trial."

"True, but you can count on it being tossed out there in the penalty phase."

Arnie nodded. "He's right, Sid."

Jaz folded her hands on the table. "I don't believe they can tie that pistol to Djuan Burden. Mrs. Ransom told us there was no way he could have put that gun where they found it after he got home from Prime Medical Equipment. It had been put away for years."

"We'll see," Vandenberg said with a skeptical shrug. "They have a witness who'll testify Burden fled the scene in a major rush. He left a paper on the desk showing his grandmother owed the company several hundred dollars. If this goes to trial, my reading is he'll face lethal injection."

Arnie Bailey leaned his elbows on the table. "Let's hear what Sid and Miz LeMieux think about the case. They obviously see things differently."

"We haven't had time to get into it in great detail," Sid said, "but we have some angles to pursue. It appears the store was a front for Medicare fraud. We're looking into the possibility the murder is tied to the criminal activity."

"Is Metro onto that?" Arnie asked.

"No. Detective Grimm is so certain Djuan is guilty, he's not about to look anywhere else."

Although he had appeared totally disinterested up to this point, Hersholt suddenly came alive. "You talked to him?"

"Grimm?" Sid said. "Yeah. Unfortunately."

He recounted their experience at the medical supply store.

"Since I don't normally get involved in criminal law, the only time I've run into that officer was when he testified in a civil case of mine," Arnie said. He added with a chuckle, "As I recall, he doesn't take kindly to having his actions questioned."

"Bart Masterson warned us about him," Jaz said. "But Sid

and I don't take kindly to intimidation. I have trouble keeping my mouth shut."

Arnie grinned. "I don't recall you being reticent about expressing your views."

Sid looked across at the two young lawyers. "I think our next move should be a meeting with your client. We need to hear what he says about all of this."

"We can set that up for you with a letter giving our authorization," Vandenberg said. "I need to warn you, though, I've read a lot of murder trial transcripts and talked to many capital case attorneys. We'll have to see some incontrovertible evidence before I'll accept that we can win this case in the courtroom."

THE METRO JAIL contact visitation room appeared as bleak as Djuan Burden's outlook as he shuffled in from the lockup. It contained only a small table and four chairs. There was video monitoring but no audio, since Sid and Jaz were representing the attorneys. His five-eight frame filled the orange jumpsuit, though he looked shorter with his head leaned forward. Dreadlocks hung limp about his downturned face. He wasn't handcuffed or shackled. He looked up when Sid spoke.

"I don't know if you were told, but we're private investigators hired by your grandmother to help your lawyers."

Burden spoke slowly in a soft, deep voice. "Those lawyers, they looked like they didn't believe me when I said I didn't shoot that man."

"Some lawyers won't take a case if they think you're guilty," Sid said, though he didn't know about Hersholt and Vandenberg. "Our job is to find the real killer. You can help us by describing exactly what happened that afternoon."

He shook his head, the dreds coiling about like woven snakes. "Man, I'm not sure about anything anymore. I thought

I was done with barred cells and prison cots.”

"This shouldn't have happened to you," Jaz said.

"The Big Man must think I ain't paid enough for what I did all those years ago. It'll be like with me the rest of my life."

"You were just a kid."

"I don't know why I shot that man. I really don't. It was a long time before the impact of what I'd done began to sink in. At first it was just a big joke. Everybody knew how serious it was but me."

"I guess you've had plenty of time to ponder over it."

"Damn right. Sittin' in that cell, I spent a lotta time thinking about that night. Took me years to start feeling sorry for the guy's family. I thought about my own life. My mom never had time for me. She didn't know whether I was shootin' baskets or out stealin' cars and she didn't give a damn. I didn't know any better. It was just what we did."

Jaz looked him in the eye. "Your granny told us that you vowed to change your life when you came out of prison."

"Granny's my angel. She let me move in with her. If I'd gone back to the hood, I'da got mixed up with the same guys I ran with before. The ones that aren't in jail or dead. I just hope Granny don't think I've let her down."

"What have you been doing since you got out?"

"Looking for a job, mostly. But nobody wants to hire me. I was sittin' on the porch one day and some kids came up, trying to make out I'm something because I did time for murder. I told them the real heroes are the guys who get jobs and work to make something of themselves. Kids just don't understand."

"Did you get any career counseling in prison?"

"I got my GED. Took some courses that would help me open a center for kids like me. But I can't do anything without money, and I can't make any money without a job. Now this."

He rubbed hands as rough as a scratchy blanket down the sides of his face. "That fat cop kept saying 'you killed that man; you killed that man just like you killed the one fourteen years ago.'"

"You denied it, didn't you?" Sid asked.

"Damn right. I told him I never fired that gun. But I knew better'n to say anything else."

He'd learned how to stonewall the cops during his prison stay, Sid thought. "Getting back to what happened Tuesday afternoon, think about it. Concentrate on what you saw and what you heard when you first entered that store."

Burden closed his eyes for a moment, his face twisted as if in pain. When he opened them, he said, "I saw junk scattered all around. It was a mess. As I walked in, a box turned over and stuff clattered onto the floor. Oh, and I smelled gunpowder. Then I saw the man at the desk."

Sid pictured the scene as he remembered it. The fallen box lay in the doorway to the back room. At the time, Valdez would have been dead already. Who knocked the box over?

"Did you hear any other sounds?" Sid asked.

Burden looked puzzled. "What sort of sounds?"

"If you smelled gunpowder, Valdez must have just been shot. Did you think someone was in the back room?"

"At the time I wouldn't have cared...wait." His eyes widened. "Yeah...I remember now...a noise, a clicking noise. Was there a back door?"

"There was."

"Damn! I see what you mean. The killer must've left just as I got there, and I never saw him."

"Maybe somebody else did," Jaz said.

6

BY LATE AFTERNOON, the bright spring day had turned sour, with knotty dark clouds smudging the blue canopy overhead. Sid dropped Jaz off at a downtown garage where she'd left her red Lexus. She had an accountant to meet at her company headquarters before the office closed. Sid drove out to Green Hills to find who might have had a view of the rear door at Prime Medical Equipment.

A paved alley behind the building provided access for delivery and garbage trucks. A large gray dumpster sat between the rear entrances to the former medical supply store and the florist shop next door. Sid stopped beside the trash receptacle and looked around the area. Trees in the process of leafing out and tall wooden fences blocked the view from houses beyond the alley. A tire store-automobile service shop bordered the alley on a side street. Its overhead doors in back opened onto a parking area where cars awaited servicing. As he watched, a mechanic climbed into a pickup truck and drove it inside the service bay.

Sid parked in front of the shop and entered the office area, where two neatly-dressed women chatted in cushioned wrought iron chairs at one side. A couple of suited business types wandered around looking at tires on display racks. Behind the counter a scruffy-looking man in tan coveralls greeted him with a toothy smile. "I got some great tires just the thing for that Chevy," he said.

Sid returned the smile. "I'm sure you do. Maybe some other time, though. That's not what I'm here for now. Are you the manager?"

"Quint Nevins," he said, nodding. "You don't look like a salesman."

"Good observation." Sid introduced himself and showed his PI card. "Were you here when the murder took place yesterday afternoon at the medical supply place across the alley?"

"You better believe. Spooked people around here, I'll tell you. Cop cars all over the place. Heard it was that black boy just out of prison."

"He was charged with the murder, but we're looking into another possibility. It looks like somebody left by the rear door about the time of the shooting. If any of your employees were out back at the time, they could have seen something."

Nevins scratched his nose. "I guess it's possible."

"Mind if I talk to them and see if anyone remembers anything?"

"Not a good time. We're awful busy today. Gettin' behind and these folks are waiting."

"I could come back later."

"Let me ask around when I get a chance. You got a card? I find anybody who knows something, I'll give you a call."

Sid wasn't happy with that prospect but handed over a business card and hoped for the best. He didn't trust other people to ask questions the way he would. He drove back to Hillsboro Pike and pulled up to the florist shop. The fragrance of flower blossoms scented the air. Something springy, maybe daffodils or hyacinths. They had been his mother's favorites. Several plants were displayed around the small lobby in wicker baskets. Vivaldi's "The Four Seasons" flowed like a sprightly summer rain from a speaker in the ceiling. A silver-haired woman in a flower-bedecked smock stepped out from behind the counter.

"Can I show you something?" She had a strong voice that reminded him of Mary Virginia Chance. His mother had been an English teacher who specialized in American Literature. That was how he came to bear the name Sidney Lanier Chance.

Sid explained who he was and asked if she had been in the shop when the murder took place next door.

Her thin brows pinched toward her nose. "I'm afraid so."

"I guess it was rather traumatic when you found out what had happened."

"It certainly was. I started this shop twenty years ago, and I can't remember anything like this in the past."

"Were you acquainted with the people who ran Prime Medical Equipment?"

"I'd met them but never really got to know them. Mr. Valdez wasn't much of a communicator."

"How about Ms. Ortiz?"

"She was friendly enough, though I only saw her on a few occasions. She bought some potted plants once to decorate the front of the store."

"Were you aware that they were moving out?"

"I had no idea. I hadn't seen many cars around, but I never did. I presumed they did most of their business by mail or by phone. I get lots of phone orders."

"Did you hear the gunshot?"

"No, even though it happened on the other side of this wall." She nodded toward the medical supply store. "The police asked about that. I told them I supposed the music could have drowned it out."

"Did you have a loud song playing?"

"I never play loud songs."

It could mean a suppressor, popularly called a silencer, he

thought. "Were you in a position to see anyone going into the store, or coming out?"

She pondered that for a moment. "I stay busy in here, Mr. Chance. I could have been back in the workroom. Anyway, I don't do much window gazing. I don't recall seeing anyone."

Sid turned, looked out toward the parking lot, and nodded. "I imagine it would be difficult to see someone from here. And you probably won't see anyone for awhile. The real estate agent let us in there this morning after the police were finished examining the scene. They won't be cleaning the mess out for a while yet."

He gave her a card and asked her to call if she thought of anything else.

Moving next door to the clothing store, he found it a shop that specialized in what he called funky clothes for teenagers. Stacks of brightly colored tops and jeans with stringy threads covering fake holes were arrayed on tables. The two clerks had seen and heard nothing after the murder except all the police cars that crowded the parking lot. An officer came in to question them, but they were completely in the dark as to what had happened. Sid gave up and started back to his office in Madison. While creeping along I-440 in the homebound traffic that slowed even more with a drizzling rain, he got a call from Quint Nevins at the tire store. None of his employees had reported noticing anyone behind Prime Medical Equipment on the afternoon of the crime.

AFTER DINNER IN THE spacious kitchen with Marie and John Wallace, Jaz retreated to her office. Before her father died, the Wallaces had lived in a small house behind the mansion, but she finally convinced them to move into the big house with her. Turning to her computer, she logged onto a comprehensive search site used by private investigators and entered "Omar

Valdez" with his Nashville address. She found scant current information on him other than his position as president of Prime Medical Equipment, Inc. In the past he had lived in Albuquerque, New Mexico, where he worked at Casa Rosa Restaurant. Even if he had been the manager, and there was no indication what job he held, no way would it have provided him with the designation of "veteran medical supplier." He had no criminal record, no judgments against him. He appeared about as plain vanilla as they came.

Next she tried Elena Ortiz, who currently lived at the same address as Valdez. There was no shortage of information on the secretary- treasurer. She had worked in accounting at an orthopedic clinic in San Antonio, Texas. Thirty-five years old, she was born in El Paso of legal immigrant parents from the Mexican state of Chihuahua, which bordered on the Rio Grande. Ortiz had no criminal record. There was a note, however, to "see entry for Pablo Francisco Ortiz."

When Jaz checked on Pablo, she found he was Elena's brother. He had a lengthy criminal record around El Paso, including drug trafficking. It was an interesting development, but brother Pablo's wicked ways didn't appear to have any relationship to his sister's evident involvement in Medicare fraud.

Considering where to turn next, Jaz recalled finding a crumpled deposit slip on the floor beside Omar Valdez's desk. Though the slip was blank, she reasoned that the bank involved would be the one where the company had its account. The good news was that she had a close friend from her police department days who now worked in security for the bank. She picked up the phone and punched in Hattie Jordan's cell number.

"Hello, Sunshine, where you been hiding?"

As rookie cops, they had faced similar hurdles, though

Hattie's problems were doubled. Not only was she a woman, but a black woman. Jaz replied with a smile in her voice. "Sorry I've been out of touch lately. It's been a hectic month."

"I understand. How can anybody believe you'd do something like that?"

"I'm sure it was the work of a rival company we're having problems with."

"Well, you just give me the word, honey, and I'll tell 'em where they can shove that stuff."

"Thanks, Hattie."

"What you up to now?"

"Just doing a little computer trolling for a new case I'm working on with Sid."

"That big hunk, huh? You'd better grab him before some slinky babe snatches him away."

"A tall, slinky number like you?" Her friend was five-eleven, a real charmer with skin as smooth as a chocolate shake.

Hattie Jordan laughed. "I'm not immune to the charms of oversize guys."

"I've told you it's just a business arrangement with us."

"Of course it is, baby girl. Doesn't mean you can't work in a little monkey business."

"Speaking of business," Jaz said, quickly shifting the conversation, "are you keeping the bank as secure as ever?"

"Actually, I'm at the office right now. And since you mentioned computer trolling, we've had a hacker trying to do a bit of that on us lately. Goes on all the time, of course, but this one is a little more sophisticated."

"You cut him off at the pass, I hope."

"He didn't do any damage, and we're on his trail."

"I need a little assistance, Hattie," Jaz said. She explained about the Djuan Burden case, that they were looking into the possibility of Medicare fraud.

"Isn't that the Feebs' job?"

"Right. We turned over some stuff we found to an FBI agent, but they're not interested in the murder angle. What I need to know is if Prime Medical Equipment, Incorporated has an account with the bank. They were located on Hillsboro Pike in Green Hills. Names associated with the account would be Omar Valdez or Elena Ortiz."

"You wouldn't want to get a girl in trouble?"

"You're on your cell phone, Hattie. Nobody knows the trouble you see."

She laughed. "Okay, smartie. Let me get on my computer."

Jaz listened to the sound of keyboard clicking, her friend doing a bit of *um, hmm*ing, and then she was back.

"The murder took place yesterday afternoon, right?"

"Correct."

"First thing this morning, Miz Ortiz closed out the account and departed with a check for several thousand in Uncle Sugar's currency. You might want to talk to her...if she's still around."

<h1 style="text-align: center;">7</h1>

WHEN HE GOT BACK TO the office, Sid checked his email. He found a message from a potential client searching for a missing heir to a small fortune. During his limited time in the business, he had earned a reputation for his ability to locate hard-to-find people. This job sounded like it had the potential for big bucks, which was always an intriguing prospect. Not that he faced any financial difficulties. He had a tidy egg resting in his nest. It was managed by Mike Rich, a financial wizard who had been one of his mother's prize students back when.

Sid started entering notes on the day's activities into his computer, but the ringing phone interrupted him. It was the owner of the florist shop next to Prime Medical Equipment.

"I thought you might be interested in what I saw when I was locking up the store," she said.

"What was that?"

"A black car parked in front of the medical equipment place, and a man got out. It was a Dodge Avenger. I know because my sister has one. He went into the store and I left then, so I don't know how long he stayed."

"It was probably somebody from the real estate agency," Sid said, "but thanks for calling." She was a good observer. He wished she had been out back at the time of the shooting.

After printing out the case notes, he crossed to the small refrigerator in the corner and pulled out a bottle of Sam Adams, a Boston brew he had developed a taste for. He popped the cap and returned to his chair. Leaning back, he scanned the list of areas they had probed so far. He was almost convinced now of Djuan Burden's innocence. A big question mark still hovered over the ballistics test, but he would press Bart Masterson on what the TBI lab might have turned up. Glancing at the clock, he saw he still had time to catch part of the local news. He switched on the TV across from his desk.

Turmoil in he Middle East brought interviews with Nashville citizens who were concerned about the safety of relatives back home. As he nursed the Sam Adams, he turned back to the printout on his desk. Hearing the name "Djuan Burden" snared his attention and his eyes snapped back to the TV screen where he saw a familiar sight, the front of Prime Medical Equipment. Victor Grimm and a smaller man whose face was turned away, no doubt his partner, busily removed crime scene tape while the reporter updated the story. From what the real estate agent had said, the pictures must have been shot that morning.

He turned off the TV and returned to his notes, thinking about what he and Jaz would face in the days ahead. A major concern was how the confrontation with Detective Grimm might affect their investigation. They would have to use the backdoor approach through Bart or some other source to dig out what the police knew. Running his finger down the page, he stopped on the interview at Bailey, Riddle and Smith. The lawyers had been reluctant to consider going to trial, but he felt confident he could handle them. Confirmation of a person leaving Prime Medical by the rear door at the time of the murder appeared the most promising bit of information they could unearth, though at the moment it seemed totally out of reach.

When the phone rang, he saw Jaz's number on the caller

ID. He lifted the phone and said, "What's up, partner?"

"Just thought I'd relate a conversation I had with an old banking buddy." She gave him the gist of her conversation with Hattie Jordan.

Sid drained the last of his beer. "Sounds like I have another missing person to chase down. Since Ortiz came from Texas, it's likely she would head back there. We need to find out a little more about her first."

"They lived on my side of town. I'll check around their apartment first thing in the morning."

Sid dropped the bottle in his wastebasket. "Sounds like a plan. Call me with what you find."

After backing up his computer files, he shrugged into his jacket, grabbed his Titans cap, and glanced around to see if he'd forgotten anything. though he rarely took work papers home. Jaz, who possessed a computer science degree as well as an MBA, had him set up where he could access the office computer from home. As he reached for the light switch, the phone rang.

"Thought you'd be there," Sgt. Wick Stanley said. "You still have cop work habits."

"Just on my way out the door. Got to restock my beer cooler before the poker game."

"Good. I'll probably be thirsty."

"I just finished a Sam Adams. I'll have the usual variety. So what's the hot news in the West Precinct?"

Wick paused a beat. "That's really why I called."

"Oh?"

"Bart told me you were shaking the bushes on this Djuan Burden murder."

"I guess you could call it that. Jaz and I've been digging around for leads all day."

"Just thought I'd give you a word of warning."

Sid leaned back against his desk. "What have I done to deserve this?"

"Do you know a detective named Ramsey Kozlov? Sometimes known as Ram, though cops usually refer to each other by their last name."

"No."

"He's paired with Grimm on this case."

"Short fellow, young guy with a Clark Gable mustache?" It must have been the one he had seen on TV.

"You've met him."

"No, but Burden's grandmother mentioned he was with Grimm when they came to arrest the boy. What about him?"

"He's the son of Deputy Chief Kozlov. In my opinion he's a troublemaker. Maybe worse."

"Meaning?"

"I'd rather not get too specific. This comes under the heading of rumor. But informed rumor. The important thing, old dad is very protective."

"Okay, got it."

"If you ask me, Ram Kozlov is a predator. He likes to manipulate people. He's a watcher and a listener, always on the lookout for a deal. Just remember your training, Sid. Watch your ass and expect the worst."

8

JAZ THOUGHT ABOUT the case as she went through her exercise routine in the rec room Wednesday morning. She had always been athletic, battling to play boy games when she was a little girl. She took up basketball in high school, frowned upon by her mother but encouraged by her dad. It resulted in a college scholarship where she played on a championship team. After a new coach's incompetence and favoritism left the team in disarray, she quit in disgust and joined the Air Force, infuriating her elitist mother. An assignment with the Security Police sparked her interest in law enforcement.

After showering and dressing in a casual white shirt and tan slacks, she checked with John Wallace about a fallen tree on the back lawn. John had been in charge of maintenance and landscaping around the estate since Jaques LeMieux hired the couple more than thirty years ago. John told her the tree would soon be turned into logs for the large stone fireplace in the living room. With everything under control at home, she pointed her Lexus down the winding driveway toward Franklin Road and headed for Granny White Pike, the location of Ortiz and Valdez's apartment.

The street hardly resembled the old buffalo trail that ran south out of Nashville two centuries ago. It was named for a white-haired woman known as Granny White who, in her sixties, ran a popular inn along the trail until her death in 1815.

Now mostly residential except around David Lipscomb University, the street gradually changed from large, expensive homes out toward the county line to more modest houses the farther into town you drove. Jaz found Ortiz's address at a nondescript rectangular brick structure that hardly resembled the groups of modern buildings that comprised Nashville's newer rental communities. It had entrances on either end and a corridor down the middle, with apartments on both sides. Jaz thought it looked more like a motel than an apartment building. She found number 208 and moved on to number 210 before knocking.

An elderly woman with short white hair, wearing a yellow wool cardigan over her plain white dress, opened the door and gave her a curious look. She had a one word greeting. "Yes?"

Jaz held out her ID and gave the woman a friendly smile. "I'm Jasmine LeMieux, a private detective with Sid Chance Investigations. Are you acquainted with your neighbors in two-oh-eight?"

"He's dead and she's gone," the woman said.

Jaz was tempted to grin at the succinct reply but maintained her composure. "Do you mind if I ask you a few questions about them?"

She shrugged. "I guess not."

"Did you know them very well?"

"They weren't too neighborly. I don't think he ever talked to anybody. Missus Ortiz would speak to you now and then."

"How long had they lived here?"

"Six or eight months, I think."

"Did they say where they came from?"

"She mentioned something about Texas."

"What else did she talk about?"

The woman gave an open-handed gesture. "Everyday stuff. The weather, the price of grapes. Last time I talked to her, she was telling about some country singer she'd made friends with recently."

"Did she mention the singer's name?"

"It was a girl with some Mexican-sounding name. I'd never heard of her before. I don't care for country music." The woman cocked her head and squinted her eyes. "You know you ought to talk to the police. They were here a couple of days ago asking the same sorts of questions."

Jaz smiled. "You'd think that would be the simplest thing to do, but the police aren't too eager to share their information. We work for a law firm involved in the case. We have to conduct our own investigation."

"They say that boy murderer did it. Those people just can't be trusted."

Jaz decided it was advisable to take a different tack. "How did you know Elena Ortiz had left?"

"Saw her go out of here with her bag packed. Her car is gone, but his is still parked down there in the lot. Don't know if she's coming back or not."

"Which car belonged to Omar Valdez?"

"The gray SUV with the Arkansas license plate."

"Was there any talk about his coming from Arkansas?"

"Not that I heard."

"Did they have many friends drop by?"

"Nope. Like I said, they weren't very neighborly."

After getting a few more terse negative replies, Jaz decided she was unlikely to learn anything further. She thanked the woman for her help and went around knocking on a few other doors, getting no answer. She headed out to the parking area and searched for the gray SUV. It sat by itself off to one side. Though it appeared to be in good shape, it was not a recent model. She jotted down the license number and returned to her Lexus.

Sid answered as soon as she punched in his number. "Got a license tag to check out," she said.

"You find Ortiz?"

"No. I found Valdez's car, and I got a lead on where to look for Ortiz." She told him about her conversation with the neighbor.

"So we need to look for a Mexican-sounding country singer," Sid said.

"Sounds like the best way to go."

"I'll see what I can chase down on that. Why don't you ask Bart or Wick to run the tag number?"

"Will do."

"One other thing you need to know. Wick called me last night to warn about Detective Grimm's partner."

He told her about the rumors involving Detective Ramsey Kozlov.

"Oh, crap," she said. "I remember that one well. He came on the force before I left. He was one shifty cop, your best buddy one minute and your worst enemy the next. Thank God I never got tangled up with him. A friend on my shift did, though, and wound up transferred to a desk job. Ram's dad was a lieutenant back then, but he knew where all the bodies were buried and how to pull all the strings."

"That's what I suspected," Sid said. "Just keep your eyes open if we encounter him."

"Don't worry. I will."

Before starting her car, she called Bart Masterson.

"Hey, there, lady," he said in his usual breezy manner. "You ready for tomorrow tonight?"

"I'm always ready for the next good hand. I trust you plan to deal off the top of the deck this time?"

"Oooo...that cuts to the quick. You know I'm honest as the day is long."

She laughed. "I may do like your namesake and draw a six-shooter if you get out of line."

"Old Bat may have been a bit reckless as a lawman, but he damned sure knew how to handle the cards."

"How about putting on your lawman's hat for a moment and checking a tag number for us. It's from Arkansas." She read off the number for him.

"You guys are starting to work me harder than Metro."

"Just want to get our tax dollar's worth."

"Ha...with that big house you probably wouldn't get close. Let me run this and I'll get back to you."

Jaz was about to back out of the parking spot when a car pulled across behind her, blocking her path. As she looked around, she saw a short man with a small mustache separated in the middle walking toward her door. Although she hadn't seen him in years, she had no trouble recognizing Ramsey Kozlov. She lowered her window as he approached.

"Have I done something wrong, Detective?" she asked.

His cold black eyes made a stark contrast to the smile on his face, though she thought of it more as an evil grin. "Well, if it isn't my old police colleague, LeMieux."

"Detective Kozlov," she said, showing no emotion. "You've come up in the ranks."

"Not as much as you. But I can brag I knew her back when she was just a plain old patrolman. Which makes me wonder why you decided to start playing cop again?"

"You should know the answer to that. It gets in your blood. That's why you're still around, isn't it?"

He laughed. "Don't know about the blood, but it keeps money in my pocket."

Was that a Freudian slip? "What brings you here?"

"Same as you." He looked up at the apartment building. "Omar Valdez and his girlfriend lived here."

"And you know that Sid Chance and I are investigating the Valdez murder."

"That's right. I understand my partner got a little upset that you all were tinkering around in the case. I'm not concerned, though. I'm sure you haven't found anything of importance we didn't already know about. In fact, I can't imagine why you're even bothering with it, it's such a clear-cut case of murder."

She stared at him with the hint of a smile. "You really don't know why we're doing this?"

"Nope."

"Then let me enlighten you. The way you and Detective Grimm have manipulated the facts in this case is a clear invitation for someone to step in and set the record straight."

His mood shifted from sociable to antagonistic. "*Your* record seems pretty straight, LeMieux. I've read all about the way you treated that black woman at your truck stop."

"That's another example of manipulation."

"Yeah. You manipulated the hell out of her, didn't you?"

Jaz drew in a deep breath. She didn't have time to count to ten. "We're sure she was paid to do that. It was a setup, just like what you're doing to Djuan Burden."

"You're full of shit, lady. You'd better wise up to the fact that things are different now than when you were on the force."

"You get away with whatever you want, huh?"

His eyes narrowed to slits. "I'd hate to see those pretty teeth slammed back into your mouth. It could happen if you don't stay out of the way."

He stalked back toward his car, climbed in, and sped off.

Bart Masterson called about the time she arrived home to report the car in the parking lot was registered to Omar Valdez in Little Rock ten months ago using a fictitious address.

Though it made her wonder, Jaz was not surprised at that bit of detail. A veteran homicide detective, Bart taught a basic criminology class at the local community college.

"How did you find out the address was fictitious?" she asked

"I called a buddy in the Little Rock PD and asked him to run the tag for me and see if they had anything on Valdez. He said he didn't find any record on the guy, but he noticed the address listed for his registration was nonexistent. I'd pass that along to Grimm, but I doubt he'd give a big fat rats' ass."

"Not if it might throw a cloud on his case."

"Yeah. Y'know, it's a real shame how the job has messed him up. When Grimm first came to Homicide, he wasn't a bad guy. Had a tendency to be bossy, but he took an interest in people, delivered groceries we'd collect at Thanksgiving and Christmas. After a few years of working homicides, he seemed to harden like a block of ice. All he cared about was getting convictions, whatever it took."

"I just had an encounter with his partner, Ram Kozlov," Jaz said. "He made some nasty threats if I don't stay out of his way. I'm determined they're not going to get a conviction on this one. Have you heard anything from your TBI contact?"

"I'll try to have something for you tomorrow night. But I'd steer clear of Kozlov. He's bad news."

9

BACK IN JANUARY, Sid had located a long lost cousin for Art Yancey, a producer on Music Row. Yancey sounded like his best bet for finding information about a country singer with a Mexican-sounding name. A call to the music executive's office brought word that he was in a recording session and wouldn't be out until around lunchtime.

Sid used the morning to work on his new missing heir assignment. It involved a woman in her thirties whose last known address was in Kansas City. That had been nearly twenty years ago. He saw it as a challenge and an opportunity to hone his search skills. The satisfaction of uniting people concerned over each other's whereabouts for years made the job extra rewarding. He began by surfing the databases, utility and courthouse records, both online and by telephone.

Jaz called around eleven to report her conversation with Bart.

Sid thought about it for a moment. "If Valdez used a fictitious address in Little Rock, I wonder how much else about him is fake?"

"Good question."

"Didn't you mention having a friend who recently went to work for the Medical Examiner?"

"An old college basketball teammate."

"Is she an M.D.?"

"A forensic pathologist. Her husband is also a doctor. They

moved here when he got a position with the Vanderbilt School of Medicine."

"How about giving her a call and see what the autopsy showed, where they sent the body?"

Jaz paused. "If she'll agree to talk. We haven't been all that close in years. I did take them out to dinner when they first came to Nashville. Wanted to introduce them to the town as I know it."

"Can't hurt to try."

"I'll check with her and see what happens."

"Good. I hope to catch my music producer client, Art Yancey, at lunchtime and see if he can steer me to the Mexican singer Elena Ortiz's neighbor mentioned. Let's compare notes this afternoon."

Sid drove along Music Row West, known to most Nashvillians as Seventeenth Avenue, past record companies, music publishers, licensing firms, recording studios, and dozens of other music-related businesses. Some occupied vintage residences, others were located in fancy new office buildings. He pulled into the parking lot where Art Yancey worked and found a vacant slot. He entered the reception area and asked for the producer.

"He was just through here a few minutes ago," a pert redhead said. "Let me find him. What was your name?" Sid handed her a business card. She spent a few moments on the phone, then smiled at him. "He'll be right out."

A modest-sized man with unruly brown hair and a restless manner of moving about strode into the room. He grinned when he saw Sid.

"I was thinking about you last night," he said. "I had another long chat with my cousin. We're planning a trip to Cozumel, on the Yucatan Peninsula, this summer. I sure appreciate your finding him for me. We were really close as kids."

"Glad I could do it," Sid said.

Yancey's expression sobered. "Is anything wrong? You got my check, didn't you?"

Sid grinned. "Sure did. Thanks. The reason I dropped by is I've got a little project you might be able to help me with."

The producer looked relieved. "Hey, anything you need. Come on back to the office."

He led the way to a small room with a desk, a few chairs, an electronic keyboard and all sorts of audio equipment, plus a large flat screen TV monitor. He slipped behind the desk and Sid took one of the chairs.

"Whatcha got?" Yancey asked.

"I'm trying to find a woman for an investigation we're involved in. The only clue I have is she told a neighbor she had a friend who's a country singer with a Mexican-sounding name."

"Was the singer male or female?"

"Female."

Yancey tapped his fingers for a moment. The slim, articulate fingers of a musician. "Nothing comes to mind in that category. Of course, we have no shortage of Mexicans around Nashville."

The recent census had showed Nashville with more Hispanics than any other city in Tennessee, the state with the highest percentage increase during the past decade.

"Lots of them in Madison where I live," Sid said.

"She's most likely an aspiring singer. Wannabe's appear along Music Row like cicadas popping out of the ground." Nashville would be deluged in a couple of months with the thirteen-year variety of the insects and their incessant buzzing. Yancey chuckled. "I'll have to say the singers have a lot more pleasant sound."

"You have to listen to a lot of them?"

"I only get the ones recommended by somebody in the industry. Band leaders, studios, backup musicians."

"I guess if you're lucky you find one who turns into a hit maker."

"And if you don't, you turn into another guy with a guitar pounding the pavement along Sixteenth and Seventeenth Avenues."

"I don't want to put you to any trouble," Sid said, "but could you ask around, see if anybody has run across a singer recently with a Hispanic name?"

"Sure. No problem. There's a big party Friday night over at Loews Vanderbilt—music people are about the biggest partygoers around—and everybody who's anybody should be there. I'll see what I can find."

Back in the car, Sid called Jaz's cell phone.

"Where are you?" he asked.

"At the company office. I came by to check on a couple of things."

"Want to meet me for lunch at South Street?"

"Ahh...we're making amends."

"Just a normal business luncheon. We were going to compare notes, remember?"

"Will I have to talk to Mike Rich and get him to release a little cash for you?"

In addition to being Sid's financial adviser, Mike had been a friend of Jaques LeMieux and also handled Jaz's investments.

Sid grinned, knowing she couldn't see it. "I think my credit card can handle it."

"Okay. How does one o'clock sound?"

"I'll be there."

Its official name was South Street Original Smokehouse, Crab

Shack and Authentic Dive Bar. The rambling, triangular shaped building sat on Twentieth Avenue South near Vanderbilt University. Crowded by large trees, it featured a Tree House Oyster Bar on top. A marquee-like red signboard ran the length of the structure in front, emblazoned with such tasty delights as shellfish, ribs and PoBoys. Sid arrived a little before one, saw nothing of Jaz's car, and strolled into the restaurant.

A few people waited near the door. Sid checked with the hostess and headed back outside. With the sun hidden behind billowing clouds, the day had taken on a look as dull as pewter. A chill hung in the air. He walked to the pointed end of the building, adjacent to the parking lot, and soon spotted the red Lexus turning off Division Street. She paused while someone backed out of a nearby spot, then eased into it. As she walked toward him, Sid grinned at the confident stride, the sure step of a woman in her prime, in full control.

"Right on time," he said, ushering her toward the door.

"Do I get extra points for punctuality?"

"'I know no point to which she sticks; She begs the simplest questions.'"

"Oh, brother. Who wrote that?"

"Alfred Cochrane, English cricket player, sports writer, and creator of humorous verse."

"Never heard of him."

"Not a lot of people have. He was a contemporary of P.G. Wodehouse but hardly as prolific with the pen."

"If you say so."

As soon as they entered, the hostess walked up and smiled. "Your table is ready, Mr. Chance."

Jaz arched her brow. "I'm impressed."

They were seated next to a wall of windows divided into smaller panes. Afternoon traffic rumbled along the street below. Sid opened his menu and glanced at it, grinning as always at the location statement:

CONVENIENTLY LOCATED BETWEEN GRACELAND AND GATLINBURG

"Would you like something from the bar?" a cute blonde waitress asked.

"I'll have a glass of Cabernet Sauvignon," Jaz said.

Sid cut his eyes. "No South Street Rita or Red Snapper?"

"You know I'm not a hard liquor girl. I'm a wino. What are you having?"

He looked up at the waitress. "Do you have Sam Adams?"

"I think we can find one for you," the girl said with a smile.

After she left, Sid related the details of his discussion with Art Yancey.

"So we're stuck on that score until after the Music Row party?" Jaz asked.

"Looks that way. Did you talk with your Medical Examiner friend?"

"I did. Her name is Reagan Abrams. She was reluctant to talk about it at first, but after I explained the situation, she loosened up a bit. She said they placed the time of death around three-thirty. As you suspected, the bullet ricocheted about the skull. It destroyed his brain, killing him immediately. She said the lead wound up considerably misshapen."

"Might prevent ballistics from getting a match."

"Maybe Bart can tell us tonight. Reagan said Elena Ortiz arranged for the body to be sent to Spring Valley Funeral Home."

"Did she say when they released the body?"

"I understood it was just done today."

"Good. I'll check with the funeral home and see what kind of contact info they have on Ortiz."

The waitress brought their drinks and took orders. Jaz

chose the shrimp platter. Sid opted for a crabcake sandwich and a large salad, which he said would help maintain his girlish figure.

"I haven't seen too many six-foot-six girls around," Jaz said.

"Were you a basketball player?" the waitress asked.

"I played football in high school." He pointed to Jaz. "She's the athlete. She not only played big league basketball, she was a champion boxer."

"Really?" Her eyes widened.

"That was a long time ago," Jaz said.

"You don't see me challenging her to a match," Sid said. He had absorbed one of her non-lethal punches when she showed her displeasure over one of his stupid decisions.

After the waitress left, Jaz took a sip of wine and looked across at Sid. "Why don't you call the funeral home while we're waiting?"

He looked around. The crowd was thinning out, leaving a decent space between them and the nearest occupied table. He didn't like having others privy to his conversations. "I'd have to check information for the number."

"Not if you used up-to-date technology," she said, pulling out her smartphone. She slipped out the mini-keyboard and punched in the information. "Here's the number for Spring Valley."

He entered the numbers on his phone as she read them out. When the funeral home answered, he asked for a funeral director he had met there on a previous case. A new voice soon came on the line.

"This is Sid Chance," he said. "We talked not long ago about the Gladstone burial."

"Sure, I remember you. You're the big guy who's a private eye."

Sid recalled the undertaker as a small man with a big mustache. He figured the contrast likely gave himself the appearance of giant proportions. "That's me. I'm told by the Medical Examiner that you have the body of Omar Valdez, the murder victim from last Monday. Do you have funeral arrangements yet?"

"There won't be any funeral."

Sid frowned. "How so?"

"His fiancée, Miz Ortiz, signed all the papers to have the body cremated. The remains will be transported to Texas."

Sid squinted his eyes in disbelief. Miz Ortiz was full of surprises. He thought of what they had learned about her background. "Shipped to San Antonio?"

"Right. The Alamo Mortuary."

"Did she give a local contact address?"

"No. I understood she was leaving town. She paid for everything in cash, said she had closed her bank account."

What did this mean, Sid wondered? Was the cremation intended to hide something, or was it designed to keep Ortiz from being in the spotlight, allow her to fade out of the picture?

"You mentioned ashes." Jaz said after he had ended the conversation. "What's going on?"

He told her what he had learned about Valdez's fate and Elena Ortiz's apparent plans to skip town.

"As you predicted, it looks like she's headed back to San Antonio," Jaz said. "If we need to go down there and search for her, we could bum a ride on our company plane. It makes frequent trips to Houston for oil industry contacts. I can check and see if there's one coming up."

"Let's hold off on that for now. I'm not so sure she's left Nashville. If this murder is related to the Medicare fraud, Ortiz might be as much at risk as Valdez. If she had been at that store Monday afternoon, she could have wound up dead, too."

The waitress stopped to inquire if they needed drink refills and said their food would be ready shortly.

"I see what you mean," Jaz said. "She could be hiding from a potential murderer as much as from the cops."

"Right. And whoever was after her would probably know about her Texas connection. She might feel safer hiding out here."

Jaz appeared to contemplate this new turn of events as she toyed with her wine glass. "Your man Yancey may be our only hope."

Back in his office, Sid got a call from Special Agent Baron Eggers.

"Just touching bases to see what you've come up with on the Prime Medical Equipment case," the FBI agent said.

"Did you hear they were cremating Omar Valdez's body?" Sid asked.

"Yeah, and Elena Ortiz has pulled a disappearing act. We have Metro keeping an eye out for her car."

"I hadn't checked into what she drives," Sid said.

"It's a two-thousand and nine white Toyota Carolla. She bought it before coming to Nashville, but it has Tennessee plates."

"Do you think she's still in Nashville?"

"Could be, but our people in Texas are looking for her, also. How's your murder investigation going?"

"We're looking into the likelihood that someone left the store by the rear door about the time Djuan Burden came in the front entrance."

"Interesting. Got any suspects?"

"No. I'm stymied at the moment. I was hoping to find someone who might have seen him in the alley, but nothing so far."

"Good luck with it. We're still tracking down Omar Valdez's background. Seems he came from Albuquerque, but he hasn't used his Social Security number around here, so he's obviously been camouflaging his movements."

"What about his driver's license?" Sid asked.

"It was a fake."

"Did Metro tell you that?"

He laughed. "Grimm hadn't checked it."

"Was it from Tennessee?"

"No, Arkansas."

"His car was registered in Little Rock with a bogus address."

"Where did you find his car?" Eggers had a note of excitement in his voice.

"It was parked in front of his apartment this morning."

"On Granny White Pike?"

"Right."

"Thanks. Let's keep in touch." He sounded anxious to get moving.

10

THURSDAY MORNING Sid sat at his desk, staring at the windowless wall at one side as if all the answers to his questions might suddenly appear there. He knew that wasn't likely, though, as the montage of photos assembled on the wall represented his triple careers as a Green Beret in Vietnam, a National Park ranger for nineteen years, and as police chief in Lewisville for a decade. But he also knew all that experience should count for something.

Considering what they knew about Omar Valdez, it just didn't add up. Some element was missing from the equation. He ticked off all the facts they had gathered about the man, which amounted to a pitiful few. None of it triggered any flashes of insight.

Sid turned his attention to the missing heir case, hoping the distraction might allow some insight to float up from his subconscious. He'd hardly opened the file when Quint Nevins, the tire store manager, called.

"Sorry if I led you astray," Nevins said. "I didn't think about the fact that one of my guys was off Tuesday when you came by. He was talking to one of his buddies this morning and learned that I had asked if anybody saw anything across the alley that afternoon. Seems he did."

Sid felt a surge of excitement. "What did he see?"

"He couldn't remember what time it was, just along the middle of the afternoon."

Sid gripped the phone. "And?"

"He said a man came out the back door and got in a car parked near the dumpster."

"Did the man appear to be in a hurry?"

"He didn't mention that. Just said the car started up and drove off down the alley."

"What kind of car?"

"He wasn't sure. Said it was shiny black. That's all I know."

"Thanks. Give me your guy's name. We may need to talk to him later."

Sid jotted the name on a pad, turned the phone off, then called Jaz. "Looks like we have a break, tenuous as it is."

"What happened?"

He told her about the mechanic's sighting.

"Wish I knew one of these psychologist types who can hypnotize people and come up with details they didn't know they'd seen."

"Yeah," Sid said, "that would be nice, but I'm afraid that's wishful thinking. We could go back out there and look around the area for possible clues."

"After three days, it would be highly unlikely we'd find anything. Particularly since we have no idea what to look for. I could stop by there on my way to your office this afternoon and check it out."

"Okay. Just don't be late for the game."

After lunch, Sid got a call from Hardy Vandenberg at Bailey, Riddle and Smith. "Have you caught the murderer yet, Mr. Chance?" he asked.

Sid didn't like the way the lawyer put the question. "We aren't ready to arrest anyone, but we have a report of a man exiting the rear of the building around the time of the murder."

"Any identification?"

"He left in a black car, but that's all we have."

"I hardly think that will be enough. The District Attorney is ready to go to the Grand Jury with this case. The forensics laboratory reports the gun found at Mrs. Ransom's house had been fired recently."

It was the information he had dreaded getting. He was at a loss to explain it, considering what Burden's grandmother had told them and what they had learned about the man leaving the medical supply store by the rear door. Regardless, he realized he needed to call his client and report what they had done so far. As soon as he identified himself, Rachel Ransom asked about her grandson.

"Did you talk to Djuan? How's he taking it?"

"We saw him Tuesday afternoon," Sid said. "He was depressed, but he's a strong young man. I think he'll hold up okay."

"Have you found anything that might prove he didn't shoot that fellow?"

"Nothing conclusive, but we have some leads to follow."

He told her what they had learned at the medical equipment store, about the man seen leaving through the rear door."

The elderly woman's voice sounded more animated. "Do you think he's the one who fired the shot?"

"Yes, and we're working to gather the evidence to prove it. Have you thought of anything else that might be of help?"

She paused as if uncertain. "I don't know if it means anything, but I was thinking this morning about something I heard those detectives talking about after they found George's gun."

"What was it?"

"They were in my bedroom and I had walked back that way to see what they were doing. I stopped just outside the door. I saw they'd been going through my cedar chest. It must have been right after they found the gun. The big man was talking in a low voice, but I could hear him all right."

"What did he say?" Sid asked, trying not to sound impatient.

"He said something about it looking like an old gun, would it still work? And the other fella said sure, when we get away from here I'll demonstrate. As soon as they saw me, they got real quiet and acted like they were embarrassed."

Sid wasn't sure how to take that observation. Had Mrs. Ransom really just remembered it this morning, and realized it might be significant, or was she giving her grandson a way out if the gun proved to have been fired recently, which it had? He wanted to believe she hadn't lied to them about any of this, but he just didn't know. If it had happened the way she described, the implications were startling.

When he mentioned the cremation plans for Omar Valdez and that the victim's partner, Elena Ortiz, was missing, Mrs. Ransom posed a hopeful question.

"Will that help Djuan?"

"I don't know. It may indicate the murder had something to do with them being involved in a Medicare fraud scheme, but we have a lot more digging to do."

"I wish there was something I could do to help."

"Just keep giving him your support," Sid said. "He's afraid you'll think he let you down."

"I'll straighten him out about that when I go see him tomorrow. I've been praying for him. For you, too, Mr. Chance. I pray you'll find who really did this."

Sid put the phone back on his desk with the hope that he'd prove worthy of her prayers.

LATE THAT AFTERNOON, Sid scurried about preparing the reception area for the Miss Demeanor and Five Felons Poker Club session. He brought out a round folding table from the supply room and set it up after pushing the furniture against the wall. He was dragging out the beer cooler when the door opened and retired reporter Jack Post and former Criminal Court Judge Gabriel Thackston walked in. Post doffed his ever-present felt hat and looked around.

"You mean we beat the Police Department?" His round, owlish face bore a slight smile. A short, stocky man in his seventies, he had covered police beats for both Nashville and Memphis newspapers.

Sid glanced at his watch. "You're a few minutes early. How's it going with you, Judge?"

"I can't complain," Thackston said. "Every day brings a new set of problems. The legal profession is as disordered as ever."

"Are you familiar with *The Devil's Dictionary*?"

Thackston nodded. "Written by Ambrose Bierce?"

"Right. He defined litigation as a machine which you go into as a pig and come out a sausage."

Post bent over laughing.

"Come on, Jack," Sid said. "It wasn't that funny."

"Not the joke. The Judge's face."

Thackston did the rolling eye gesture, rubbed a hand over his prematurely white hair and took his seat in the usual place. Each player had a traditional seat which was considered bad luck to change. A few minutes later, Jaz arrived, followed by Bart Masterson and Wick Stanley. Everyone exchanged greetings while Sid passed out beers for the guys and a Coke for Jaz. She had never cultivated a taste for the brew.

"I suppose you know Jaz and I are working with a couple of Arnie Bailey's guys on the Djuan Burden case," Sid said after everyone had taken their seats.

"News to me," Post said. He pushed his fedora back to reveal a widening stretch of slick scalp.

"You must be out of the loop these days," the Judge said. "I picked up hints of it around the Courthouse."

"Do you want to talk about it here?" Bart asked, a note of caution in his voice. The lanky six-footer leaned his elbows on the table.

Sid rumpled his brow. "Frankly, we can use all the help we can get. The lawyers tell me ballistics reports indicate the gun had been fired recently."

"I find that un-believable," Jaz said, dragging out the word.

"I don't think the TBI lab has any interest in fabricating test results," Bart said. "I suppose there is some good news, though. The bullet was in too bad a shape to identify the gun it came from. Also the weapon had been wiped clean of any prints."

Sid picked up the new deck of cards he'd laid on the table and shuffled it absently. "That sounds odd. You wouldn't think Mrs. Ransom would have wiped it clean."

"I could tell she's a very tidy housekeeper," Jaz said. "Tell them about the sighting behind the building."

"Yeah, that's our most promising lead." He turned to Jack Post. "Remember, none of this goes outside this room."

Post shrugged. "I know."

"Burden recalls a box falling off a stack in the doorway to the back room of the medical supply store. He saw it right when he came in. He also smelled gunpowder. Then he heard a clicking noise in the back like a door being closed, which we took as an indication the murderer had just left. Turns out a mechanic at a tire store around the corner saw a man come out the rear door and get into a car around the same time."

Wick Stanley, dressed in his habitual blue jeans and Titans jacket, perked up. "Did he give you a good vehicle description?"

"Just a black car."

"Bummer," Wick said. Sid figured the twenty-five-year

veteran patrol officer could empathize, having encountered his share of myopic witnesses.

Jaz folded her hands and tapped her thumbs. "I went by there this afternoon and searched around the area between the back door and a trash dumpster. That's where the mechanic saw the car. I didn't find anything useful."

"I'm familiar with the area," Wick said. "There's a bank on the corner, if the car went in that direction. Some of our guys moonlight as bank security guards, but even if they were outside, they wouldn't have noticed a car going by unless it had done something unusual."

"Doesn't look like we can help you out on that score," Bart said. "Any other loose ends we might be able to tidy up?"

"There's a woman we'd like to question, if we could find her. Name is Elena Ortiz. She was apparently a partner and probably lover of Omar Valdez."

"We got a BOLO on her," Wick said.

Sid pushed the cards to the middle of the table. "The FBI asked for it. They're also looking for her in Texas, but I have a hunch she's hiding out around Nashville."

"You are an astute observer of the darker arts, Sidney," the Judge said in his best courtroom demeanor. "Surely you have some idea of where this lady might be concealing herself." Thackston had been an erudite jurist, well thought of until he got voted out of office after reports of injudicious sexual behavior.

Sid told them what Jaz had learned from Ortiz's neighbor about the country music singer with a "Mexican-sounding name" and that a music producer believed she was probably a wannabe.

"Wick and I may be able to help," Bart said after emptying a roll of quarters onto the table. "We're frequently in contact with the Mexican community. We could get our Spanish-speaking officers to ask around, too. We have a unit called El Protector that works with the Hispanics."

Thackson cleared his throat noisily and turned to his male cohorts. "Before we get started, gentlemen, I think we should express our full support for Jasmine in her time of trial. We know that what has been alleged against her is pure rubbish. She, of all people, has demonstrated her unquestioned loyalty to people of African-American heritage."

"Amen," Wick said.

"Thank you, Judge," Jaz said with a pained smile. "It has been distressing, but I'm coping. I appreciate you guys' support." She picked up the cards. "Now let's get down to business."

She spread out the cards and each in turn chose one and turned it face up. Sid's ace took the deal. He wondered if this might be a good omen?

THE GAME ENDED around ten when Sgt. Stanley had to head home and get ready for his shift in the West Precinct. Jack Post wound up with the largest pile of quarters. It left him in an unusually gleeful mood for a born skeptic. After Jaz helped tidy up his office, Sid locked the door and walked out to the parking lot with her.

"I hope you didn't lose too much," he said.

She laughed. "I think I have enough left for lunch tomorrow."

"Good. Did you come up with any new insights into our case?"

"It would really help if we could find somebody else who saw that car behind Prime Medical."

"I agree. I may take another run by there tomorrow and look around," Sid said as Jaz opened the door of her Lexus. "And I'm going to question that mechanic myself. Take care."

Jaz shook her head with a grin as she slid onto the seat. He knew what she was thinking. She had expressed it often enough: quit worrying about me; I'm a big girl perfectly capable of taking care of myself. Which he knew was true, but she was a special person.

As Sid pulled out of the parking lot, he noticed a car approach slowly on the street behind him. With the mall closed, the area saw little traffic this time of night. When he stopped to turn onto Gallatin Road, he recognized it as the same model Dodge used by Metro detectives. Driving toward the Neelys Bend section where he lived in the home his mother had left him, Sid caught an image in the mirror he felt sure was the same car, though it lagged back a respectable distance.

Sid's house sat near the street's dead end at the Cumberland River. He pulled into the driveway far enough for the sensor to trigger the eve lights to come on. It was part of the security system he had beefed up after a nasty experience that plagued a previous case. Normally he would have circled around to the garage in back, but he stopped in the driveway as the car eased to a halt near the mailbox. He opened the door, stepped out, and looked back to see the window on the car's passenger side lowering.

As he approached, he saw Detective Victor Grimm's face displaying a surly half-smile. In the dim light he could barely make out Ramsey Kozlov behind the wheel.

"Looks like you've been waiting for me," Sid said as he walked up.

"Just thought we'd bring you up-to-date on the situation, Mr. Chance. It looks like all that nosing around you've been doing was in vain."

"How do you figure that?"

"The great homicide investigator Sidney Chance has been digging in a dry hole. We wanted to let you know there's no point in your continuing to muddy the water around town."

"Besides tossing around clichés, Detective, what news do you bring?"

"The DA is ready to feed Burden to the Grand Jury. The TBI forensics people say their tests show Burden's gun was fired recently after he claimed it hadn't been."

"A slight correction, Detective Grimm," Sid said in a pedantic tone. "Djuan Burden said *he* had not fired the gun. His grandmother confirmed there was no way he could have returned the gun to her cedar chest after he got back from the medical equipment store."

"She's an old woman. She's obviously mistaken."

"I think not." The words could have been coated in ice. It had suddenly come together in his mind, Grimm's confident gloating and the conversation between the detectives Rachel Ransom had heard, her insistence that Djuan could not have had possession of the gun.

The detective's face reddened. "Then who the hell pulled the trigger on that gun?"

Sid had never been more sure than he was now.

"I think you know the answer to that, Detective. Mrs. Ransom heard your partner say he could demonstrate that the gun still worked."

Sid turned abruptly and stalked back toward his car.

"You can't prove shit!" Grimm screamed.

Sid slammed the door, started his car, and raced down the driveway, almost skidding off the pavement as he turned toward the garage. He breathed hard as the anger churned in his stomach. He was ready to fight dragons to prove Djuan Burden's innocence.

11

FRIDAY MORNING, Sid drove to Green Hills and stopped at the tire store. He figured a personal interview with the mechanic should be more productive than a second-hand report from the manager. He hit it lucky this time. The worker who had spotted the murder suspect was not tied up on a rush job. Sid talked to him in the service bay beside a grease-stained work bench. A short man with a paunch he'd have difficulty maneuvering beneath a car chassis, the mechanic appeared eager to help.

"I remember seeing him come out over there," he said as he wiped grime from his hands on a blue shop rag.

"Could you describe him for me?" Sid asked.

"I couldn't really tell how big he was, but he looked to be more my size than yours."

"How was he dressed?"

He twisted his mouth in thought. "Best I remember he had on dark clothes. Like maybe blue jeans and a dark jacket."

"What about a hat?"

"Nope, don't think so."

"Could you see any facial features?"

"No, he was too far away for that."

"You said the car was black. Remember anything else about it?"

"May have been a Ford. Could've been a Chevy. Looked shiny new, though."

"And it drove off toward the bank at the other end of the alley?"

"Yeah."

"Okay, thanks," Sid said and headed back to his car. It wasn't a lot, but it was more than he'd coaxed out of the manager.

The weather had taken a turn for the better. A beaming sun now cast sharp shadows as it drifted higher in the sky. Spring had begun to cut a colorful swath across Nashville with the awakening of redbuds, Bradford pears with their snow-like petals, and the first shoots of soon-to-follow dogwoods, both pink and white. Sid lowered the window as the sun had already left the car stuffy.

Before he pulled away from the tire store, he got out his phone and called Jaz. She was just leaving for a meeting at the company office with a group of Welcome Home Store managers from across the country. They were all concerned about false accusations against the chairman.

"I got a little more info on our killer," he said, covering what he'd learned from the mechanic. "I also have some more sobering news," he added.

After listening to his description of last night's encounter with Grimm and Kozlov, she spoke in an incredulous voice. "You think those detectives fired Mrs. Ransom's pistol?"

"I don't have any doubts about it, especially after what Rachel Ransom heard them say. But as Grimm bellowed at me, there's no possible way I could prove it."

"I can't believe a policeman would stoop that low."

"Believe it, Jaz. I suspect Kozlov might be the more culpable, according to what Wick said. They're both into it."

"That's disgusting. This racism business plus these dirty cops is really getting to me, Sid. Maybe a little shopping spree at the mall would put me in a better mood. I think I'll head out that way after my meeting. Do you have any other ideas I can pursue?"

"Not at the moment. Hit the mall and enjoy yourself."

THE MEETING LASTED longer than she'd anticipated and it was late afternoon before Jaz could get away. She drove out Hillsboro Pike along with several hundred other homebound workers and pulled into the garage at the Green Hills mall. She found a parking spot near an entrance to Macy's and sauntered in. As she wandered through the stores, picking through bargains in clothes and jewelry, her problems with the Welcome Home Stores employee and the Burden case drifted out of her mind. She stopped in an electronics shop and checked out the latest techno gadgets, browsed in a fragrance shop, and spent a little time looking at shoes. In the end she wound up with a couple of blouses and a pair of slacks. Toting her shopping bags, she took the escalator back down to the floor that opened onto the garage.

After pulling out onto the street, she decided to make a last reconnoitering run past Prime Medical Equipment. Twilight had settled in while she wandered about the mall, and now the street lights had come on. They cast a soft glow that painted thin yellow lines on the walkways where signposts stood along Hillsboro Pike. She drove slowly past the small strip center and turned in at the corner. That was when she noticed the bank Wick Stanley had mentioned was a branch of Hattie Jordan's employer.

Jaz drove around to the back and pulled in. There was a drive-in window accessible from the alley, also an ATM machine. She let her gaze roam over the structure until she found a small camera mounted where it would likely pick up an image from the alley. She pulled out her phone and called Hattie.

"Hi, this is Hattie. I'm not available—did I say that? Leave me a message and see."

Jaz snickered. She never knew what to expect from her friend. She left a message asking for a return call.

JAZ SAT IN HER REC room facing the large screen TV. She had redone the room since her father's death, removing all but one of the casino card tables. She kept the wet bar and added exercise equipment. She had just turned on the ten o'clock news when Hattie called.

"Been having a night on the town?" Jaz asked.

"Thought I had a hot date, but it didn't turn out so hot."

"Wrong guy?"

"Too possessive. Nice dinner, though."

"Wasn't all bad then."

"Hey, girl, I can always make sausage out of a sow's ear."

Jaz laughed. "That sounds like a pretty mixed metaphor, Hattie. Doesn't the saying have something to do with a silk purse? Before you get me any more mixed up, let me ask you something."

"Be my guest."

"Do you keep the tapes from your branch surveillance cameras for awhile?"

"We keep the digital files for ninety days."

"So if a car passed one last Monday afternoon, you should be able to find it?"

"Give me the time and the place."

"It's the one in Green Hills down the block from the former Prime Medical Equipment store."

She told Hattie about the black car a mechanic had seen going down the alley toward the bank around the time of the murder.

"And when was that?" Hattie asked.

"Based on the nine-one-one call, approximately three-thirty Monday afternoon."

"Shouldn't be any problem to find, but I can't guarantee what it'll show of the car."

"I studied the setup when I was by there earlier tonight," Jaz said. "According to my calculations, it might even show the license plate."

"Don't bet your boobies on it, baby girl."

"Don't worry. That's where I draw the line on wagering."

Hattie had a raucous laugh that would trigger a seismograph. When it diminished, she said, "You're too much, Jazzie. How soon do you need this great spycraft revelation?"

"Would it be possible to do something tomorrow?"

"Sorry, I'll be gone all day tomorrow. How about Sunday? After noon. My momma'd be all over me if I missed church."

They agreed to meet at the bank Sunday afternoon at one. When Hattie was off the line, Jaz called Sid to advise him of the plan.

"I have some news for you," she said on a hopeful note. "It may be a break. May not. We'll just have to wait and see."

"What have you got?"

"I went shopping at the mall this evening and afterward took a look at the bank Wick mentioned, the one at the end of the alley behind Prime Medical."

She told him what Hattie Jordan said about the surveillance tapes, that she would be there Sunday at one.

"I agree with Hattie. I wouldn't get my hopes up too much," Sid said. "But I'll be there."

12

SATURDAY WAS NO different than any other day for Sid Chance. Up early, he donned his sweats and headed out for his morning run. This early rising and physical conditioning routine dated back to his time in Army Special Forces. After Vietnam, his love of the outdoors led to a career with the National Park Service. The years had not dimmed his delight in the crisp morning air that greeted him as he began his trek around the neighborhood. His mood was buoyed by Jaz's news last night regarding the possibility of finding something on the bank's surveillance footage.

While most people slept, Sid ran through the quiet streets past modest ranch style houses like his own, as well as more elegant homes with fancier cars in the driveways, primarily along the riverfront. He knew the sun had risen when landscape details sharpened, but the sky remained a dark, murky void. He settled into a quickened pace, his lungs filling with the ripeness of the spring air. By the time he finished his four miles, the anger that lingered from rehashing the Grimm/Kozlov incident had given way to the exhaustion of a strenuous workout.

He languished under the shower, dressed, and ate breakfast, feeling renewed and ready to tackle whatever lay ahead. Since it was too early to deal with a sleeping public on a Saturday morning, he went into his home office and booted up his computer. Jaz had copied him on everything she had dug up regarding Omar Valdez, Elena Ortiz, and Prime Medical Equipment. He started going through all the notes, including his own, looking for anything he might have overlooked the first time around.

When he reviewed what he had learned about Valdez from Agent Eggers and the funeral director, he was struck by a feeling that he might be looking at something he couldn't see. As he read on, he kept checking the clock and wondering if he dared call Art Yancey yet.

At around seven-thirty, the phone rang. He grabbed it off the desk and answered it.

"Good morning, Sid," said the familiar voice, "this is Art. I hope this isn't too early for you. I remember your telling about your early morning runs."

"Just sitting here at my desk. I've been up for hours."

'Well, I have something for you."

"Great. You found a girl singer?"

"She's only been in Nashville a short while. That's why I hadn't heard of her. She's Cuban, comes from Miami."

"What's her name?"

"Rosario Diaz. She plays a flamenco guitar and wants to adapt the style to country music. She says flamenco came from Southern Spain, so why wouldn't it work in the Southern U.S.?"

"What do you think?" Sid asked.

Yancey laughed. "I'm not so sure you can combine the two, but in this business, you never know what will catch on next. The way some of our country stars have caught on in Hollywood never ceases to amaze me."

More classically inclined than country, Sid voiced a philosophical view. "I think every music genre has the power to move people in one way or another."

"You know the old saying, 'music soothes the savage beast.'"

Sid chuckled. "Actually, that's a popular misquote. William

Congreve, the English playwright and poet, wrote: 'Music has charms to soothe a savage *breast.*'"

"You're getting too literary for me."

"No problem. I think the idea works both ways, breast or beast. Did you get an address for Rosario Diaz?"

"She lives in the Greystone Apartments on Bell Road. Apartment Twenty-two Thirteen."

When he got off the phone, Sid called Jaz. She sounded a bit sleepy but said it was time to get up. He gave her the good news on Rosario Diaz.

"We'd better get busy where things look promising. If Elena Ortiz is hiding out with Rosario Diaz, I'll find her. Greystone Apartments isn't all that far from me. I'll go check her out as soon as I can get some breakfast. Do you have a phone number?"

"Yes, I do, but it would probably be best to hit her cold. You can get a better reading on her reactions that way. Good luck."

JAZ DRESSED CASUALLY in a stylish denim jacket and blue jeans. She drove south on Franklin Road to Old Hickory Boulevard, then followed the circumferential highway as it crossed the southern section of Nashville until it changed names to Bell Road. Her mind buzzed away at putting together a plausible story for the interview as she drove.

The Greystone Apartments occupied a hillside site, a group of two-story wood-and-brick buildings with entrances for each cluster of apartments. The heavy overcast gave the complex a gray look as Jaz parked in front of the 2200 building and gazed about for a white 2009 Carolla. She saw none.

After walking up the wooden stairway, she pressed the buzzer at 2213. A couple of minutes later the door opened and an attractive young woman with long black hair and a bright smile looked out. She had the coloration of a well-tanned tennis player.

"Miss Diaz?" Jaz asked.

"Yes?"

"I'm Jaz LeMieux. I'm working on a story for The Country Reporter about aspiring country music artists who are fairly new in town. Your name was suggested. Mind if I come in and ask you a few questions?"

"Please come in," she said, excitement glowing on her face. "You'll have to pardon the looks of the place. I haven't had a chance to straighten up."

Jaz detected only a slight accent.

Rosario Diaz held the door open, then followed Jaz into a small living room that appeared well lived in. Newspapers and music-related magazines lay strewn haphazardly about the sofa. She gathered them up to make room for Jaz.

"Do you live by yourself?" Jaz asked after they were seated. She pulled a small pad and pen out of her handbag.

"Yes. I considered finding a roommate to help with the rent, but I didn't run across anybody I felt comfortable with. Then I got so busy trying to promote my music that I just gave up. I had saved enough money to live for a year in Nashville without any outside income."

"You were smart to do that. Most musicians who come here to try the waters soon wind up waiting tables." Jaz looked around the room. "This is really a lovely apartment. Would you mind showing me around?"

"Be happy to," Diaz said.

She led Jaz through her small kitchen, two bedrooms, and bath. Rosario Diaz' bedroom showed no signs of another occupant, and the second bedroom had no bed, only a desk, a small portable electronic keyboard, her guitar, and the case she carried it in. A few boxes still to be unpacked sat against the wall. Jaz knew it was highly improbable that Elena Ortiz had used this apartment as a hideaway.

Back in the living room, Jaz asked several questions about Diaz' music and what she had accomplished in Nashville. After describing her fruitless jaunts around Music Row, she added, "I've managed to play at two night clubs. I'm hopeful it will lead to something bigger."

Jaz decided on one more try at establishing a link to Elena Ortiz. "Have you made any friends in the local Hispanic community?" she asked.

Diaz smiled, displaying a perfect set of shiny white teeth. "I've acquired a boyfriend. I don't know if he'd want me to mention his name."

"No problem," Jaz said. She asked a few more questions and wound up the interview.

She sat in her car before leaving Greystone Apartments. It was close to nine o'clock when she called Sid.

"How did it go?" he asked.

"She's a lovely young woman, and I hope she succeeds in the business, but she's not Elena Ortiz's 'Mexican-sounding' country music singer."

"You're sure?"

"Positive."

Sid's voice took on a note of discouragement. "I should have known this wouldn't work out. It looked too easy."

"I know how you feel. Where does that leave us?"

"Back to the proverbial square one. We can't find Ortiz, we've hit a dead end with Valdez, and we have a killer without a face."

"But a black car. And maybe more if Hattie's tapes pan out."

"Let's hope so. Meanwhile, as my old football coach used to say, if all else fails, punt."

"Guess you'd better get out your kicking shoes, Sid."

THE CLOUDS SHOWED no sign of breaking up, but by early afternoon the mercury had risen enough to give the day a spring-like feeling. Jaz moved to a cushioned rocker on the front porch with a clipboard and pen. Following the pattern she had picked up from Sid, she checked off the varied bits and pieces of information they had accumulated on the case. As she pondered where they might search next for Elena Ortiz, John stepped out the front door and called to her.

"Miss Jasmine, Detective Masterson is on the way up."

"Thanks, John," she said, glancing down the tree-lined driveway. John took care of visitors who called from the gated entrance when Jaz was not in her office. She wondered what Bart wanted. He could have called if he had any new information for her.

A few moments later, she saw the unmarked black Metro police car approaching. That meant he was on duty. She watched as he pulled into the parking area in front, opened the door and swung his tall frame out.

"Come on in," she said as Bart walked up. "I'm working out here, enjoying the nice weather."

"Glad to hear it."

She noticed his face appeared singularly lacking in gladness. "Have a seat," she said, motioning to the chair beside hers.

Bart turned his chair so that he was facing her. "This isn't a social call, Jaz. I have to ask you a few questions."

She sat up with a sudden queasy feeling. "What's going on, Bart?"

"Just answer the questions, okay? I have to establish something first."

She didn't like the way he was acting, so formal and official.

Something was definitely wrong. "All right, Bart. Ask your questions."

"Where were you this morning before eleven o'clock?"

"Oh, my God, Bart. Am I being accused of something? Do I need a lawyer?"

"Nobody is accusing you of anything, but I need to know where you were this morning."

She looked down and rubbed her forehead. "I was here until I left to interview a country singer at the Greystone Apartments on Bell Road. Rosario Diaz, Apartment Twenty-two Thirteen. She was not the Mexican-named girl we were looking for. Then I drove over to I-40 and took Briley Parkway to the late Opry Mills Mall. I picked up a jacket at Bass Pro Shops Outdoor World for John."

"John Wallace?"

"Correct."

"Then what?"

"I drove on over to Gallatin Road and headed downtown."

"On Gallatin Road?"

"Of course. Is that against the law?"

Bart stood up and crossed his arms defensively. "I'm not enjoying this any more than you are, Jaz. It sounds like you were in the Inglewood, East Nashville area sometime between nine-thirty and ten-thirty. Right?"

Jaz pushed up from her chair. "Closer to nine-thirty than ten. But I didn't run into anybody or run over anybody. I didn't even hit a neighborhood dog. What is this all about, Bart?"

"Earline Ivey was shot to death this morning at her house near Gallatin Road in Inglewood."

Jaz gasped and her heart nearly stopped. Earline Ivey was the Welcome Home Stores employee who had accused her of using the "N" word and making racially disparaging remarks.

13

J AZ SLUMPED BACK into her chair, pulse pounding in her ears. A cold chill ran over her. It took a few moments before she could speak.

"Surely you don't think...you know I would never..." Her voice trailed off.

"I think it's highly unlikely you would do something like this, and I hope to hell you didn't, Jaz. But I'm just doing my job. You know what it's like. I had to ask, and you admit you were in the area."

"Purely by accident." She was getting her wits back now, her ire stoked. "I didn't stop except at a drugstore to get some headache pills for Marie. I should have taken Ellington Parkway, but I was in no hurry and used the time to think about Sid's case. We have enough problems on our hands without this. What happened to Mrs. Ivey?"

Bart shoved his hands into his pockets. "She was found around noon by her daughter, who had spent the night with a friend."

Jaz held her hand to her face. "Oh, my God, the poor girl. How old was she?"

"Thirteen."

"That's awful."

"I need to talk to her, but she was a basket case when I got there."

"Where is she now?"

"An aunt came after her. She's staying at their house."

Jaz just shook her head. "What a trauma that must have been."

"Yeah. It's something she'll have to live with the rest of her life."

"You said Mrs. Ivey was shot?"

"A bullet through the back of the head."

Jaz winced. "Was it a twenty-two?"

"Why do you ask?"

"It's what Omar Valdez was killed with. At least Mr. Grimm and Mr. Kozlov can't accuse Djuan Burden of this one."

"It might be better for you if they could," Bart said.

"That's a bunch of crap. It's preposterous to think I had anything to do with it." She was getting steamed.

"At the moment there's no evidence that you pulled the trigger, but you could have hired it done."

He spoke in a calm, matter-of-fact voice, but Jaz had heard enough.

She jammed her hands against her hips. "That's the most ridiculous thing you've said, Bart Masterson. I may not need a lawyer, but I don't have to stand here and listen to absurd, asinine accusations from somebody I thought was a friend."

Bart held out his hands as if to ward off a blow.

"Calm down, Jaz. You know what's involved. As soon as I arrived at the scene, I got a call from the department's PR man. He pointed out that this was the woman who'd been causing all the trouble for you, as if I didn't know. I had to come talk to you or I'd be answering to the chief."

"I know you're on the spot," she said, still breathing hard. "But you obviously have no evidence against me because I was not near that woman's house."

"You just said—"

"I said I was on Gallatin Road. Does she live on Gallatin

Road? I have no idea where she lives, and who could have done this is beyond me. I'm just as shocked as everyone else."

Bart spread his hands in a peacemaking gesture. "Let's leave it at that for now, Jaz. I'm sorry I've upset you so."

"You certainly have."

"Maybe we can close this out in a hurry and take the pressure off. I'm sure the next thing you know we'll be hearing from the NAACP."

"They've already been onto the Earline Ivey complaint. I don't know how this will affect the anti-discrimination hearing I'll probably face, but I'm certainly not looking forward to it."

Bart backed off.

"I need to go check on what the forensic guys picked up, if anything. Maybe they'll have something I can use."

He hurried out to his car. Jaz picked up her notes and went inside. She found Marie and John waiting for her.

"I heard some angry sounds out there," Marie said, her face clouded. "What did he want?"

Jaz hugged her. "Don't worry about it, Marie. It was just a misunderstanding. Everything's okay."

Marie gave her a dubious look, then turned toward the kitchen.

Of course, everything was not okay. Jaz headed for her office, called Sid, and blurted out what had happened.

"What a crock of—"

"I let him have it with both barrels."

"Good. He ought to have his head examined."

She had calmed down a bit and her tone showed it. "I felt sorry for him after he left. Bart was only doing his job, Sid. Don't you get onto him, too. I gave him a hard enough time about it."

"But to even think you'd do something like that."

"What would be the purpose?"

"The only reason would be to shut the woman up, and it was a she said-she said situation to start with. You could bring in a passel of black women who'd swear you'd never say anything like what she claimed."

"I've had plenty of them call or write me. Including some Welcome Home employees. But any way you consider it, this affair doesn't make me look good. I wouldn't wish anything like this on anybody. And the worst part is her thirteen-year-old daughter found her."

"That's brutal." Sid was silent for a moment. "Did you go to the company office when you got downtown? Maybe somebody there could pin down the time."

"I intended to stop by the office, but there's hardly anyone around on a Saturday morning. I wound up driving past the place, then went on home. Anyway, the murder probably happened before that."

Sid paused. "That shot to the head is worrisome."

"Too much like the Valdez murder?"

"Right."

"But what does Prime Medical have to do with an employee of Welcome Home Stores?"

"Nothing. That's what makes it so worrisome."

"Well, I hope Bart can solve it in a hurry. It would be best for Earline Ivey's family as well as for me. You might give him a call and see if you can be of any help."

Sid grunted. "Right now I'd be more inclined to give him a punch in the nose."

Next Jaz called the chief operating officer of Welcome Home Stores to see what they could do in support of Earline Ivey, who was still an employee. He had just heard about the shooting and was both shocked at the violence and concerned about how it might affect the company. They agreed on a statement for the media and a wreath to be placed at the store where Ivey had worked. Employees would be let off to attend the funeral.

When she got off the phone, she felt like the bell had just rung for the last round in a tough boxing match. She wasn't sure if she could make it to the finish.

14

SINCE HE DIDN'T have the luxury of a John Wallace to manicure his lawn, Sid had spent most of the morning cleaning up his yard. Twigs and sticks of various sizes had blown off the trees. Left over leaves, many carried by the wind from the riverbank, had to be piled up and disposed of. He didn't realize how long he had neglected the job.

After Jaz's call, he sat at his desk, fuming over what he had heard. Looking at it logically, he could understand where Bart was coming from. But where Jaz was concerned, he tended to view things more from an emotional standpoint that pure logic. He knew he could not have appeared as dispassionate about the situation as Bart had. But what should he do?

He picked up the phone and punched in Bart's number..

"Masterson." His typical I'm-busy-what-the-hell-do-you-want voice.

"It's Sid. Jaz just told me what happened."

"Aw, Christ, don't you get on my case, too. You know what I had to do."

"Yeah. I also know she couldn't have had anything to do with it."

"I can only deal with the facts, Sid."

"So what kind of facts do you have? Anybody see a car, a guy around the house?"

"Not that we've found. The place is not far off Gallatin Road, a little cul-de-sac with only two houses. There's a wooded area behind it. We found the back door wide open."

"Footprints?"

"Negative. The ground was dry. This area didn't get any rain yesterday."

"Any shreds of clothing caught on a fence or bush?"

"That's all I'd better say about it, except it looks like we got lucky."

"How so?"

"A crime scene officer found a latex glove on the back porch. It must have fallen out of his pocket."

"Good," Sid said. "You're using 'his,' not 'hers.'"

Bart laughed. "Whatever you say. If they can pull a print, maybe we can put this case to rest in a hurry."

"I hope you're not going to mention Jaz to the press."

"They've already showed up, but I'm not talking. I made it clear any statements would have to come from the PR section, and I haven't told them anything about Jaz."

Sid clicked off and called Jaz to tell her what he had learned.

"That glove business sure sounds promising," she said.

"I agree. TBI came up with an excellent glove print for us in Lewisville once that cinched a conviction. It may be Monday before they can get to it."

"The sooner the better as far as I'm concerned."

"I may take a run over to Inglewood and check out that house."

"Just don't get afoul of the media."

Sid decided he might as well act like one of the media and take his camera along. He found the address in the phone book, an area not far from where he lived. Briley Parkway formed the demarcation line between Madison and Inglewood. As he approached the street that lead to Earline Ivey's cul-de-sac, he saw a few commercial properties on Gallatin Road next to it. He started to make the turn but a conglomeration of traffic including police vehicles and TV trucks clogged the road ahead. He pulled into a parking area at a store near the corner and set off on foot.

Older houses, probably dating from the end of World War II, lined the street. The cul-de-sac featured a short stretch of pavement not quite as wide as a single house with two modest-sized ranch style structures bordering the turn-around. Yellow crime scene tape circled the house on the right. Two men with shoulder-mounted TV cameras stood around just outside the tape, where a couple of rookie-looking cops kept them at bay. Sid paused nearby and studied the scene. Standing back to one side, two women in casual dress talked with arms folded.

He approached them with what he hoped was a pleasant, non-threatening look. "Pardon me, ladies, but do you live around here?"

One of them, whose wind-blown white hair reminded him of how his grandmother had looked, nodded and pointed over her shoulder at the house on the left. "I live there."

"I'm with an insurance company," he said, inventing a cover story as he talked. "I wonder if you'd mind my going into your back yard to shoot some pictures of the rear of the Ivey house?"

"What for?" she asked.

"Apparently we may have some liability. I don't really know. I was just told to come take the photos. I won't bother anything. Would it be okay?"

She turned to her friend with a look of uncertainty. "I guess it would be all right, wouldn't it, Martha?"

Martha shrugged. "Suit yourself."

Sid didn't wait for further comment. "Thank you very much. I really appreciate it. I won't be long."

He started around the house on the opposite side from the Ivey residence. The yard looked about like his had before he cleaned it up. There was a small out building in back. He moved beside it to where he had a good view of the rear of the dead woman's house. Two concrete steps lead from the small back porch down to a brick patio. There appeared to be no line-of-sight from any of the nearby houses. A clump of trees began no more than ten feet back. When he looked around, he saw a line of trees that ran up to the businesses on Gallatin Road.

Sid walked close to the yellow tape that spanned the Ivey yard and started snapping photos of the area.

"Hey! What're you doing?"

Sid looked around to see a young cop hurrying toward him from between the houses.

"Taking pictures," Sid said.

"I don't know...hey, Sarge!" he yelled toward Earline Ivey's back door.

A Metro three-striper stepped out, followed by the familiar inverted V mustache of Detective Bart Masterson.

"What's the problem?" the sergeant asked.

Before the young officer could reply, Bart stepped forward. "I'll take care of this."

He ducked under the tape and walked toward Sid.

Sid grinned and waved his camera. "Just taking some pictures."

"What the hell for?" Bart asked, frowning.

"That's what investigators do, when they don't have crime scene techs to do it for them."

"I thought you were one hundred percent sure Jaz had nothing to do with this."

"I am, but as long as she's the subject of a police investigation, I'm going to be looking into the big picture."

"Like you're doing with Djuan Burden."

"Correct. Particularly since both murders involve the same MO."

"You're not suggesting—?"

"I can't imagine any connection, but if there is one, I intend to find it."

He saw nothing to be gained by bringing it up at the moment, but he had begun to wonder if somehow this murder could involve an attempt to get him and Jazz off the Burden case. The possibility was nebulous at the moment, but he tucked it back in a mental file drawer for later consideration.

Bart laid an arm on Sid's shoulder. "You are one persistent dude, buddy. I admire the way you attack a problem. I just hope it doesn't backfire. Incidentally, I've been asking around about your Mexican singer."

"Thanks." Sid motioned toward the house. "Find anything new in there?"

"No. The guy was pretty careful."

"Except with his gloves."

"They all make mistakes sooner or later. Homicide detectives would be in bad shape if they didn't. Right?"

Sid nodded. He hoped they would soon find one made by the Omar Valdez murderer.

He stopped by his office to download the photos he'd shot, then headed for a nearby steakhouse for an early dinner. He got home just in time for the six o'clock news.

JAZ LAY CURLED UP on the sofa in her recreation room, devouring the latest Bangkok mystery novel by Tim Hallinan in a valiant effort to get her mind off of Earline Ivey. The phone rang beside her.

"Have you been watching the news?" Sid asked.

"No, I've been reading. What did they show?"

"Some shots of the cops around Earline Ivey's house. They showed her sister's place where the daughter is staying, but no pictures of her."

"Somebody in human resources checked her file and said the girl's name is Vanita."

"The TV story gave the background of who Ivey was and how she had accused you of racial discrimination. They read a short statement from your company deploring what had happened."

"Nothing about me personally?"

"No. I talked to Bart over at the Ivey house this afternoon. He assured me he was saying nothing to the media."

Jaz sat in silence, the pain of the accusation and its aftermath palpably coursing through her body. "This whole thing is so unfortunate. I didn't deserve what happened to me, and for whatever reason it was done, Earline Ivey certainly didn't deserve to be the victim of a cold-blooded shooting. I'm sure it was devastating to her daughter."

"I looked over the scene behind her house this afternoon," Sid said. "I took some pictures. Bart told me he's still asking around about a Mexican-named singer."

"Be great if he could find our girl."

"Other than that, sounds like our best bet is that tape Hattie plans to show us tomorrow. I'll see you at the bank."

Jaz punched the phone off and stabbed the TV remote. She saw a smiling, snappily-dressed young man pointing out what was happening weatherwise in Middle Tennessee. The details didn't register in her mind, though. What they might learn tomorrow at the bank and what might happen to her credibility as a result of the Ivey murder kept her thoughts in a jumble. She let her gaze wander around the room where Jaques LeMieux had decorated the walls with hunting scenes. What would her dad have done faced with a situation like this? She knew. He would have sucked it up and faced the snarling tiger with confidence in his ammunition. Though Canadian by birth, he was not a royalist. He revered Oliver Cromwell and would quote his advice to "put your trust in God, but mind to keep your powder dry."

She'd have to hold her powder high as the troubled waters rose.

15

URING HIS RUN SUNDAY morning, Sid puzzled over the slaying of Earline Ivey. He had seen the TV news reports last night, and this morning the carrier had thrown his newspaper onto the driveway just before he started out. There was no husband or boyfriend in the wings, the two most likely suspects. The police found no evidence of a robbery and made no suggestion of a motive. Acquaintances of the woman offered none either. Neighbors reported seeing no one around the house. The murderer apparently entered through the back door, as Bart indicated. Had Earline left it unlocked? Had someone knocked and been let in, or had they picked the lock? There was no mention of the glove found on the porch.

This morning appeared a clone of the previous day, with dark folds of cloud making the landscape resemble a dawn that wouldn't break. It gave Sid an idea. As soon as he got home, he took a quick shower and dressed in black pants and a black sweater. He headed out to the garage and climbed into his vintage brown pickup, the transportation he preferred to use when it wasn't necessary to appear the competent professional. A few blemishes in the paint job gave it the look of a workingman's vehicle.

Gallatin Road would soon bustle with worshippers on the way to services at the area's many churches, but for now traffic moved sparsely along the thoroughfare. He drove to the commercial area where he had parked yesterday and pulled in at the side of a small market. Seeing no one around, he locked the truck and walked behind the building. Locating the line of trees that ran through the neighborhood, he began picking his way between the trees, moving slowly to avoid attracting attention. He encountered a couple of fences, but neither blocked his path.

It took only a few minutes to reach the rear of Earline Ivey's house. Yellow crime scene tape still circled the yard, but he was able to move close enough to see where a stalker could have crossed to the rear door. Looking around the area, he found nothing that might indicate who had been here. Of course, had there had been anything, Bart or his crime scene crew should have found it.

He turned around and made his way back through the trees to the market. Instead of returning to his truck, he walked around to the front and entered the building. It was a typical convenience store with gas pumps out front. Beer and soft drinks and an assortment of grocery items lined the shelves. A young man, early twenties, dressed in jeans and a plaid shirt, stood behind the counter, cleaning it with a large rag. His look was one of pure boredom.

"Were you working here yesterday morning?" Sid asked.

The man paused in mid-swipe. "Yeah. I open at seven in the morning six days a week. I'm a glutton for punishment. What's the problem?"

"No problem." Except for me, Sid thought. What he was about to ask would hardly even qualify as a long shot. But when you had absolutely nothing, anything was worth a try. "Do you recall if somebody came in here around this time yesterday morning? Maybe wearing an outfit like this?"

The clerk glanced up and down Sid's full height, then continued wiping the counter. "He wasn't nearly as tall as you. Had a black baseball cap, though."

Sid felt his heart kick into overdrive. "Could you describe his features...hair, eyes, anything unusual?"

"Are you a cop?"

"Private investigator. Think about it for a moment. What did he look like?"

"Jeez, he wasn't here all that long. Just bought a pack of Salems and left."

"If you remember the brand of cigarettes, surely you can recall something about his looks."

The young man stopped swiping the rag and stared. "Squinty eyes, oval-shaped glasses, wide mouth. He was black. That's about all I remember."

"Did you see what kind of vehicle he drove?"

"A black car pulled out into the street after he left, but I didn't see him get in so I don't know if he was in it."

"Thanks," Sid said and headed back to his truck.

He thought about calling Bart but drove home for breakfast first. Normally he'd eat after his run and shower. He was starving now. His time in Special Forces, when he could exist on hardly any food for days at a time, was only a distant memory. As he sat at the kitchen table downing a bowl of oatmeal, he thought about what he had just done and what might have happened if some homeowner had spotted him and called the police. But nobody did, which proved to his satisfaction that some murderous individual had made the same trek through the trees.

It was around nine when he got Bart on the phone. "You working today?" Sid asked.

"What do you think?"

"I think you're probably pulling your hair out trying to get a handle on this case."

"Are you peddling handles?"

Sid laughed. "I might be."

He told Bart what he had done and the information the store clerk had given him.

"You realize if we'd gotten a call, you and Jaz both would now be persons of interest."

"I know. And I know it's long odds, but this guy could be your man."

"So all I have to do is find a black guy wearing a black outfit, squinty eyes, glasses, and a wide mouth, smoking Salems, and I've got my murderer."

Sid's voice had a cheerless ring to it. "You're hard as a walnut this morning, Bart. Must have been a rough night."

"Yeah. We walked our asses off and talked our heads off in that neighborhood. Checked tree lines and sight lines and came up with nothing. Your market boy must only work mornings because he wasn't there for us."

"Most likely. He said he opens at seven o'clock six days a week."

"I don't want to sound ungrateful, buddy, but it'll take a lot more than that sighting to pin the tail on this donkey."

16

THEY MET AT THE BANK'S main office in a downtown high-rise. Hattie Jordan unlocked the door to let them in.

"Hi, Sid, good to see you again," she said with her usual exuberance.

She opened her arms and Sid moved into her embrace, remembering she was a major league hugger. He'd only seen her a couple of times but knew all about her from Jaz.

Hattie reached out with one arm and pulled Jaz in. "Don't think you're gonna get left out, girl."

"I didn't expect to," Jaz said, grinning. "Lead us to your lair."

They followed her down a long corridor to an office labeled SECURITY, where she slid her badge through a card reader and opened the door. The room held several desks and banks of monitor screens. A young man in slacks and an open-collared dress shirt sat in front of a computer.

"Hi, John," Hattie said, "what's up?"

"All quiet on the western front," he said without looking up.

"Let's stir things up then. Meet my friends Jaz LeMieux and Sid Chance, private investigators par excellence."

The young man spun around in his chair, stood, and stuck out his hand. "Glad to meet you."

"Don't let us disturb you," Sid said as he shook hands.

"You don't know disturbance until Hattie Jordan gets on your case." He grinned as he said it.

"Back to your knitting," Hattie said. "We got work to do."

She led them over to a console where she consulted a directory and pulled up the Green Hills Branch cameras on a screen. She punched in an ID and the view outside the drive-in window appeared.

"This is a live view," Hattie said. She pointed to a light pole in the background. "That would be the alley there, wouldn't it?"

"Right," Jaz said. "If the car turned away from Hillsboro Pike, we should be able to see the license plate."

Sid rubbed his beard. "I'd think that would be his choice, taking the less traveled route out of there. Lower the odds of being noticed."

"But the license plate image won't be very big, and these videos are compressed, so they get distorted when you do much enlarging." Hattie started typing on the keyboard. "They're backed up daily. Let me put in last Monday's date and we'll start at three o'clock."

After a couple of false starts, a picture appeared with the date-time stamp showing 15:00:00, three p.m. on the 24-hour clock. A car sat beside the ATM. Hattie began scrolling forward slowly and the car moved out of view. After a lull period, three vehicles in succession shuffled up to the drive-in window, paused, then moved on. When a car suddenly appeared beyond the driveway in the alley, she slammed her finger onto the keyboard and the video paused.

"It was black," Jaz said from a chair beside Hattie. "But it's already gone."

Sid leaned forward over her shoulder. "Hardly slowed when he got to the street."

"Okay," Hattie said, "let's back up."

The picture began reversing, frame by frame. The car slowly backed into view. When it reached the point where the rear bumper showed squarely, Hattie hit pause again.

"There you go. You can see the tag, but you can't read it. Let's enlarge it a bit."

She kept hitting a key to enlarge and shifting the picture to keep the license centered. When it got large enough to see detail on the plate, the image was too distorted to read the letters and numbers. The colored squares on the right edge looked like the state and county decals that would show the year on Tennessee plates.

Hattie replayed the scene backward and forward again. A few frames caught the driver looking to the left before he entered the street. He had a full head of black hair and a beard to match. Sid thought he looked white but well-tanned. One thing appeared certain. The car was a black 2011 Ford Fusion. The time stamp showed 15:24:34.

"If you'll put that sequence on a disk," Sid said, "I'll see if Agent Eggers can help us out. The FBI has a program to enhance moving images. Maybe it can make the license number readable."

"That must be the one NASA developed," Jaz asked.

"Right. It's called VISAR—Video Image Stabilization and Registration. It can really make a difference."

Hattie transferred the surveillance video to a DVD and gave it to Sid.

"Anything else the bank can do to re-establish law and order in our fair city?" she asked.

"I wish you'd had a branch across the street from Earline Ivey's house yesterday," Jaz said, a wistful look crossing her face.

Hattie raised a sculptured brow. "I wasn't going to mention that."

"I guess I'm a person of interest, since I happened to drive down Gallatin Road around the time of the murder."

"Anybody would be crazy to think you had anything to do with that," Hattie replied.

"And there's no reason they should," Sid said. He told them what he had done that morning, about the man who came into the market.

Jaz reached across and squeezed his hand. "Thanks."

"Just doing my job," Sid said with a grin. "Can't have my partner locked up in the hoosegow."

"Methinks there's more here than meets the eye," Hattie said.

Sid ignored the comment, pulled out his phone, found Baron Eggers number, and pressed "Call." When the agent answered, he reminded him of the reported sighting of a man in the alley behind Prime Medical Equipment. "I think we have him on a bank surveillance video."

"Congratulations."

"Trouble is we can't read the license plate. If I give you a disk of the footage, could your people enhance the image with the VISAR program?"

"I'm sure they could, if they have the time."

"Would you have to send it to Washington, or could you do it here?"

"It can be done locally, but unless it's of interest to the Bureau, I can't guarantee how soon."

"If a Medicare scammer was the victim of a professional hit, wouldn't that be of interest to the FBI?"

"I see your point. Bring it to me in to morning and I'll see what can be done."

After they left Hattie at the bank, Sid walked out to the parking lot with Jaz, talking about where their investigation to clear Djuan Burden might turn next. "I'd say we should concentrate on tracking down Ortiz and learning all we can about Valdez," Sid said.

His cell phone rang. When he pulled it out and answered, he heard Bart Masterson's voice. "Got something for you, Sid. Don't know if it's what you're looking for but should be worth a try. Haven't got an address, but there's a girl singer named Cristina Torres, works as a waitress at Las Flores Restaurant in Madison."

After thanking Bart, Sid closed the phone. "How are you on Mexican food?" he asked Jaz.

"I've already had lunch, but dinner sounds fine. What's the deal?"

He told her that Bart had found a singer who might be the one they were searching for. With no address, they'd have to identify the waitress and follow her home. They agreed to meet at Sid's office at six.

17

MADISON, THOUGH NOT officially a town, was one of the largest communities within Metropolitan Nashville. According to the Madison-Rivergate Area Chamber of Commerce, the population totaled more than 35,000. It stretched from Briley Parkway north to the Sumner County Line. Over the past decade, it had become a popular destination for Mexican immigrants. The community's main street, Gallatin Road, featured many Hispanic businesses, ranging from markets to auto repair shops to restaurants. Taco wagons plied their trade in the main business district.

A small restaurant tucked in between an alteration shop and a jewelry store, Las Flores lived up to its name as soon as Sid opened the door. Flowers littered the place. Baskets around the walls, vases with red and white roses on the tables. Red, white and green banners, representing the national colors of Mexico, hung from small staffs around the room. Mariachi music rolled from speakers on either side, toned down so as not to drown out conversation at the tables.

A young woman in a red dress and green shawl greeted them. "Welcome to Las Flores," she said with a heavy Spanish accent. She ushered them to a table near the front window and left menus at their places. "Cristina will be right with you."

Sid looked around when she left. Three other tables were occupied, two by obvious Hispanics, the other anyone's guess. "Sounds like we hit the jackpot," he said.

Jaz nodded. "Sure does. This must be her."

A girl in a flowered bolero blouse with long black hair cascading over her shoulders approached their table. Hazel eyes above high cheek bones highlighted an attractive smile. "What can I get you to drink?" she asked in nearly flawless English.

They ordered iced tea, and she left for the kitchen.

"What do you think?" Jaz asked.

"If her singing voice is as pleasant as her speaking voice, she may have a good chance in the business."

"But would she be the type to hide Elena Ortiz?"

"We'll have to find out."

She picked up her menu. "So what do we eat while waiting?"

Sid scanned the entrees. "I'm not big on the hot stuff. The chicken quesadilla sounds good to me."

"I think I'll try the beef enchiladas."

Cristina Torres brought their tea and took their orders. After she left, Sid picked up the conversation.

"Now that we have Ortiz on hold, where do we stand on Valdez?"

"We know he's ashes by now," Jaz said. "And they're headed for Texas."

"But he came from New Mexico, according to the background check."

"Ortiz came from Texas, and she's in charge now."

"Okay, so what do we know about the man? He worked at Casa Rosa Restaurant in Albuquerque. Maybe he was the manager, or assistant manager. How did he get involved in a Medicare scam? He'd have to have studied the medical equipment business and procedures used by Medicare in approving and paying claims."

"Elena had experience in the medical arena. As for Omar, we know he likes to mask his moves and use fake documents."

Sid added a little sweetener to his tea, then looked up. "A fake address in Little Rock and a fake driver's license. What if he was fake all the way?"

"What do you mean?"

"What if the man who's now reduced to ashes isn't really Omar Valdez?"

Jaz looked at him with narrowed eyes. "We could call the restaurant in Albuquerque."

"But that wouldn't tell who he really is."

"The Medical Examiner routinely fingerprints victims."

"But do they submit them to the police with the autopsy?"

Jaz shrugged. "Maybe not, unless requested."

"Detective Grimm would not likely have requested it. He had Ortiz identify the body."

"And he had a driver's license, which it took the FBI to prove was a fake."

"Why don't you ask your friend, Dr. Abrams, about the prints, whether they have been checked with AFIS?"

The FBI's Automated Fingerprint Identification System should tell them precisely who the victim was.

When Cristina brought their food, Sid asked her what time the restaurant closed.

"We quit serving at eight," she said, "but it's usually eight-thirty before everybody is finished."

They were out long before eight. Sid had chosen to use his truck tonight, feeling it would attract less attention in areas they were likely to go. It was not Jaz's favorite mode of transportation, but she agreed with his thinking. He moved the truck to a far corner of the parking area where they could see Cristina when she came out. He had checked the rear of the building earlier to be sure there was no parking in back.

"Reminds you of the old stakeout days," Sid said as they waited in the dim light from a nearby pole.

"I didn't have to do much of that in patrol."

"While chief in Lewisville, I worked as patrolman, detective, whatever was needed."

"Do you miss those days?"

It had been more than three years since he resigned in disgust, feeling disgraced, after the widely-publicized reverse "sting" when the sheriff charged him with taking a bribe from a drug dealer. Using a young man he'd arrested on a possession case, Sid had set up a buy from the dealer to catch him in the act. When the dealer learned what was coming, he went to the sheriff and made a deal, claiming Sid had approached him about a bribe. He was wired when he met Sid for the buy and handed him an envelope.

"What's this?" Sid asked.

"The five thousand bucks you asked for, Chief. Now keep your cops off my back."

After a long silence while the past played out in his mind, Sid looked around at Jaz, a sadness in his eyes. "Yeah, I enjoyed the work. I had planned to keep at it until I retired. You've heard the rest of the story."

"Not a good way to go out," she said. "You know how I felt yesterday when Bart talked like I had something to do with the Earline Ivey murder."

"It's a real downer."

After a brief pause, she asked, "How does the PI job stack up against being police chief?"

"Different animals. I'm learning to enjoy it more. In a way it's tougher, a real challenge."

"How so?"

"As a cop you've got the law behind you. Either they cooperate or go to jail. As a PI, you have to learn to finesse things, be more tactful, diplomatic."

"You learn that in the business world, too," Jaz said.

They took turns keeping an eye on the restaurant entrance while chatting. It was Sid who finally saw the young waitress come out.

"There she is," he said. "Watch where she goes."

She walked between two cars out to the second row of parking spaces next to the street. As soon as she unlocked her door and climbed in, Sid started his truck. He pulled out to follow when she headed down the side street away from Gallatin Road. She drove an older model Honda Accord, dark colored. Hanging back to avoid arousing suspicion, he trailed her to Old Hickory Boulevard, the four-lane highway that bisected Madison east and west. She turned onto Myatt Drive, which would come out near Sid's office at RiverGate Mall, though along the way were several streets that ran off to either side with lots of small, older houses.

When she took a darkened street, Sid switched off his headlights and pulled in after her, easing to the curb. They watched as she turned into a driveway in the middle of the block. After she got out and walked toward the house, Sid inched forward to park behind a car two houses away.

"How do you want to handle this?" Jaz asked.

They both wore dark-colored outfits to make them less obvious at night. With the moon hidden by clouds and the nearest streetlight at the end of the block, chances were good they could move about without attracting attention. But Sid remained cautious.

"I'd like to check the back of her house to see if Ortiz's white Carolla might be hidden there," he said.

"Think the neighbors are nosy enough to stare out their windows at night?"

"You never know, until one calls the cops or comes out with a shotgun."

"The houses aren't too close together and it looks like most drapes are drawn. If you want to give it a try, put your phone on vibrate and I'll warn you if I see anything."

Sid took out his phone and set it to vibrate. "Okay. Keep a sharp eye out."

He reached up to switch off the overhead light, scooted out of the seat, and closed the door softly. He looked around and saw no one. He strolled casually toward Cristina Torres' driveway. It was graveled, and part of the gravel had worn away. He turned in and slipped past her car. Lights shone behind shades in the house next door. He heard no sound. As soon as he moved beyond the back corner of Torres' house, however, a dog started barking in the backyard of the next house beyond.

Sid darted toward the street before the lights could come on. He had seen what he came to look for. A white 2009 Toyota Carolla with Tennessee plates sat behind the Hispanic girl's house.

18

S ID PULLED HIS TRUCK around the car ahead of him and parked in front of Cristina Torres' driveway. A small frame structure with a wooden porch that stretched halfway across the front, the house hadn't been exposed to a paint brush in quite a while. A small placard on the door said BIENVENIDO. Sid ignored the button and knocked.

The porch light came on. After a few moments, the door opened and Cristina looked out, her eyes large and questioning.

Sid smiled. "You waited on us at Las Flores tonight. We're Sid Chance and Jasmine LeMieux."

"Is something wrong?" she asked, still wary.

"No, the meal was fine and the service was excellent. We're here to see Elena Ortiz."

Her mouth dropped open and she covered it with her hand. "How did you...?"

"Her car is parked around back," Sid said. "A neighbor at her former apartment said she was a friend of yours."

"What do you want with her? You're not police—"

"We're private investigators looking into the murder of Omar Valdez. We need to know who she thinks killed him."

Torres looked confused. "It was that man who had been in prison."

"That's what the police say. We know better. Djuan Burden's grandmother hired us to find the real murderer. Elena Ortiz should be able to help us."

Sid heard another voice behind Torres. The girl looked around and said something, then pulled the door open. "She will talk to you."

Sid and Jaz walked in. They faced a small woman about five-foot-five wearing jeans and a blue denim shirt. She had dyed her hair a golden blonde, as if that would hide her identity. She looked from Sid to Jaz with indigo eyes, a blue so dark they were almost black.

"Why do you think this Burden person did not kill Omar?" Elena Ortiz asked.

"Simple," Sid said. "The gun the police found at his grandmother's house had not been fired in twenty years. The man who called nine-one-one saw Burden leave the front of the store. Just prior to that, a man was seen leaving by the back door. That was the murderer."

Ortiz slumped into a chair beside a small TV. "How would I know who it was?"

"You were living with Valdez," Jaz said. "You knew him well. You knew who had something against him, who would have wanted him dead. This looked like a contract killing. Somebody hired a professional assassin to kill Omar."

She shook her head. "No. They have their own people who do that."

"Who does?" Sid asked.

"I can't tell you. They will kill me."

"Who are they?"

She shook her head again. "They will find me."

Sid squatted down in front of her to make eye contact. "We know you were involved in a Medicare scam. The FBI is onto this. If you cooperate with them, they could put you in the witness protection program, give you a new identity, and help you start a new life in a different area of the country."

He knew he couldn't guarantee anything, but it was a good

possibility if she had information that would incriminate others. From her remarks, it sounded like she was referring to a large operation.

Ortiz's eyes had turned watery now. "He didn't think they would find him here."

Jaz moved beside the chair and put an arm around her shoulder. "You've been through a traumatic few days, Elena. You had to identify the body, make arrangements with the funeral home, then find a place to hide out. It's been tough. At the moment, we're the only ones who know where you are, but what we did others can do. The FBI can put you up in a safe house where you'll be protected until they work things out. Help us and we'll help you."

Ortiz rubbed her hands together nervously, then dabbed her eyes with a tissue. "I don't know. If I...I just don't know."

After glancing at Sid with a determined look, Jaz turned back to the teary-eyed woman. "Tell you what, Miss Ortiz, while you're making up your mind, I can guarantee your safety at my place. I have a large house out Franklin Road with security and an electronically-monitored gate. You can stay with me for a few days until this gets straightened out." She handed the woman one of her Welcome Home Stores business cards. "That's my primary position. I only work with Sid occasionally because I enjoy detective work."

Sid frowned. "Are you sure you want to do this?" He didn't like the idea of her taking in a woman who had been involved in Medicare fraud. How far could she be trusted?

Jaz nodded. "She's had a rough time and she needs a break, Sid. I think it'll work out for us."

He knew what she meant. She thought that in the setting of her home she could talk Elena Ortiz into helping find the man who killed Omar Valdez.

Jaz turned back to the woman. "How about it?"

She looked at the card, then at Jaz. "I read about you in the newspaper."

"Not the bad part, I hope." Jaz grinned.

"What about my car?" she asked.

"I can send somebody tomorrow to pick it up and take it to a garage. They'll keep it out of sight until you're ready for it. You were smart to keep it out of sight. That car's the easiest way they can track you down."

"All right," Ortiz said. "I'll go. I don't want to put Cristina in danger."

While she packed her bags, Sid took Jaz by his office to get her car. Back at Cristina Torres' house, they loaded Elena's belongings into the Lexus. She had brought only enough clothes for a week and used Torres' washing machine to keep a fresh outfit. Sid followed them across town to Jaz's house. With the women safely inside, he returned home.

He found a message on his answering machine in a distorted voice.

"A word of warning, Chance. You could be next."

19

S ID SHOWED UP at the FBI's Nashville Resident office on Elm Hill Pike at eight o'clock Monday morning. He met Agent Eggers and gave him the disk from Hattie Jordan, along with a print-out of the frame from the video showing the license plate.

"You're sure this is the guy seen coming out the back of the store after the murder?" Eggers asked.

"It fits the time line. The nine-one-one call came in at three-thirty. The time stamp on the getaway frame is three twenty-four. That works out perfectly. The video showed the car coming up the alley from the direction of Prime Medical."

"We deal with security camera footage all the time. Shouldn't be a problem to target in on the license tag."

"There's a good shot in there of the driver's face, for what it's worth."

"If he's a pro, it's altered with a disguise."

"That's what I figured."

"I can't promise you anything, but since it's at least peripherally tied in with an active case, maybe If I can get it done. If so, I'll let you know who the car's registered to. It would help my case if you had something good for us on Prime Medical's owners."

Sid knew the best thing he could provide was Elena Ortiz, but he was reluctant to give her up until Jaz had gotten her to talk. "We're following up on a couple of things. I may have something for you later today. I'm still trying to get a handle on Omar Valdez."

"I've asked our Albuquerque Field Office to check with the restaurant where Valdez worked. Let me know if you turn up anything."

If things went as he suspected with the Medical Examiner's fingerprint record, Sid figured the FBI would find Omar Valdez still worked at the restaurant, had died, or was unknown. He counted on Jaz's friend Dr. Abrams to come up with the Prime Medical president's real name.

When he got out to his car, he called Jaz. She was on the way downtown to meet with a company attorney to discuss the Earline Ivey case.

"I called Reagan Abrams," she said. "She confirmed that no one had requested a copy of Omar Valdez's fingerprints. She said she would ask for a check with the FBI database and let me know what they found. Did you see Agent Eggers?"

"I did. I gave him the disk and print. He wouldn't promise anything. He's reluctant to get out on a limb with us, but I think I convinced him it was something the FBI would like to have." He also told her about the request to the Albuquerque Field office on Valdez.

"So one way or the other, we should soon have something definite on Ortiz's boyfriend."

"How are you making out with Elena?" Sid asked.

"I'm working at it, but she's still holding out. She's definitely scared of what might happen to her, but I get the feeling there's something else involved."

"Like what?"

"I can't put my finger on it. I'm hopeful Marie can warm her up for me. Turns out Elena likes to cook, so they should get along fine. I'll make another try at winning her over as soon as I get back from the lawyer's office."

THE SHELVES BEHIND K.C. Urban's desk were lined with rows of imposing legal tomes, state and national codes, court decisions, books on civil procedures, contracts, consumer protection, criminal law casebooks. Jaz wondered if he had one on how to keep corporate chairmen out of trouble. She sat across the neat desk from the tall, hefty lawyer who exhibited the incongruous look of a short Marine Corps haircut and large Barry Goldwater-style hornrims. She began with the key question.

"How do we get this mess cleared up, K.C.?"

His name was actually Cayce Thornton Urban, but he didn't like either of his given names so he chose to call himself K.C.

"This murder business complicates things," he said. "Earline Ivey's supporters talked about going to the E.E.O.C., but this isn't really a case for them. She alleged an isolated incident, not a pattern of activity by the company. But she gains a lot of sympathy because of what happened to her."

"I can understand that. It was anguishing to me. Did you know she had a thirteen-year-old daughter?"

"I saw that. And the kid found her mother dead."

"It must have been terrible. I wish there was something I could do for her."

"Maybe later. Certainly not now. Her family would either refuse it or take it as an admission of guilt."

"I feel so helpless, so frustrated."

"Don't let it get to you. It may not be as bad as it first seemed."

"In what respect?"

"She filed a complaint with the Tennessee Human Rights Commission. I know their general counsel. She said they would have to investigate it, but on the surface it sounded like a pretty weak case."

"We didn't do anything in retaliation," Jaz said.

"Right. That's why she didn't have much of a case. As you know, we've been looking into the possibility she had received a big payoff from one of our rivals. What happened Saturday changes the landscape."

"It would be nice to know, even if it's a little late."

"We'll find out, but there may not be anything we can do about it," he said, absently rapping his knuckles on the desk.

"So what should our position be?" Jaz asked.

"I think we lay low, make as little noise as possible, and see what happens."

"That suits me fine. I'll be happy to stay out of the limelight."

"I thought you would."

"If I weren't committed to helping Sid Chance on an investigation, I'd probably take a long vacation."

K.C. smiled. "Might not be a bad idea."

"I was afraid I might have to call you to bail me out on Saturday."

He pushed the hornrims down and stared over them. "Why on earth...?"

She told him what happened when Detective Masterson came out to talk to her about the murder.

"It's unfortunate you happened to drive through the area," he said, "but that's absurd. You haven't done anything wrong. Why would you want to kill her?"

"Exactly. It makes no sense."

"Call me if you have any more problems with the police. I started out practicing criminal law, you know."

"I wasn't aware of that."

"It was after I graduated from law school and went to work for a Knoxville legal firm. I took the full course in the college of hard knocks."

"Why did you give it up for civil law?"

"I got burned out on criminals after awhile. You come across some interesting cases, but I couldn't stomach dealing with clients whose innocence claims were about as valid as Charles Manson's. Civil law can get really gritty at times, but it's basically a gentleman's sport."

Jaz grinned. "I like that. But I'll keep your name on my speed dial."

20

When he left the FBI office, Sid checked for the possibility of anyone following him. It had become routine since the visit Friday night by Detectives Grimm and Kozlov, but the call on his answering machine last night added urgency to the mix. Though he had no idea who had initiated the call, it undoubtedly concerned the Prime Medical murder case.

He saw no evidence of a tail as he pulled out onto Elm Hill Pike.

Thinking about the .22 caliber pistol the TBI lab had tested, he decided to drop by Rachel Ransom's house. He parked behind the blue Ford, walked to the door, and knocked. While he waited, a boy with a somber look and beady eyes who should have been in school ambled down the sidewalk, one hand gripping pants that hung perilously below his waist. Sid gave a slight shake of his head. This could be one of those boys Djuan Burden would have helped, given the chance.

Mrs. Ransom opened the door and looked up at Sid. The same sad expression he had seen last Tuesday seemed etched onto her face.

"May I come in for a moment?" he asked.

She pushed open the screen door. "Please do."

After taking a seat in the living room, he spoke in a gentle voice.

"I wish I could say I had found the answer to Djuan's

dilemma. Unfortunately, I haven't. But I think we're getting close to answering some significant questions."

"What sort of questions?"

"About the identity of the man seen leaving the back of the medical equipment store right after the shooting. The FBI is helping us out on that."

"You think he was the real murderer?"

"Yes, but we can't prove it yet."

"Is Miss LeMieux all right?" The lines in her face seemed to deepen as she spoke.

"She's fine. We don't always work together on a case. She's taking care of some business at her company today."

"I just wondered. Poor thing. Marie Wallace told me what happened about that woman who was killed."

"It was very unfortunate for everybody. But I'm sure everything will work out." He said it with conviction, though he was beginning to have some doubts.

"I sure hope so. She's a very nice woman."

The telephone rang on the table beside Mrs. Ransom. She picked it up and answered. As she listened, her face became more drawn; her mouth pulled into a taut line. After a few moments, she said, "Thank you," and hung up.

She blinked back the tears, her voice shaky. "That was Mr. Vandenberg, Djuan's lawyer. He said the Grand Jury had indicted Djuan for the murder."

Sid crossed to where Rachel Ransom sat, got down on his knees, and held her hand. "That only means the District Attorney thinks he has a case. I promise you he doesn't. When was the last time that pistol from your cedar chest was used to fire a bullet?"

"Not since it left California."

"And that was what, fifteen years ago?"

"About that."

Sid released her hand and she pulled a tissue from a box on the table beside her, dabbed her eyes with it.

He stood and looked down at her, feeling some of the same agony that showed in her wrinkled face. "We'll prove that man did it," he said. "That's a promise."

As he walked out to his car, he thought of that promise. He hadn't make it idly. He wanted to prove Djuan Burden innocent more than anything. His personal integrity was at stake, and that was a major incentive.

JAZ ARRIVED HOME to find Marie in the kitchen teaching Elena Ortiz the delicate art of making meringue for a chocolate pie. She waited as Elena carefully placed the pan in the oven under Marie's watchful eye.

"Is this some new Mexican dish?" Jaz asked.

Elena smiled. "I've had chocolate pie before, but it never looked like this. She has magic in her fingers."

"I've known that for years," Jaz said.

"Next time I cook something Mexican, you can show me how," Marie said.

Elena shrugged. "I'm not all that good a cook, but my mother was."

"Does she still live in El Paso?" Jaz asked.

Elena cut her eyes sharply. "You must know all about me."

"Quite a bit. I know you worked at an orthopedic clinic in San Antonio. Let's go in my office and chat a few minutes. Call us when that pie is done, Marie."

"You know it's not proper to eat pie just before lunch."

Jaz grinned. "Okay. Call us when lunch is ready."

She led Elena into her office, provided a chair beside the desk and turned hers around so they faced each other. "Did you meet Omar in San Antonio?" she asked.

Elena paused a moment, as if trying to decide how much

to divulge, then nodded. "He came to the clinic as a patient with a sprained ankle. He had turned it when he jumped off a porch. I happened to be in the reception area when he was leaving. I helped him out to a friend's car."

Jaz smiled. "Sounds like the beginning of a fairy-tale romance."

Elena closed her eyes and winced. "Fairy-tale romances don't end this way."

"That's true." Jaz leaned forward in a gesture of urgency. "You would like to see the person responsible for this punished, wouldn't you?"

"I doubt that he will be."

"We can make it happen if you'll help us."

"You don't know these people."

"You keep referring to 'these people.' Is it a criminal gang?"

With lips firmly closed, Elena nodded.

"Are they involved in Medicare scams?"

"No."

"Then what?"

She squirmed uncomfortably in the chair. "I'm sorry. I can't talk about it."

"You're safe here now," Jaz said. "The FBI can assure your future safety."

Elena spoke so softly Jaz could hardly hear the words. "It could hurt others."

What others could she be concerned about, Jaz wondered? Then she recalled what she had read on the internet regarding Elena's brother, Pablo.

"Might it hurt Pablo?" she asked.

Elena's eyes flashed. "What do you know about my brother?"

"I know he's been involved in several drug arrests. Was Omar's murder carried out by a drug gang?" As she thought about it further, she added, "A Mexican drug cartel?"

Elena covered her face with her hands and sobbed. Jaz put an arm around her shoulder and handed her a box of tissues. She felt terrible for having inflicted the pain, but it appeared the only way to get the information they needed. Did the end in this case justify the means? She wasn't sure, but she was convinced Elena had confirmed a key piece of the puzzle..

21

AN OVERWHELMING SENSE of helplessness continued to plague Sid after he returned to his office. He had promised Rachel Ransom they would prove who committed the murder of Omar Valdez, but they were still a long way from reaching that goal. He remembered what Jaz had said when she first called him about Djuan Burden's arrest.

"If he's innocent, you'll prove it."

It was time he lived up to his reputation.

When the phone rang, he saw FBI Agent Baron Eggers' number on the caller ID.

"Is your fax turned on?" Eggers asked. "I'm about to send you a copy of the enhanced photo. You owe me on this one, friend. I had to call in a marker to get it done."

Sid's voice took an upbeat turn. "Just name your price. Can you read the plate number?"

"Yeah, but there's a slight problem."

"What's that?"

"The plate doesn't belong on that car. It was stolen from a Mustang in a parking lot at a shopping center."

Sid gave a sigh of disgust. He felt like someone had dumped a bucket of cold water on his head. It was hardly the ecstatic feeling a football coach got when his players doused him with Gatorade.

"Which shopping center?"

"The Mall at Green Hills."

"He must have switched plates shortly before going to the medical equipment store."

"Probably. He would have ditched the stolen one when he finished the job for sure. Sorry. You win some, you lose some."

Sid turned his chair and looked out the window where the sky had turned as gloomy as his mood. "I'm getting tired of being on the losing end."

"I know the feeling. Before I came with the Bureau, I worked homicide in Kansas City. We had a case like this with an obvious hired killer. The victim had been accused of raping a young woman whose father was a wealthy businessman. The crime scene offered practically nothing. The killer fired three shots. There was no brass, no fingerprints, nothing. When people in the area were questioned, we got one description of a guy going toward the scene, a different description of a man leaving the scene."

"Did you find him?"

"Not a chance. He was a skilled disguiser, a real pro. He probably used multiple identities. The father denied any knowledge of the murder, and we couldn't find any trail leading to him."

"I suppose it's a stroke of luck that we got a picture of this guy, although he probably doesn't really look like the photo. Maybe I can get something from the car."

"I'll go ahead and fax the photo to you," Eggers said. "And I sympathize with your frustration. We've struck out so far in finding Elena Ortiz."

They had to give him Ortiz, Sid thought. If Jaz hadn't come up with any answers, they'd be forced to let the FBI give it a try. He thanked Eggers and punched off the phone. A couple of minutes later, the fax part of his all-in-one printer activated and began to crank out the picture. He walked over to retrieve it and laid it on his desk.

He had no trouble reading the license number, for all the good it did. As he studied the photo, though, he noticed something odd down in the lower right corner. The image had been enlarged so it showed the tag and part of the rear bumper beneath it. What he saw in the corner appeared to be a portion of a small sticker, maybe a logo. It had no lettering, only three stars along a diagonal line. The photo was black and white, but two of the stars were shaded, apparently indicating different colors. The shape had a familiar look.

He pulled out a drawer where he kept his financial records and searched a couple of months back, when he had used an airline for a quick trip out of town. He located the date, thumbed through papers for a rental car receipt, finally pulled it out. The symbol—red, white and blue stars above a blue line—appeared just to the left of "TriStar Car Rental."

Sid checked the phone book. It showed only one local office for TriStar, located at Nashville International Airport. He took it as a clear signal they were dealing with a hired killer. He flew into town, rented a Ford Fusion, switched the license plate in case he was seen, and checked out Prime Medical Equipment. When he was ready, he parked in the alley, probably picked the lock, sneaked in, and murdered Omar Valdez, or whoever the scammer might turn out to be. Then he stopped somewhere on the way to the airport, replaced the original license tag, tossed his gun into the weeds, and caught a flight back to his home base.

Sid locked up the office, climbed in his car, and drove through Madison to Briley Parkway, which would take him to I-40 one exit below the airport. As he passed the sprawling Opryland Hotel, recently re-opened after a $270 million face-lift necessitated by Nashville's disastrous spring floods, he saw buses lined up to transport conventioneers to some local tourist venue. Just beyond the hotel stood the sadly vacant wings of the Opry Mills Mall and its vast empty parking area, one victim of the 2010 floods that hadn't been restored. Only the small section occupied by Bass Pro Shops Outdoor World had been re-opened.

Sid thought about the errand that had brought Jaz here Saturday morning, leading to her fateful drive downtown that took her past the neighborhood where Earline Ivey was murdered. He knew from her comments Saturday night that the confrontation with Bart Masterson had caused her a great deal of agony. And his work Sunday morning to find a possibe witness had made little impression on the detective. Sid put it out of his mind to concentrate on the more pressing problem Djuan Burden faced.

He pulled into the short term parking garage, wound around until he found a vacant spot, and crossed to the moving walkway that led to the ground transportation level. His mind filled with questions, he dodged passengers heading out to the pickup area and looked for the auto rental counter with the three stars on its logo. When he found it, he stepped up behind a customer who had obviously flown in from somewhere to the north, his fur-collared jacket lying on the roller bag at his side. When the man turned away with his vehicle contract in hand, Sid approached the counter.

"I'm Sid Chance," he said to the pert redhead dressed in blue. He held out his PI card. "I'm a private investigator looking for a man who committed a serious crime in Nashville a few days ago. I'd appreciate it if you would check your records for the driver of a black twenty-eleven Ford Fusion. He turned his car in late last Monday afternoon. He probably rented it a day or two before."

She read the card slowly, frowning, then handed it back. "I'm not allowed to give out information on customers except to the police."

"I'm working with the police." It was close to the truth. The FBI had given him information on the car.

"I don't know," she said. "Let me check with my manager."

She got on the phone, turned her back, and talked a few moments. She looked back at him and shook her head. "I'm only allowed to give out that kind of information to the police."

Sid took out his phone and called Bart. He explained where he was and what he had asked for.

"Where did you get the information about the car?" Bart asked.

"FBI Agent Baron Eggers took a shot from the bank surveillance tape and enhanced it until the tag was readable."

"Did you give the rental agent the license number?"

"No. Eggers said it was a stolen plate, but the bumper showed a TriStar Car Rental logo."

"In that case, your hit man wasn't too professional."

"He probably didn't want to deface the car and have TriStar come after him." Bart was right, of course. The guy had let down his guard.

"And you want me to do what?"

Sid repeated what he had asked the redheaded agent.

"When are you gonna put me on the payroll, buddy?"

Sid chuckled. "I'll find a portable time clock you can punch."

"Let me talk to the lady," he said.

Sid handed her the phone. "This is Metro Homicide Detective Bart Masterson."

She took the phone and listened a few moments, then asked, "How do I know you're really a Metro detective?"

She listened again, a little longer this time, wrote something down, and handed the phone back to Sid.

"What's the verdict," he asked Bart.

"I told her to call the precinct to verify my identity. I have to go, buddy. Good luck."

Sid noticed the agent looking over his shoulder as she made the call. He turned and saw a couple with frosty hair standing behind him, large bags resting at their side. A nearby baggage kiosk rumbled noisily, bringing more passengers and likely more car rental customers.

"This will take some digging," the agent said, returning to the counter. "I'll have to look it up between customers. Give me a number where I can reach you."

He handed her a business card. "Use the cell number. I'll be in a restaurant upstairs." He didn't want to give her an excuse to delay things.

Sid had become friends with the airport police chief during a recent case involving insurance fraud. Snagging a passing airport cop, he arranged to meet the chief in the ticketing area. He explained his situation and got escorted past security into the concourse area, where he wandered into a restaurant that specialized in Italian food. He ordered a spinach and cheese Stromboli with a side salad and carried his food to a back table. People-watching had always fascinated him, even when he wasn't looking for somebody in particular. As he observed the flow of passengers in and out of the restaurant, he tried to guess who they were and what their mission might be. At one point he saw a young man saunter in, middle to late twenties, casually dressed in denims and a nondescript tee shirt, a carryon bag clutched in his left hand. He wore an Atlanta Braves baseball cap pulled down on his forehead. Sid watched his eyes make a careful sweep of the area before he ventured up to the counter.

This guy mirrored the description Sid had imagined for the man he now felt certain had murdered the Prime Medical Equipment owner. He looked about the right age and physical condition for the men he had been associated with in Army Special Forces forty years ago in Vietnam. A few of them, he recalled, could easily have slipped across the line into forbidden territory. They had the skills and the guts to be hired assassins, and the monetary rewards could have been hard to pass up. The cap could be a decoy. He probably came from the Southwest or Northeast.

Sid ate slowly. When he'd finished his meal, he went back for a cup of black coffee and returned to his vigil. He thought of calling Jaz to find out how things were going with Elena Ortiz, but he decided to wait in case the rental car agent should call. After nearly an hour, he decided to hell with it and punched in Jaz's number.

"Any luck with Elena?" he asked.

She told him how the interview had gone.

Sid glanced around the room as he talked. The man in the Braves ball cap had long since departed. The crowd stayed in a constant state of flux. "So she as much as admitted the murder involved drugs, maybe a cartel?"

"That's my take on it," Jaz said. "She broke down and I couldn't see pushing her any further. She's been in her room ever since. She wouldn't come down to lunch."

"What did you work out in your session with the lawyer?"

"He thinks we should lay low and see what happens. When I told him about Bart questioning me on the murder, he said he used to be a criminal lawyer, call him if I needed any help."

"Hopefully it won't come to that," Sid said. "Matter of fact, I got a little help from Bart this morning."

He told her what Agent Eggers had found from the enhanced license plate photo and how Bart had helped with the rental agent, that he was waiting in an airport restaurant for her to finish her search.

"We have to get this cleared up soon, Sid," Jaz said when he mentioned his visit to Rachel Ransom. "That woman has suffered enough."

"Yes, and this situation is getting too complicated for my comfort. We're going to have to turn Ortiz over to the FBI."

"Why?"

"For one thing, I owe it to Agent Eggers. Also he's getting frustrated at not finding her. If he should trace her to your house, you could be charged with harboring a fugitive."

"That I don't need," she said. "Let me try to talk to her again."

22

SID DECIDED TO WAIT another five minutes, then return to the car rental counter if he hadn't heard from the agent. He was already out in the terminal corridor when his phone rang.

"Mr. Chance, this is TriStar Car Rental," she said. "I think I have what you're looking for."

"Thanks. I'm on my way down."

He headed for the escalator and the long descent to the ground transportation level. Observing the man in front of him whose toupee had gone askew made the trip more interesting. The agent at the car rental counter gave him a thin smile.

"It's been a busy time, but the search wasn't as difficult as I was afraid it might be." She removed a pad from the desk and laid it on the counter. "We only have one black twenty-eleven Fusion. It's a popular car, though."

"Was it turned in last Monday afternoon?"

She looked at the pad. "Four-oh-five p.m."

He recalled the 15:24:34 time stamp on the surveillance photo. Forty-one minutes would be time enough for the suspect to change license tags, ditch the gun, and remove his disguise, then make it to the airport and turn in the car.

Sid took out his pen and pocket-sized notebook. "What's his name and address?"

"Your detective was very persuasive," she said with a grin. "I have it all here for you."

She ripped a sheet off the pad and handed it to him. It contained all the information from the rental application: name, address, driver's license number, even the credit card number. He knew he'd have to put everything they had accumulated in a report and get it to Vandenberg and Hersholt.

"You've been most accommodating," he said, saluting her as he turned toward the garage.

On the way to his car, he sorted through the information that was piling up on his mental hard drive. He had lots of facts, but each one seemed to lead to a question mark. By the time he sat behind the wheel, he had decided it was time to get straight with Agent Eggers and see if that might be productive.

"This is Sid Chance," he said when Eggers answered. "I really appreciate what you did with that photo. It provided us with a real breakthrough."

"How did that happen?"

"I'll tell you in a minute, but first I have something for you."

"I hope it's a good one."

"How about Elena Ortiz?"

"You found her?"

"Jaz is currently grilling her. She's already come up with a pretty good indication that the murder was drug related. Probably a Mexican gang."

"I'll need to get that to the DEA. Where is she?"

"I'm about to go meet with Jaz. When I get there, I'll call and let you know where to pick up your prize."

"Okay," Eggers said. "I'll give you a little tidbit that just came in from Albuquerque. They say Señor Valdez, he doesn't speak the English too good. Still works as a bus boy at Casa Rosa Restaurant. He had no idea someone was using his Social Security number. What did you come up with from that license plate photo?"

Sid told him what he had learned at the airport.

"That sounds promising. Apparently the guy's getting a little careless."

"Right. And if he was hired by a Mexican gang, it should give us some leverage with Ortiz."

"I definitely need to look into this. Give me the information you got from TriStar Car Rental. I agree it was probably all fake, but I'll check it out. We'll interview the clerk who dealt with him and try to get a good description. Then maybe we can track him back to his point of origin."

MOST OF THE BEDROOMS were on the second floor. Jaz found Elena sitting by the window, looking down at a succession of robins, red-winged blackbirds, and cardinals pecking away at a triple-decker bird feeder atop a post in back of the house. Her mother would never have admitted to such a plebeian pastime as bird watching, but Jaz remembered many times seeing Gwendolyn LeMieux sitting beside the window just like Elena.

"Wouldn't you like to come down and eat something?" Jaz asked, leaning against the bed post near where the dyed blonde sat.

Elena looked up, her face expressionless. "In a little while, maybe."

"I wish you'd tell me how you got involved in all of this. Maybe I could help you find a way out. I'm almost certain the FBI would drop any charges against you if you cooperated and helped sort this all out."

"I don't think it will be that easy."

"It might not be easy, but it's sure a lot preferable to the alternative. Before I joined my father's company and prepared myself to take over, I did a lot of things I'd have been better off skipping. I enlisted in the Air Force and served in the Security Police. It's like being an Army MP. After that I spent a few years as a professional boxer, living from hand to mouth on meager earnings. Then I joined the Metro Nashville police force and worked as a patrolwoman. I know the criminal justice system, Elena, and I know you don't want to get tangled up in it."

"Whatever happens, it's too late to help Omar."

"True, but you're still young. You have a lot of life to live."

The phone on the bedside table rang, followed shortly by a tone that indicated the call was for her. She picked up the phone. "This is Jasmine."

Sid's voice mirrored his upbeat mood. "The FBI is onto this big time now," he said. He briefed her on the information he'd learned at the airport and what FBI Agent Eggers had told him about the real Omar Valdez.

"I'm talking to Elena now," Jaz said.

"I'm going to head that way. It won't take long. I promised to call Eggers and let him know where he can pick up Ortiz. Maybe we can get a little more out of her with this new information before he gets there."

She put the phone down and turned to Elena. "Sid is on his way over here. He has some interesting information to talk to you about."

After Elena finally agreed to let Marie fix her a late lunch, Jaz followed her downstairs and across to the kitchen. Marie took over, seated the tawny-skinned fake blonde at the table and began questioning her on what she would like to eat. Jaz returned to her office, where she called her friend Dr. Reagan Abrams at the Medical Examiner's office.

"Hi, Reagan, it's Jaz. Have you had a chance to check on those fingerprints of Omar Valdez?"

"No, and it's really odd. I was tied up all morning with an autopsy and didn't get to look into it until this afternoon. When I did, I found everything involved with the case had been sequestered."

"Why on earth—?"

"Sealed by order of the District Attorney's office."

"I wonder what brought that on?"

"I heard it was requested by the police. Seems a deputy chief was the one who called in the instructions."

Deputy Chief Kozlov, no doubt. Was this something requested by Detectives Grimm and Kozlov? What were they trying to hide? She was satisfied that they would get their comeuppance when the anonymous hit man was brought to light, but this really galled her.

"Did you tell your boss there was a suggestion that Valdez might not be his real identity?"

"She said it was out of her hands. I'd have to tell the police about it."

"I suspect they don't want to know," Jaz said. "The FBI is onto it, though."

"I think they've already been by here, Jaz. You're really into this private detective business, aren't you? How do you find the time for it with all your Welcome Home Stores involvement?"

"My dad was a very astute businessman. He set the company up with some great people in the key spots. He had phased out of most of the hands-on operation before he died. I keep a close watch on things, but the guys and gals in charge really know what they're doing."

"I'm glad everything worked out so well for you. We were all worried when you left school."

"After I calmed down, I hated that I had let you guys down without an experienced point guard."

"We understood."

"Thanks. I appreciated everybody's concern, but you do what you have to do."

"Well, I'm sorry I couldn't be any more help on this Omar Valdez situation."

"You were a big help, Reagan. Thanks. Incidentally, were you involved in the Earline Ivey autopsy?"

"Yes, that's the one I spent this morning on. I don't like the way the news people keep bringing up your name in the story. It doesn't fit you. What that woman claimed you did was disgusting."

"I know. Now I won't get my chance to face her and see who was lying."

"What was strange about the case is Ivey's wound was almost exactly like the one on Valdez, except the bullet entered her head from the rear instead of the front."

"Was it a twenty-two round?"

"Yes. It was in a little better shape. They can probably get a match with this one."

"Good. That should help the detectives. Let me know if you hear anything else over there, Reagan."

"I will. You take care."

Sid had nearly reached Jaz's place when his phone rang. He saw Bart's number on the ID. He flipped open the cover and said, "Got anything new for me?"

"Where are you?"

"Nearly at Jaz's house."

"Good."

"Why good?"

"You need to talk to her. I don't think it would be a good thing for me to do it."

Sid pulled off the street into the edge of Jaz's driveway and stopped. "Talk about what?"

"I've been taken off the Earline Ivey case."

"You've what?"

"I just got the word this afternoon."

"Why?"

"The lieutenant said there was new evidence regarding Miss LeMieux and they decided I was too close to her."

"How'd they figure that?"

"The Miss Demeanor and Five Felons Club is no secret."

"I know, but that's no—"

"I told the lieutenant that was bullshit. I've been doing this for over twenty years now and nobody's accused me of being biased."

"So what's their excuse?"

"The word came from the CJC."

The Criminal Justice Center, Police headquarters. "I wonder if it was the deputy chief."

"Kozlov. He's the likely suspect. But I don't know why."

"What's this new evidence involving Jaz?" Sid asked.

"I don't know. Tommy Fagan, the detective they gave the case to, said he was sworn to secrecy. This whole business stinks. Tell Jaz to expect the worst."

Sid closed his phone and stared up the driveway, dreading what he had to do. He recalled the confrontation with Grimm at the Prime Medical store, the warning Wick Stanley had given him about Ramsey Kozlov, and the episode out by his mailbox with the two detectives Thursday night. He approached the gate and watched it swing open, then drove slowly toward the house, trying to think of an easy way to break the bad news.

Jaz stood at the door when he walked across the brick-paved entrance from where he'd parked. "Come on in," she said. "You won't believe what Reagan Abrams told me."

What Bart had said seemed hardly believable, as well, but he decided to hold off for the moment. "She get a match on the prints?"

"She got nothing."

Sid stared at her. "The prints should have been perfect."

Jaz repeated what Reagan had said about how all the files

on the case had been sealed on orders from the DA, a message relayed by the deputy police chief.

"Kozlov." Sid groaned. "I hate to be the bearer of bad news, but it gets worse."

He told her how Bart had been pulled off the Earline Ivey case. "He suspects the order came from Chief Kozlov."

She stopped in the hallway to her office and looked up, eyes wide. "Evidence about me? What on earth could it be? Since I haven't done anything, how could they possibly have any evidence?"

"Bart had no idea. The detective they gave the case to wouldn't tell him anything. But considering what we know about Grimm and Kozlov, and what they did with Mrs. Ransom's gun, it doesn't sound good."

23

SID CALLED AGENT EGGERS before they began their final
shot at Elena Ortiz. He gave the address of Jaz's mansion
and said they would be waiting for him.

"You might be interested in the results of the fingerprint
check on the late Omar Valdez," Eggers said. "His real name
is Estefan Perez Delgado. He's been involved in drugs before."

"I'm not surprised."

"Hang on to Miz Ortiz. We'll be right out."

When Siz closed his phone, Jaz suggested they use the rec
room as a neutral, non-threatening place to interrogate Ortiz.
Such things usually went better when conducted informally in
a somewhat friendly atmosphere. She led the way to the
kitchen, where Elena had finished eating and stood with Marie
beside a preparation table.

"Did Marie give you enough to eat?" Jaz asked.

Elena smiled, a good sign. "I'm stuffed."

"Let's go to the recreation room," Jaz said, "where we can
be comfortable and chat."

The walnut-paneled room had a cozy appearance with its
soft recessed lighting. Photographs from Jaques LeMieux's
hunting trips graced the walls, including a large elk and a
ferocious-looking tiger. A firm believer in wildlife conservation
after his National Park career, Sid was happy there were only
photographs and not stuffed animal heads. Jaz had kept one
of her father's casino card tables and the wet bar, adding her

own exercise equipment to one corner. A sofa and two comfortable chairs faced a large screen TV. Jaz and Elena took the sofa, Sid one of the chairs.

"Sid has learned some new information he wants to discuss with you," Jaz said.

Elena gave him a guarded look.

"You say you met Omar Valdez at the clinic where you worked in San Antonio, correct?" he asked.

She nodded.

"Where did he say he was from?"

"New Mexico."

"What did he say about his experience in the medical equipment field?"

She shifted about on the sofa. "He had worked for a company that sold wheel chairs and walkers and all kinds of equipment."

"Where?"

"In San Antonio."

"And Valdez was the name he used?"

"Of course. That was his name." Her eyes flashed toward Jaz and back to Sid as she began to twist her hands.

She's lying, Jaz thought.

"According to the Social Security number he used, the name belongs to a man who works for a restaurant in Albuquerque, New Mexico," Sod said. The FBI is on the case now. Using fingerprints from the autopsy, they've identified him as Estefan Perez Delgado."

Tears welled in her eyes and she bent forward, a hand covering her mouth.

Sid continued in a calm, deliberate voice. "Your brother was connected to a drug gang, wasn't he? Did he break away from them when he came to Nashville? Why were they after him?"

She looked up, tears rolling down her cheek. "I can't talk about it."

"You can either talk to us or the FBI, Elena."

She pushed herself forward on the sofa as if to get up, those indigo eyes flashing. "I thought you were going to protect me."

"The best way we can protect you is to put you in the custody of the FBI. They have all the resources."

She was standing now, the look changed from anger to fear. "They will torture me to get the information."

Sid stood, too, towering over her. "Sit down and be sensible, Elena. The FBI isn't the cartel. They don't torture people. FBI Agent Baron Eggers is on his way here now. Do you want to tell us about Estefan Perez Delgado?"

"No," she said, remaining tight-lipped. She stood again, looking defiant. "I don't have to stay here. You can't stop me."

"On the contrary," Jaz said. "Have you heard of a citizen's arrest? Under Tennessee law, a citizen can arrest and hold a person believed to be guilty of a felony. I'm sure Medicare fraud falls under that category. The law requires the person to be turned over to the nearest law enforcement officer."

John Wallace appeared at the door a moment later and announced that the FBI agents were here.

"Bring them back, John," Jaz said.

Sid took Eggers aside to fill him in on what had occurred earlier.

"It was Ortiz's reaction to questions about her brother Pablo's involvement in drug trafficking that gave us the clue."

"It appears likely that Delgado was connected with Pablo Ortiz," Eggers said. "I've turned most of that over to DEA. There's been a big jump lately in the flow of heroin into the Nashville area. First I need to make sure the murder doesn't have any connection to the Medicare business. The drug people have learned that Medicare fraud is a lucrative racket."

"I asked her if Delgado broke away from a drug gang when they came to Nashville. Her only answer was 'I can't talk about it.'"

"We'll get the truth out of her."

"Have you turned up anything from the car rental link?" Sid asked.

"We're just getting into it. The surveillance camera showed him with black hair and a black beard, but the agent who rented him the car said he was clean shaven with light-colored hair. He obviously uses disguises. These guys are usually so cautious it's impossible to pin them down, but this looks like we might have a halfway decent chance of nailing him."

They went into the rec room where Elena Ortiz sat with Jaz. The other agent stood in the doorway. Ortiz looked as nervous as a caged lion. Eggers took out his Bureau identification and showed it to her. "I'm Special Agent Baron Eggers of the FBI," he said. "We need you to come down to the office and answer some questions."

"Am I under arrest?" she asked.

"No."

Ortiz looked around at Jaz. "She said I was under citizen's arrest."

"I said under Tennessee law we had the right to make a citizen's arrest," Jaz replied. "But I never said you were under arrest."

Eggers spoke to Ortiz again. "I need to talk to you about a matter that on the surface doesn't appear to involve Prime Medical Equipment."

Which meant he intended to question her about Estefan Delgado and why someone had sent a hit man to end his life, Sid thought.

24

AFTER THE TWO FBI agents had left with Elena Ortiz, Sid and Jaz returned to her office. Jaz slid into her chair behind the desk.

"Now that we know she's been lying to us, she doesn't sound quite the innocent tool that she seemed at first," Jaz said.

Sid dropped into a chair across from her. "I considered her a full participant from the start. The way she took the money and ran the morning after the murder cinched it for me."

Jaz turned to her computer. "Let's see what's out there on Mr. Delgado."

Sid watched as she logged onto a background search site. "According to Eggers, Delgado was another El Paso product."

"I'll put that in," she said as her fingers danced over the keyboard.

After making a few refinements to the search, she pointed to the screen. "This looks like him."

She turned the monitor so Sid could see it better. Estefan Perez Delgado had been arrested for drug dealing in San Antonio. A brief newspaper story explained how a key witness had failed to appear in court, resulting in dismissal of the charges. Following a link, Jaz turned up an item that showed Delgado appearing in a photo with a ranking member of a Mexican drug cartel.

"It looks like he was definitely involved in drug

distribution," Sid said. "Eggers wants to find out if the drug folks were taking part in Delgado's Medicare scam. The big question is why did they decide to cut their ties with him in a fatal manner."

"I can understand Elena being scared to death they'd come after her," Jaz said. "If she's smart, she'll make a deal and tell everything she knows."

Sid sat back in his chair and nodded. "I think we have enough to throw Grimm and Kozlov's case out the window. I need to put it all on paper and get it to the lawyers so we can get Djuan out of jail."

As he pushed up from the chair, an electronic beep notified Jaz of a visitor at the gate. Glancing at the monitor, he saw a stern-faced man at the window of a black sedan.

Jaz keyed the microphone on her desk. "Can I help you?"

"We're here to see Miss Jasmine LeMieux," he said.

"Can I tell her who's calling?"

"Metro Police."

She pressed the button to open the gate and turned to Sid. "I wonder what they want?"

Sid had a bad feeling about it, but he only shrugged. "They're detectives. More questions, I guess."

She called John Wallace on the intercom and asked him to bring the officers back to her office. A few minutes later, John appeared at the door with two average looking guys who appeared to be in their thirties. They could have been a couple of young businessmen, but the one in front took out his identification and showed it to Jaz.

"I'm Detective Thomas Fagan, Metro Police Department." He nodded his head toward the other man, a sharp-eyed black officer in a snappy gray suit that appeared a cut above the one Fagan wore. "This is my partner, Detective George Quarles. Are you Miss Jasmine LeMieux?"

"I am," Jaz said. "What can I do for you?"

"You can come downtown with us," he said in an all-business voice. "You're under arrest for the murder of Earline Ivey. You have the right to remain silent. Anything you say can and will be used against you in a court of law..."

Sid listened in shock as Fagan continued with the Miranda Warning. Jaz stood with her mouth half open, her face contorted in a look of total disbelief. When he got to the part about "do you understand," she shook her head vigorously.

"I don't understand any of this," she said. "You could not possibly have any evidence connecting me to her murder."

"We have the evidence," he said. "If you need anything before you leave, Detective Quarles will accompany you."

"Have you looked into the possibility this could be a professional hit?" Sid asked in a sharp voice.

Fagan looked across at him. "You must be Mr. Chance. I was told you might be here."

"By whom?" Sid asked.

Fagan ignored him, turning back to Jaz. "If you need anything, please get it now. We need to get downtown."

Sid wasn't one to be ignored. "What's the rush?" he asked. "Is Chief Kozlov pulling the strings?"

"He's just doing his job, Sid," Jaz said, her voice calm though she looked anything but. "I was once a police officer. I'm familiar with how it goes. I'm sure we can get this straightened out shortly. Call K.C. Urban and have him meet us at the Criminal Justice Center. Here's his card. He should be at the company office."

She picked up a business card off her desk and handed it to him.

Sid could hardly believe what he was seeing. It was too reminiscent of what had happened to him in Lewisville. He couldn't imagine what kind of evidence they had trumped up.

If this was some sort of retaliation for the way he and Jaz had "tinkered" with Grimm and Kozlov's homicide case, he would rattle cages until somebody paid a price for it.

Jaz put on her jacket and started toward the door, but Fagan stopped her. He pulled out a pair of handcuffs and snapped them on one of her wrists.

"Can you put them in front?" she asked.

He cuffed her hands in front as Sid protested.

"She's a highly respected businesswoman. Is that necessary?"

"It's department policy. We do it to every murder suspect, regardless of who they are."

"If you'd called and asked, she would have come in voluntarily."

Fagan looked uncomfortable but made no reply.

John and Marie were standing in the hallway when they came out of the office.

"I shouldn't be gone long," Jaz told them. "Don't worry about it. I'm sure we can clear up this misunderstanding quickly."

Sid knew she was putting up a brave front for their benefit, but he doubted her confidence was all that great. He followed them as they walked toward the door. Out on the porch, he hailed Jaz.

"I'll call Urban and follow you downtown. Keep a stiff upper."

As soon as he got into his car, he punched in the lawyer's number. As he headed down the driveway behind the police car, he told Urban what had happened.

"The way she talked this morning, I was afraid there might be more to it than she thought."

"Can you get over to the Criminal Justice Center and meet her?"

"I'll be there."

The detectives sped through the late afternoon traffic along Franklin Road as if they were on an emergency call, though they used no lights or siren. Sid stayed on their tail, letting them run interference. The gloomy skies looked ready to cry, and he shared the feeling. As they approached police headquarters, across James Robertson Parkway from the back of the Metro Courthouse, Sid saw the crowd of news people, including several TV cameras, waiting in the broad, tree-lined plaza outside the Criminal Justice Center.

Anger rose in his stomach like a flaming torch. He could have chewed a railroad spike. Somebody had tipped off the media. This had Kozlov written all over it, a setup from the word go. Sid slowed as the black vehicle pulled to the curb. Detective Fagan got out of the car and opened the rear door for Jaz as the reporters and cameras closed in.

25

JAZ SAW THE CROWD in front of the building and dreaded what was coming. After the publicity brought on by Earline Ivey's accusations, she had been skittish about talking to anyone in the media. They had carried her denial, but the Ivey story garnered much more coverage. Now they would be going for the jugular.

Detective Quarles stopped the car near the walkway leading to the Criminal Justice Center entrance, and Tommy Fagan stepped out onto the sidewalk. She saw the crush of news-people coming as he held the door open for her. Camera lights glared and flashed in the gloom of the afternoon as she struggled out with her hands bound, looking and feeling like a common criminal.

Fagan grasped her left arm and started to move her forward when another hand clutched her right arm. She glanced around to see the formidable presence of K.C. Urban. As the reporters began to shout questions, K.C. countered in a booming voice.

"Miss LeMieux has no comment at the moment. We'll give you a statement later." He looked across at the detective. "I'm her attorney. Let's get her in out of this free-for-all."

It all felt unreal as they hurried Jaz through the mob into the building. Fagan led them back to an interview room.

"Make yourselves comfortable while I go find Detective Quarles. Be back in a few minutes."

The lawyer stopped him as he started out the door. "Don't turn on the microphones. I need to speak to my client."

"Okay." He walked out and closed the door, leaving Jaz and K.C. Urban in a small room with three chairs and a table.

"I feel like a wanted criminal," Jaz said with a sigh. "This is much more embarrassing than the dispute over the accusations of racism."

"Sit down and try to relax. Do you have any idea what prompted them to make such an accusation?"

"Not the slightest," Jaz said as she dropped into one of the chairs. It felt uncomfortable, which she knew was part of the game between cop and suspect. "They haven't told me a thing."

"With your stature in the community, I'm sure the District Attorney would require some significant evidence before making this charge."

"I certainly don't know where it would have come from. I was nowhere near Earline Ivey's house, except driving along Gallatin Road. From what Bart said, she was already dead by then."

Urban shifted his weight to find a more comfortable position. The chair had not been designed for a man of his size. "What do we know about the time of death?"

"According to the Medical Examiner, it occurred between seven and ten a.m."

"What time were you driving in the area?"

"It was somewhere around nine-thirty."

She told him about Sid's hit-man theory, that the suspicious character had visited the market on Gallatin Road sometime after seven that morning.

"Did he tell the police about this?"

"He talked to Bart Masterson, who had the case until they took it away from him this morning."

While she was relating their problems with Detectives

Grimm and Kozlov, the door opened and Fagan and Quarles walked in. Quarles took a seat while Fagan, obviously the lead detective in the case, remained standing.

He placed a small recording machine on the table and punched a button. After giving the date and circumstances of the interview, he looked at Jaz. "Please state your full name."

"Jasmine Rebecca LeMieux."

She gritted her teeth and gave the detective a stern look. This was totally ridiculous. It was time to get the situation out in the open and quash this inquisition.

Fagan opened a folder and looked at something inside. "You told Detective Masterson that you were in the vicinity of Earline Ivey's house Saturday morning around nine-thirty."

"So were several hundred other people," Jaz said.

K.C. Urban spoke up. "I'm advising my client to say nothing further until you reveal what evidence led to this charge. If you don't want to tell us, I'll go to the District Attorney."

Fagan took a photograph out of his folder and dropped it on the table. Jaz and the lawyer leaned toward it. She saw a picture of a latex glove that had been rumpled by wear.

"Do you know what that is?" the detective asked.

"Of course," Jaz said. "It's a glove similar to what we use, as do you, in gathering evidence at a crime scene."

"It is also used by criminals who don't want to leave fingerprints. This one was found at the back porch of Earline Ivey's home after her murder."

"I was told one had been found there," Jaz said.

"But that wasn't necessary because you already knew. You dropped it there."

Jaz's chest rose as her nostrils flared. "That is the most asinine statement I've ever heard."

"That glove contains your fingerprints, Miss LeMieux."

26

S ID COULD DO NOTHING but watch as the mob of newsies swarmed Jaz on the sidewalk in front of the Criminal Justice Center. Just before he had to move on, a large man appeared to come to her rescue on the opposite side from Detective Fagan. He presumed it was K.C. Urban, the attorney.

He had to buck the homebound traffic to find a parking spot in the next block on the opposite side of James Robertson Parkway. He pulled in and checked his watch. The TV people would have just enough time to get their stories in for the evening news. He put a couple of quarters in the meter and got back in the car, uncertain what to do. They would be inside police headquarters by now. If he strode in there and said what he wanted to, he'd likely wind up in jail himself. He decided to call Bart.

"Masterson," said the gruff voice. It sounded like he'd been having the same kind of day as Sid and Jaz.

"It's Sid. Detectives Fagan and Quarles came out to Jaz's house and put her under arrest for murder. I'm parked across from headquarters. They just took her in there through a swarm of reporters."

"I suspected something like this."

"She asked me to call a company lawyer named Urban, who used to practice criminal law. I think he was the guy who intercepted them in front of the building. I don't know what I can do but sit here and wait."

"Nothing you can do, Sid. They'll question her if the attorney lets them, which he shouldn't. Then they'll book her. With her standing in the community, they should bond her out."

Sid let down a window as the car began to heat up. "Fagan wouldn't tell her what evidence they had against her."

"I found out," Bart said. "Remember the latex glove I told you about? The lab lifted her fingerprints from it."

"How the hell could—"

"Only one answer, Sid. She had worn it."

"But..." His voice faded away as his brain went into overdrive. They had both worn gloves at the Prime Medical Equipment store Thursday. He had stuffed his in the wastebasket. As he recalled, Jaz had dropped hers in the chair where Valdez-Delgado had been shot. But how could one possibly wind up on Earline Ivey's back porch?

"You still there?" Bart asked.

"Yeah. I'm thinking. Jaz and I discarded latex gloves after we searched through the junk left behind at that medical equipment store. Victor Grimm saw us with them on when he came in. He made some snotty remark about us gumshoes poking around with our rubber gloves."

"He left before you did, didn't he?"

"Right. We waited there for FBI Agent Eggers."

"Grimm is a contentious bastard, but I can't see him planting evidence like that."

"I don't think I told you what happened Thursday night after the poker game."

Sid detailed how Grimm and Kozlov had followed him home, with the burly detective taunting him about the tests that showed Rachel Ransom's gun had been fired recently. Sid reiterated Mrs. Ransom's assurance there was no way Djuan could have returned the gun to her cedar chest after his trip to

Green Hills, and that it had not been fired since she and her husband came back from California fifteen years ago. He told Bart how Grimm had replied when he said Mrs. Ransom heard Kozlov mention that he could demonstrate how the gun still worked.

"He said 'you can't prove shit'?" Bart asked in disbelief.

"More to the point, he screamed it. That was proof enough to me that the detectives had fired it before they turned it in as evidence. Of course, he was right. No way could I prove it. But now this glove business comes up."

"I see your point, but you have no proof there, either."

As Sid thought about what had happened that day in Green Hills, he remembered the call that evening from the florist shop owner. She had seen a man get out of a white Dodge, maybe an Avenger, and go into the Prime Medical Equipment store. He had dismissed it at the time, considering it likely someone from the real estate agency. But considering subsequent events, the white Dodge Avenger gave him a different perspective on the sighting.

"I just thought of something, Bart," he said. "There's a possibility I might come up with the information we need. I'll let you know if I do."

He ended the call and looked up the flower shop phone number in his notebook. He had a good ear for voices and recognized the owner as soon as she answered.

"This is Sid Chance," he said. "You called Tuesday night and mentioned seeing a man get out of a white Dodge in front of the former medical supply store. Do you remember anything about how he looked?"

"Oh, hello, Mr. Chance. You caught me just in time. I was about to lock up. Yes, I remember. I thought it was a bit odd for somebody to be going in there after business hours, so I took a good look at him. He was a short fellow, and when he turned toward me as he went toward the building, I noticed he had a mustache."

"Could it be described as a Clark Gable mustache?"

"Exactly. I hadn't thought about it, but that's exactly what it was."

"Anything else you can think of, like how he was dressed?"

She was silent a moment. "Light colored pants and a dark jacket. That's all I remember."

"Thanks very much," he said, feeling a new surge of hope. "You've been a big help."

"Happy to oblige. Let me know if I can be of any further assistance."

After closing the phone, he faced the question of what now? As he looked across at the brick building where Jaz was being subjected unfairly to a traumatic experience, his mood quickly changed to one of frustration.

27

AFTER BEING FINGERPRINTED and run through the booking process, Jaz appeared before a judge, where an assistant DA agreed she should be allowed to post bond and be released. She posed no a threat to the community, nor was she likely to flee. An NAACP lawyer, who had been tipped on what was coming up, objected. He obviously had no idea what Jaz had been involved in lately.

"Miss LeMieux should be held to the same standard as Djuan Burden, who is now confined to the County Jail," the lawyer said.

Jaz spoke up before her attorney could stop her. "Your honor, if you'll set bond for Djuan, I'll happily bail him out."

The judge gave her a judicious frown. "That is not germane to this case, Miss LeMieux. I'm setting your bond at five hundred thousand dollars. You are not to leave this jurisdiction without informing the court."

SID DROVE OVER TO the building where Arnie Bailey had his office and took the elevator up, hoping Bailey would still be there. He found the small, stocky lawyer talking to the receptionist, who appeared to be cleaning up her desk for the day. Bailey's face turned grim when he saw Sid.

"What the hell's going on?" he asked. "I've just been told there was a breaking news report on TV that Jaz was in jail for murder."

"I don't know about the jail part," Sid said, "but I saw them take her into the Criminal Justice Center. She's innocent. It's a big mess. I've got to get to the bottom of it. I need to use a computer."

"Come on into my office."

He led the way down the hall. The room appeared rather small compared to the rest of the Bailey, Riddle and Smith suite. An executive desk with a computer station angled behind it, bookshelves on two walls, a few cushioned chairs. That was it. The desk held neat stacks of papers, the sign of a well-organized mind.

"What do you need from the computer?" Bailey asked.

"Channel Five had a follow-up story about Djuan Burden Tuesday night that showed the detectives removing the crime scene tape from the front of Prime Medical Equipment. I need to see if they have the video on their website."

"That shouldn't be too difficult." He turned to his computer and started punching on the keyboard. After a couple of minutes, he looked around. "Check this out."

Sid moved to where he could see the screen. "Okay, start the video."

He saw Grimm and Kozlov removing the crime scene tape from Prime Medical just as he remembered. The shorter detective wore light colored pants and a dark jacket, though his Clark Gable mustache didn't show since his back was turned away from the camera.

Sid looked back at Bailey. "We've got a problem and I'm not sure how to handle it."

"Tell me about it."

Sid gave him the whole story, from his belief that the detectives had fired Rachel Ransom's gun to the latex glove found at the Earline Ivey murder scene.

"The problem is I have no proof that any of it happened."

"Do you think this florist lady could identify Ramsey Kozlov?"

"I could ask her, but that would only give us a circumstantial case. There's no way to show what he did in the medical supply store. I might check with whoever cleaned out the place, see if they remember seeing the gloves in the chair. But there, again, it's only circumstantial."

Arnie Bailey could only shake his head.

Sid's phone rang and he saw Jaz's number on the screen. "Are you okay?" he asked.

"No, but I'm not in jail. Where are you?"

"At Arnie Bailey's office."

"Can you pick me up and take me home?" Her voice sounded strong, though it held a definite weariness.

"At the Criminal Justice Center?"

"No, at Welcome Home Stores. K.C. Urban brought me over here. I'll tell you what happened when you get here."

JAQUES LEMIEUX HAD served in the Korean War with a Canadian Army unit involved in vehicle maintenance. His knowledge of trucks and how to maintain them impressed an American Army officer who invited him to visit Nashville after the war. The young man's father operated a truck sales franchise. When Jaz's father visited him, he talked LeMieux into going into business with him in a service station that would cater to over-the-road truckers. Jaques came up with a succession of improvements in the business, plus he saw a great future with the new interstate highway system under way. After a few years, he bought out his partner and launched an expansion campaign. It resulted in the far-flung network of travel centers now headquartered in a five-story building out West End Avenue.

Sid parked in a visitor slot behind the impressive brick and stone structure and followed signs to the reception area. He had never visited Welcome Home Stores before. After getting directions from a security guard, who called to make sure he was expected, he took an elevator to the top floor where the chairman's office was located. An attractive young redhead with ADMINISTRATIVE ASSISTANT on her desk greeted him when he entered the suite.

"You must be Mr. Chance," she said, making a show of looking slowly up to his face.

He cocked an eyebrow. "Has my reputation preceded me?"

"You're very well thought of around here. Go on in. Miss LeMieux is waiting for you."

The door to Jaz's office was half-open, but he knocked before entering. The room was almost a mirror image of her office at home, complete to the bookshelves around the walls. It had obviously been created by her father. She sat in a chair next to the large man with the burr haircut he had seen outside police headquarters.

"K.C. Urban, Sid Chance," Jaz said as the two men shook hands.

Sid took the chair across from them. "Bart told me about the fingerprints on the glove. What happened?"

Jaz briefed him on the session with the detectives and the bond hearing. "It doesn't look good."

"I could say don't worry, but that would be a little premature. I'm almost certain I know what happened. Proving it is something else. The glove was one you wore while we searched Prime Medical Equipment last Tuesday."

Jaz perked up when he told them what the florist shop owner had seen in front of the store and how he had verified Ramsey Kozlov's description with the Channel Five video.

"It might be enough to create a reasonable doubt if the woman could identify Kozlov," Urban said. "But he would probably claim he was there to continue his investigation."

"Did Jaz tell you what we suspect about Kozlov and Detective Grimm in the Djuan Burden murder investigation," Sid asked.

"Yes, and it sounds like a similar situation. But you have to realize that what seems obvious to you might not be so obvious to a jury."

Jaz gave Sid a wistful look. "This is the point in the story where you're supposed to reach into your hat and pull out a live, kicking bunny."

Sid stared at his folded hands. His bag of tricks had just hit empty.

28

D URING THE DRIVE TO Jaz's house, they talked about where things stood on both fronts, the Djuan Burden case and Earline Ivey's murder. After going over the slaying of Omar Valdez, a.k.a. Estefan Perez Delgado, Sid twisted his mouth in frustration.

"I'm certain that hired killer did it," he said.

Jaz stared at the road ahead as if looking for answers, then turned back to Sid. "But it's all circumstantial and we have no hired killer."

"I'd bet my last buck Earline Ivey was also the victim of a hired killer, maybe even the same one."

"How do you figure that? What's the connection?"

"Who do we know that's linked to both cases?"

She massaged her forehead gently, then looked back. "Detectives Grimm and Kozlov?"

"Victor Grimm hasn't poked his ugly head into the Ivey case that I know of. The same can't be said with any certainty about Ramsey Kozlov. He was alone when the florist saw him enter the Prime Medical building last Thursday."

"Surely you're not saying he hired her killer."

"I don't know. But think about it this way—he accused you of interfering in their homicide case when he stopped you outside that apartment on Granny White. You posed a high profile target. Plus the racial slur accusations made you vulnerable."

Jaz paused a moment. "He warned me to stay out of the way if I didn't want to get hurt. But what would he gain by getting me charged with a murder? He knew we couldn't prove they'd fired that gun."

"Did he know we were onto the hit man's trail?"

"I suppose he could have. Several people knew about it. Hattie Jordan, of course, Reagan Abrams, Bart and Wick. I'm not sure who else. What if Kozlov knew?"

"I'm just speculating. He could have figured we were getting too close to exposing what he'd done. Taking you out of the picture would interrupt our investigation."

"Has it?"

"I didn't even think about the Burden case when I was at Arnie Bailey's office, and that's where his lawyers are."

Jaz took a deep breath and shook her head. "Is there any other possible way that glove could have wound up on Earline Ivey's porch?"

"I can't think of any. It had to have been left there by the killer or by someone after the murder. If Kozlov took the glove from the Green Hills store, he either gave it to the killer or left it himself. Either way, he had to know what was happening."

"I'm totally confused," Jaz said. "Killing that woman just to get at me makes no sense. I guess I just don't think like a criminal."

"You didn't spend enough time on the force to get your brain twisted into a criminal mindset."

The gloomy skies turned black before they reached Jaz's house. Floodlights at the corners bathed the sprawling mansion in a ghostly glow. She invited Sid to come in, and he thought it best to stay with her for a while. They ate dinner with Marie and John Wallace. Jaz spoke candidly about what had happened, which only confirmed what the Wallaces had seen on the TV news.

"We know where the glove came from," Jaz said. "It was one I had used last Tuesday when Sid and I searched the former Prime Medical Equipment store. We just don't know how it came to be found on Earline Ivey's back porch."

"I don't how anybody could think you'd do something like this," Marie said, shaking her head.

"We're going to find who's responsible," Sid said. "That's my primary mission until I can dredge up the answer."

SID ARRIVED HOME shortly before ten. Considering how much he knew about Ramsey Kozlov, plus what he suspected, and remembering the call he'd received Sunday night, he checked carefully for any sign of tampering at his house. He felt the comforting bulk of the .40 caliber Sig Sauer on his hip, similar to the gun he had carried as a National Park ranger. It remained there during risky cases, which this one had clearly become.

He found a call from Sgt. Wick Stanley on his answering machine. Wondering why Wick hadn't tried the cell phone, he checked and found it as lifeless as the coho salmon in the freezer he'd intended to cook for dinner. In all the confusion and frantic activity of the past few hours, he hadn't noticed the battery had gone dead. He plugged in the charger and called Wick on the landline.

"What's the story on Jaz?" his friend asked. "Bart said you had some suspicions about Grimm and Kozlov."

"I took Jaz home. She's okay but pretty shaken by all this. Did Bart tell you about the glove?"

"Yeah. And that you think they fired the Burden gun. Why would they do that?"

"My guess is it's an old weapon and somebody wanted to be sure it was still in working order."

"Evidently it was."

"Right. Bart doesn't think Grimm would stoop to planting evidence like that glove. What about Kozlov?"

"I warned you about him, remember?"

"Does this sound like something he might do?"

"Maybe. I've heard he could be on the take."

"Anything you can put your finger on?"

"Not really. I know he hangs around some of the guys in narcotics. One of them told me Ram asks a lot of questions, acts like he might want to transfer over there."

Sid carried the phone into the kitchen and switched on the coffee maker. "His dad could arrange that easily enough, couldn't he?"

"Yeah, and it hasn't happened. Which makes me wonder why he's asking all those questions."

"I'd like to meet him. Does he do the bar scene?"

"Some of the guys from the precinct hang out at Nick the Greek's place over on Charlotte. I think he's one of them. If you're going over there, Sid, be careful. You could wind up next on his list."

Sid remembered that anonymous phone call. "I'm already on it," he said.

THE ACTIVITY AND NOISE level at the Olympia Restaurant and Bar & Grill hardly seemed what Sid would have expected at ten-thirty on a Monday night. Walls of dark paneling and soft lighting gave the place a subdued look, but half the tables were lively with the clamor of conversation. Sid walked in and looked around. He saw a few uniforms scattered about, and several others with the cop look. As he stood near a front table, an older woman in a long flowery dress approached.

"You need a menu?" she asked.

He raised his voice to be heard over the chatter. "No thanks. Do you know if Ram has been in tonight?"

A burly cop with white hair at a nearby table grinned as he spoke. "His daddy don't allow him to stay up this late."

The others at the table laughed. One of them turned to glance at Sid. "You from narcotics?"

"No, but I heard he buddies with them."

"They don't hang out here. Maybe at the Ram's Horn over in Melrose. I suppose Kozlov thinks it's named after him, horny little bastard."

A slick-headed man with owlish eyes across the table leaned forward. "You better hope this dude's not a buddy. You could be in deep shit at the CJC."

Sid grinned. "No problem. As yet I'm not acquainted with Kozlov or his old man. Thanks for the intel."

Sid returned to his car and sat there in the revealing glow of a nearby floodlight. He pulled out his cell phone, working again after a quick charge, and felt a grudging appreciation for Jaz's love of the latest technological gadgetry. With her phone she could punch a few buttons and get the location of the Ram's Horn. He did the next best thing. He called her.

"I hope I didn't wake you," he said when she answered in a listless voice.

"I may not sleep for a week until I can figure my way out of this quagmire."

"Don't despair, I'm working on it. How about looking up the address of a bar called the Ram's Horn? It's in the Melrose area."

"What are you looking for there?"

He told her what Wick Stanley had said about Ramsey Kozlov and filled her in on his visit to the Olympia Restaurant.

"Some of the guys used to gather at Nick the Greek's place when I was on the force," she said. "I agree with Wick. Ram Kozlov could be a dangerous character. Be really careful with him, Sid."

She gave him the Ram's Horn's location, and Sid headed for the nearest I-40 entrance ramp. He found traffic moderate as he drove beneath the eerie glow of multicolored city lights, a reflection off the giant mirror of an overcast sky. Before reaching downtown, he detoured onto I-440, which took him around the western and southern suburbs and through the three-level spaghetti scramble above Franklin Road. Though the north-south thoroughfare was his target, to get back there required swinging onto I-24, exiting at Thompson Lane, and driving west a couple of miles. Nashville's traffic patterns were not always logical.

He hit Franklin Road a few blocks south of the Melrose area. As he drove north, it brought back memories of his teen years when he had frequented the shopping center anchored by the Melrose Theater, no longer a movie house. A bowling alley at the other end had been torn down. It was a shame how many of his old haunts no longer existed. After passing the darkened center, he spotted the bar beside a sign that featured a ram's head with the familiar curved horns. He recalled it as the symbol of Madison High School, where his mother had taught before it closed in 1986.

The Ram's Horn turned out to be smaller and darker than the Olympia Restaurant. At eleven-thirty it hosted only two occupied tables and three people at the bar. The walls appeared black and the dim lights provided barely enough illumination to recognize faces. As he walked toward the bar to the accompaniment of a Britney Spears song, he saw three guys in tee shirts and a fourth in a denim vest at one table. The way they eyed him made him wonder if they might be narcotics officers. He took a stool at the opposite end from two men and a buxom blonde in spiked heels. A frilly white skirt barely hid her bottom.

"What'll you have?" asked the bartender, a young man with

more rings attached to his face than Ringling Bros. & Barnum and Bailey had in their tents.

"Got Sam Adams?"

"Nope." He rattled off a few of the more popular beers.

"Miller Light."

Sid caught a movement from the other end of the bar in his peripheral vision. He looked around to see the blonde approaching with a smile heavily enhanced by makeup.

"Buy a girl a drink?" she asked in a sultry voice.

Sid gave her a deadpan look. "Sure, honey, but you'll have to take it across the room. I'm a solitary drinker."

"What an asshole," she said, turning and flouncing away.

Sid heard the tee-shirt guys laughing above the music. When the bartender brought his beer, he asked, "Do you know Ram Kozlov?"

"The cop? Yeah."

"Has he been in tonight?"

"Earlier. That's his buddies over there." He nodded toward the quartet at the table.

Sid took a swig of his beer and set it on the bar. He walked over to the table. "I understand Ram Kozlov was here earlier. Think he'll be back tonight?"

The one in the vest looked up with a wary eye. "You a friend of his?"

Sid shrugged. "Not really. I just wanted to chat with him. I'm a private investigator working on the opposite side of a homicide case of his."

"You're the big dude he talked about," a young man with short sandy hair and a NASCAR shirt said, nodding. "He wasn't too happy with your interfering in his case."

"I wasn't interfering," Sid said. "I just wanted to make sure he had it right."

Denim vest tilted his head and looked up. "Whatever."

"If you see him, tell him I'd like to chat with him," Sid said and headed back to the bar.

He glanced back as he slid onto the barstool and saw one of the men talking on his cell phone. Sid finished his beer and ordered another. He took his time with this one, and it was after midnight when he got up to leave. Two of the narcotics guys had left, but the other pair still nursed their drinks. Sid nodded at them in passing.

As he walked toward his car, he saw the dome light come on in a sporty looking BMW convertible parked beside him. Ramsey Kozlov slammed the door, swung around the front and stopped, facing Sid.

"I heard you were looking for me," Kozlov said.

"I wanted to ask why you're still pursuing the Djuan Burden case when you know he's not guilty."

"You're kidding me, right? I'll bet you're the kind of guywho likes to make jokes."

Sid hadn't expected such an approach but recalled what Jaz had told him about her Kozlov experience. It was a clear effort to throw him off guard. He also remembered Wick's description of the man as manipulative. He kept his voice even. "You know that gun isn't the murder weapon."

Kozlov grinned. "Yeah, he didn't shoot it. He just waved it around to scare people. Scared Omar Valdez to death."

"Glad you mentioned that. We have evidence that Omar Valdez, better known as Estefan Perez Delgado, was killed by a hit man."

Kozlov's jovial mood shifted suddenly. "What evidence?"

"An eyewitness who saw him leave, plus photographs from a surveillance camera. Is he the same one you gave the glove to leave at Earline Ivey's house?"

The parking area outside the bar was poorly lit, but Sid could see the anger building in Kozlov's face.

"You're full of shit, Chance. Your girl friend is as guilty as that black boy."

"You're absolutely correct, Detective. Neither one of them is guilty, but I think you have some things to answer for."

"Oh, you do? Well, I think you're digging your grave, cowboy."

"You planning to send the exterminator after me?"

"You know what happens to people who dig around in a pile of shit? They get eaten by maggots."

With that, Kozlov spun around, stalked back to his car, jumped in, and sped off with tires squealing.

29

S ID HAD INTENDED to shake up the cocky detective enough that he might say something incriminating, but as he drove home, he wondered if he had gone too far. Wick considered Kozlov dangerous, and if he had been involved in the Ivey murder, he was capable of anything. Sid decided to be especially cautious while driving, plus doubling his alertness at home. After securing his car in the garage, he went inside and checked all of his eaves cameras and alarms, which were set to leave a computer record of any attempted breeches.

First thing the next morning he called FBI Agent Baron Eggers.

"I have something else you might pass along to your DEA colleagues," he said. "I've been getting signals that something's definitely amiss with Metro Detective Ramsey Kozlov. He's paired with Grimm on the Delgado murder case."

Sid told how his investigation led him to believe the detective was involved in shifting attention away from the hit man in the Delgado murder, that Kozlov had fired the gun to make it appear that Burden was responsible. Sid added his belief that the detective was also complicit in the killing of Earline Ivey. He recounted his confrontation with Kozlov outside the Ram's Head Bar. Although it was still mostly conjecture, he decided to lay it all out for Eggers and let the Feds run with it.

"Sergeant Stanley suspects, and I'm inclined to agree, that

Kozlov has been passing on information about Metro drug enforcement. There's a possibility these murders could be tied in with it."

"Okay," Eggers said. "I'll pass this on to the people handling the drug angle and let them sort it out."

A little later, Sid received calls from Judge Gabriel Thackston and the old newsman, Jack Post, inquiring about Jaz's situation.

"Our poker partner would never have committed such an uncivilized act," Thackston said.

"You're absolutely right, Judge. I'm devoting my full energy to proving this was a despicable frameup."

"Who do you believe was involved?"

"I'm really not in a position to say much about it at this stage."

"I understand. Reminds me of a trial I presided over once where the prosecutor introduced incontrovertible evidence the defendant had committed the crime. But before final arguments, the defense found a man who confessed to the crime. Those things happen."

"I don't know that I'll get a confession, but I intend to nail the perpetrator."

"Well, you have my blessings, Sidney. If I can help in any way, please let me know."

Post called a few minutes later. He had received a voice mail from a former newspaper colleague the night before while he was attending a Nashville Predators hockey game. "He left a message saying that media circus was a setup deal with the department brass. They tipped off the news folks about Jaz's arrival time at the Criminal Justice Center."

"Thanks for confirming it," Sid said. "I was at her house when the detectives came after her. I'm sure their hurry was to get her downtown to meet the schedule."

"The story says she dropped a latex glove with her fingerprints on the porch at Earline Ivey's house. What's with that?"

"Somebody dropped one she had used, Jack, but it wasn't Jaz. She was never close to that house."

"Then who did it?"

"I'm working on a theory, but I can't say anything about it yet." He had to be judicious in his comments to the old reporter. Post liked to talk too much.

"Let me know if I can dig up anything for you. By the way, how are you coming with that other murder case? The one where the boy just got out of prison?"

"We hope to have an answer tomorrow."

"Good. When you talk to our girl, tell her to hang loose."

Sid called Jaz to see how she was holding up.

"I'm marshalling my forces," she said. "K.C. Urban has a good friend who's one of the top criminal lawyers in town. We're meeting with him later this morning. Did you find Ramsey Kozlov last night?"

He told her about the confrontation outside the Ram's Horn Bar.

"You shouldn't have given him any ideas," she said, sounding worried.

"I hoped it might prompt him to say something like Grimm's 'you can't prove shit' remark. But it didn't work."

"Have you had any more ideas?"

"I have one I plan to pitch to Wick and Bart, see if they'll buy into it."

"Concerning what?"

"If we had some solid evidence of wrong-doing, we could take this thing to the Office of Professional Accountability, file some charges."

"But we don't."

"Right. So maybe we can play the bad guys against each other."

"Grimm and Kozlov?"

"Since it looks like Ram could be playing this Earline Ivey thing all on his own, we might try to isolate Grimm and get him to turn on his more guilty partner."

"Good luck. Let me know how it goes."

Sid got on his computer and found a recent photo of Detective Kozlov. He printed out a copy and stuck it in his pocket, intending to show it to the woman at the florist shop. But first he headed downtown to visit his client's grandson at the Metro Jail.

In contrast to the way he looked during the previous interview, Djuan came in with his head held high. He didn't smile, but he didn't look downcast, either.

"Granny told me you were close to finding the real killer," he said as they took seats at the small table.

"That's right. We don't have a name, but we know he's a killer for hire. The FBI is working on it now, so it's just a matter of time."

"Time is all I got these days."

Sid felt his jaw twitch as the thought of what two cops had done rankled him. "We'll get you out of here as soon as possible. I promise."

"After this, I'd have to be really lucky to get a job."

"This shouldn't hurt you. You'll be completely exonerated."

"That don't mean nothing to folks who won't hire cons."

Sid stared him in the eye and spoke in a calm, sincere voice. "Don't get down on yourself, Djuan. You need to focus on what you want to accomplish. Don't give up."

"You don't know what it's like, Mr. Chance."

Sid smiled. "As a matter of fact, I do. Around four years ago, I was arrested for bribing a drug dealer. It was the result of a crook and a sheriff who didn't care whose life he messed up. I got down on the world and spent three years living by myself in the woods like a hermit. Miss LeMieux coaxed me into taking an assignment for her company, then encouraged me to become a private investigator. When you believe in yourself, you can accomplish great things."

Djuan gave a slight grin. "You think I should be a private investigator?"

"I think your talents probably lie in other areas, but you have talents, and you need to apply them. We'll talk about it some more when I get you out of here."

"I hope you're right."

"I am," Sid said. "Just keep your hopes up."

BEFORE HEADING BACK to his office, Sid called Bart Masterson and asked if they could meet somewhere for a little chat about Jaz's problem. He thought it best to discuss it in person rather than on the phone. They arranged to meet for lunch at a restaurant in Madison which had a fairly high noise level, enough it was unlikely anyone would eavesdrop on the conversation.

Sid arrived early and asked for a table at the far end of the dining area where he could see when Bart came in. He ordered coffee and checked out the menu while he waited. The tall figure with the oddball mustache soon strode across the room like an Old West lawman on his way to a gunfight.

"What's on your mind?" Bart asked as he dropped into a chair across from Sid.

"It looks like it's up to us to get Jaz out of this mess." Sid rubbed a hand across his beard. "Some of your colleagues are dealing off the bottom of the deck."

"So you told me."

"But I haven't told you what happened last night."

Sid related how he had tracked down Ram Kozlov at the Melrose bar and what had been said.

"You'll never get him to admit he's done anything wrong," Bart said.

"I agree. What I have in mind is working on his partner in the Burden case."

Sid outlined his plan to use Bart, Wick Stanley and himself to get Victor Grimm's cooperation.

Bart gave him a skeptical look. "It might work, but I wouldn't put too much faith in it. I haven't been around Grimm much since they split up homicide some six years ago."

"I imagine Wick has been more involved with him since they're in the same precinct."

"As a sergeant, he'd likely have more contact than a patrolman. Talk to him and see if he'll agree to do it. How do you figure on getting Grimm to sit down with us?"

The waitress arrived with their menus, and Sid waited until she had left to answer Bart's question.

"I doubt he'd agree to anything I suggested. My idea was to have one of you, probably Wick, tell him you had someone with new information on the Djuan Burden murder, but the source would only talk to Grimm. The lady who runs the florist shop next to Prime Medical Equipment has been very cooperative. I think she'd loan us her workroom. And when we get to the glove business, I'll call her in to tell what she saw."

"I'll go along with that," Bart said. "The longer this situation smolders, the more damage Jaz suffers. When do you want to set it up?"

"Tomorrow, if possible. I'll check with Wick and find out if Grimm might be available."

The waitress came back to take their orders, but before she got to Bart, his phone rang. He turned away and spoke for a few moments.

"Sorry," he said to their server, "I can't stay." He looked around at Sid. "Shooting in East Nashville. Let me know what Wick says."

With that, he strode out of the restaurant, leaving the waitress with a baffled look.

Sid smiled. "He's a Metro detective. Stuff happens. Looks like I'll be eating alone."

30

Jaz met Forrest McGinnis at K.C. Urban's office. A chubby, pink-cheeked Irishman, the noted criminal defense lawyer took her hand in both of his with a bright, paternal smile. He had thin white hair and looked to be in his mid-to-late sixties.

"Such a pleasure to meet you, Miss LeMieux," he said. "I'm familiar with your accomplishments and your father's before you."

Jaz nodded, reclaimed her hand, and took one of the chairs in front of K.C.'s desk. "I'm afraid my dad was much more accomplished than I am."

"Don't be so modest. I'm aware of the way you rose above your adversity."

He must have known my mother, she thought. "Thank you, Mr. McGinnis. I've been blessed, and fortunately I've never run into anything remotely like what I'm facing now."

"K.C. has told me a bit about your situation, but I think it would be instructive for you to go through it with me from the start."

Jaz began with the incident at the Welcome Home Store when Earline Ivey had inexplicably accused her of racial harassment. She followed with her participation in Sid's investigation of the Djuan Burden murder case, the confrontations with Homicide Detective Victor Grimm and later with Ramsey Kozlov, leading to the realization that

Grimm and his partner had fired Rachel Ransom's pistol.

"You're certain the detectives are responsible for the gun being fired?" McGinnis asked, concern showing in the lines on his forehead.

"There's no other explanation," Jaz said and explained why.

"This is a most serious charge," McGinnis said.

Jaz nodded. "And it gets worse."

She told him about their discovery of the apparent hit man in the Burden case and Sid's belief that Earline Ivey had experienced a similar fate.

When she had finished, McGinnis could only shake his head in dismay. "This is one of the most complicated and confusing homicides I've encountered in quite a while. I can see ample opportunity to cast doubt on the state's case, but as I'm sure you know, juries can be quite fickle. That glove with your fingerprints is the most damning evidence. Your admission that you were in the area is unfortunate, even though a result of pure coincidence."

"I have witnesses to where I was that morning except for the period around nine-thirty. If I was at Mrs. Ivey's house that time of day, shouldn't some of the neighbors have seen me?"

"You would think so," the lawyer said, "but it's always possible no one was paying any attention to her house then. We can press the police on that point, ask why they were unable to place you at the scene. What do we know about the time of death?"

"I have a friend who's a forensic pathologist at the Medical Examiner's office. She told me they had calculated it as between seven and ten a.m."

McGinnis raised an eyebrow. "Experienced pathologists will tell you that methods of estimating time of death can be quite inaccurate. Nevertheless, your friend's scenario with the man at the convenience market just after seven fits their parameters."

Jaz thought about mentioning Sid's plan to pry a confession out of Detective Grimm but decided it was too speculative. "The only motive I can imagine they might claim is revenge, and nobody can say I'm a vengeful person."

"We can find an endless supply of witnesses who would testify that she has never shown any bias toward African-Americans," Urban said.

McGinnis nodded. "That would certainly be helpful. Is there any possibility of finding someone who would say they knew of Mrs. Ivey's plot to cause trouble for the company by making her accusations against Miss LeMieux?"

Jaz turned to K.C. Urban. "Has the investigation of Earline Ivey turned up anything positive?"

He reached for a paper on his desk. "I just got this. She had been delinquent in her mortgage payments for several months and was facing the possibility of foreclosure. A few days after your run-in with her, however, she was able to pay off the mortgage in full."

"Then it's pretty obvious what happened," Jaz said.

"To us, yes, but we don't know the source of the money. I'm sure it was funneled to her in a way that would be difficult to trace."

Jaz gave a deep sigh. "Earline Ivey found herself in a tough situation. I wish she had come to us when they first approached her. I'd have let her have the money to pay off the mortgage."

"People don't always make the best decisions when they're facing that kind of a crunch," McGinnis said.

"My friend told me they had completed the autopsy on her this morning. That means they'll release the body for burial. I don't suppose it would be a good idea for me to attend the funeral."

"No," the lawyers said in unison.

K.C. Uban folded his arms in a defensive posture. "I still think it best that you maintain a low profile until this business is resolved."

"I agree," McGinnis said. "We don't need to stir any more passions."

"I'm sure some of her fellow employees will want to attend the funeral," Jaz said. 'And a company official, at least her manager, should be there."

"That would be appropriate." McGinnis looked up from the notes he had been jotting on a pad. "Getting back to your problem, do you know of anyone else who has encountered difficulties with Detective Kozlov? Someone who could provide testimony that would show the officer is untrustworthy?"

"Sid Chance is working on a plan to try and get one of his fellow homicide detectives to do just that."

"Let's hope he's successful," McGinnis said. "If he can't come up with something, we could be in serious trouble."

31

S ID CALLED SGT. WICK STANLEY as soon as he returned to his office. He heard traffic noises in the background. "Are you on duty?" he asked.

"Yeah, A for Adam shift for a change. You need some help?"

"I just talked to Bart about an idea I had. I need to fill you in on it, but I'd probably best do that in person. Anywhere we could meet?"

"I'm just finishing up a situation in Green Hills. How soon could you make it?"

"This time of day it shouldn't take more than twenty-five minutes for me to get over there. Where do you want to meet?"

"Call me when you get onto Hillsboro Pike."

Sid headed out to his car and took Vietnam Veterans Boulevard toward I-65. From there it was a straight shot to the turnoff at I-440. As soon as he negotiated the corkscrew ramp onto Hillsboro Pike, he pulled out his cell phone and hit the speed dial for Wick.

"I'm free at the moment," Wick said. "You want something to eat?"

"No, thanks. I just had a big lunch. Bart didn't fare so well, though. He got called out before he had a chance to eat."

"I got a break and met a couple of my guys at a barbeque place. I'm near the mall now. Why don't we meet in front of the old Prime Medical store. It's still vacant."

A few minutes later, Sid pulled in beside Wick's patrol car.

The parking area lay vacant except for a pickup truck in front of the clothing store at the other end. He got out and climbed into the passenger seat, his large frame a bit cramped by the police computer. The speaker crackled with calls from the dispatcher.

"What have you and Bat Masterson been cooking up?" Wick asked, using the name he often used in a joking manner for his detective friend.

"Something that looks like our best shot at getting Jaz out of this quagmire."

Sid explained his plan to confront Victor Grimm in an attempt to get his admission of what had happened with Rachel Ransom's gun and what he knew about Ram Kozlov's visit to the closed medical supply store.

"I haven't had much contact with Grimm other than on precinct business," Wick said.

"At least you have a relationship that should get him to listen to you."

"Yeah, but what can I say? You admit you have no proof they fired that gun. If Bart and I were to accuse him of fabricating evidence with nothing but hearsay, he could file a complaint against us with the Office of Professional Accountability."

"We're ninety-nine percent positive they did it."

"On what basis?"

"I was convinced after what Grimm said that night when I reminded him of Mrs. Ransom's statement that the gun hadn't been fired in fifteen years. But even more convincing is the FBI's decision to treat the Omar Valdez murder as a contract killing."

"The agent you worked with told you that?"

"The Dallas office is tracking down the hit man. They have a description and a good trail to follow. Anyway, I'm not worried about the Djuan Burden case. It's this Earline Ivey situation that has Jaz in a bind. We have to find a way to show that Kozlov planted that glove at the murder site."

"What do you have in mind?"

"To protect you guys, I'll do most of the talking, but I need your presence as a moral force. Without it, he wouldn't listen to a thing I have to say. Bart assures me that Grimm is really a decent cop who got emotionally messed up by the job."

Wick tapped his fingers on the steering wheel for a moment, then turned back to Sid. "Bart agreed to this deal?"

"Right. As long as you go along with it." He looked Wick in the eye and said with as much feeling as he could put into it, "I don't know any other way we can save Jaz from a rigged murder trial."

The sergeant reached over and punched a button on the computer screen, causing a list of open calls to scroll down. "Okay. Count me in. Have you cleared this with the lady at the florist shop?"

"No, but I'll do that right now."

When he opened the door to get out, Wick called after him. "I need to get moving. Call me when it's set up."

As the patrol car backed out and turned toward the traffic, Sid walked past the vacant medical supply store, now bearing a FOR LEASE sign. He entered the flower-bedecked shop next door and looked around for the owner. The tinkle of a bell attached to the door brought her out of the workroom in back.

He smiled. "Remember me?"

"I sure do, Mr. Chance. Good to see you again."

"I have a little problem I hope you can help me out with," he said.

He outlined what he wanted to do, without going into what the problem was with the detective. She agreed to go along with the plan, which Sid hoped to get set up for late the next afternoon. With that settled, he pulled out the Kozlov photo and showed it to her.

"Have you seen this man?" he asked.

Her eyes widened. "It looks just like that man I saw go into the old Prime Medical store, the one I told you about last week."

"Just as I expected," he said. "Thanks. We'll see you tomorrow."

He walked back to his car and called Wick. "It's all set with the florist shop owner. Let me know after you talk to Grimm."

"I'll try to catch him this afternoon."

Sid returned to his office and printed out a list of the key points they had uncovered during the Djuan Burden investigation. He began putting them together in a report he would present to the lawyers at Bailey, Riddle and Smith tomorrow. A quick glance gave the impression they had accumulated enough to convince Vandenberg and Hersholt of Djuan's innocence, though what he could say about the FBI's help was limited as it involved an ongoing federal investigation. But when he considered how little of the information could be termed concrete evidence, he realized he faced an uphill battle. If all went well with the Grimm session tomorrow, though, he hoped to be able to write "Closed" on the Valdez-Delgado murder case.

32

WEDNESDAY DAWNED bright as a rosebush in the spring, a flowery sight that attracted Sid's gaze as he took off on his morning run. The smell of fresh-mown grass triggered memories of youthful chores and his mother's guiding hand. He wondered what she might counsel in difficult times like these. Today would be critical for Jaz and himself.

He got to the office early and soon had a call from Wick Stanley.

"Grimm was leery of it but finally agreed to meet us at three," he said. "He argued that the case was settled and ready for trial, but I convinced him he needed to hear this to keep from possibly getting his tail caught in a crack."

"I'll park nearby and watch for you guys to go in. After you've had time to get settled in the back room, I'll make my appearance."

"Good," Wick said. "If he saw you first, he might back out. I'll call Bart and tell him."

With that settled, Sid called Jaz and alerted her to the plan.

"I don't know what I'd do without you," she said. "Forrest McGinnis, my new defense attorney, said we could be in real trouble without some evidence to explain that latex glove."

Sid knew it was far from a sure thing, but he kept his voice upbeat. "The three musketeers will be riding to the rescue this afternoon."

He had to make one more call to put the final touches on his plan. He punched in FBI Agent Baron Eggers' phone number.

"Sorry, I'm not available at the moment," said the agent's voice. "If this is an emergency, call the office." He gave the phone number.

Sid left a message for Eggers to call him, then did the same with the man who answered the phone at the FBI office. Turning to his computer, he did a final edit of his report on the Djuan Burden case and sent it to the printer. He slipped the pages into a folder and took them out to his car.

With rush hour past, he made it downtown in short order and parked in the garage at the Bailey, Riddle and Smith building. He took the elevator up, and it stopped at the main floor. Two passengers got on. One was a young woman carrying a bag from a fast food store. The other was an elderly man neatly dressed in black slacks and an open-collared white dress shirt. He wore a ball cap with the logo of the Music City Honor Flight.

"You must be a World War II veteran," Sid said. "A friend of mine went on one of those flights to Washington to visit the World War II Memorial."

The man smiled. "It was a whirlwind tour, but I really enjoyed it. Got to talk to some fellas who'd been the same places I was."

Sid patted him on the shoulder. "You guys are the real heroes. We appreciate your service."

He looked up at Sid. "You're a big fellow. Were you ever in the military?"

"Vietnam. That was a whole different ball of wax."

The elevator stopped and the old veteran stepped off. Sid continued on to Arnie Bailey's floor, where he asked if Vandenberg and Hersholt were available.

"Mr. Vandenberg is in," the receptionist said. "I'll see if he can talk to you."

A few moments later, the short, heavy-set man walked out and beckoned to Sid. He followed the lawyer back to a windowless office, sparely furnished with a desk and chair, a couple of wooden bookshelves, a small table bearing a few magazines, and a couple of straight chairs for visitors.

Sid dropped the folder on Vandenberg's desk atop a stack of transcriptions. "Here's what we've put together on the case."

"Have a seat and let me look it over," the lawyer said.

He skimmed through the pages, rechecked a couple of points, and looked up with a grin. "I'm impressed. Finding that surveillance camera footage was a real break."

"The mechanic who saw the man drive away put us onto it. Jaz has a friend in security at the bank. We thought there'd be a good chance of finding something."

"How did you find the car?"

Sid told him about the stolen license plate and the rental car logo.

"You say the FBI is looking into the hit man's identity. Where does that stand?"

"I have a call in for Agent Eggers. If this is part of an ongoing investigation, though, he may not be able to release anything yet."

"With what you have, and confirmation from the FBI, we should be able to get the District Attorney to drop the charges against Djuan Burden. It won't matter when Mrs. Ransom's gun was fired."

Maybe not as far as this case was concerned, Sid thought, but Detective Kozlov's action mattered greatly when it pointed toward his conspiracy to get Jaz LeMieux charged with murder.

"I'll get back to you as soon as I talk to the FBI agent," he said.

JAZ FELT A STRONG SENSE of frustration at her inability to find a way to extricate herself from this appalling predicament. She knew Sid was doing his best, but she had always taken responsibility for her own fate. Sitting at the computer in her home office, she reviewed the entire affair as they had pieced it together, looking for some scrap they might have missed, something that could be exploited to her benefit. She found nothing.

When Sid called, she knew it was too early for the showdown with Victor Grimm. "Have you learned anything new?" she asked.

"I went by to see Djuan Burden this morning. He's in a better mood but still skeptical of his future. We've set things in motion to free him."

He told her about his visit with Hardy Vandenberg and the lawyer's belief that the DA would drop the charges once the FBI was willing to talk.

"That's great, Sid. Have you told his grandmother?"

"No. I decided to wait until I had a chance to talk with Baron Eggers."

"Probably a good idea." She glanced at her clock, a refurbished pendulum model that came out of a Western Union office years ago. "It'll soon be time for you to head for Green Hills, won't it?"

"Right. I'm keeping my fingers crossed on that one."

"I racked my brain for some way to help," Jaz said, absently watching her screensaver rig bounce about the monitor. "Can't think of anything."

"Don't waste your worry. I've rehearsed this in my mind like planning for a military operation. Barring some unforeseen glitch, all should go well."

"Isn't that a contradiction of Murphy's Law?"

Sid laughed. "That's just another law to be broken."

Sid's phone call left her pleased that their efforts would soon save a young man's life, but looking over her notes on the Earline Ivey case reminded her that a young girl was still at risk. The murdered woman's daughter, Vanita, was only a year older than Djuan when he went to prison. With what had happened to her mother, the just-turned teenager could easily see her life destroyed, not in the same way as Djuan's but with the same effect.

Jaz called K.C. Urban. "I want to do something for Vanita Ivey, Earline's daughter. It has to be completely anonymous."

"What do you have in mind?" Urban asked.

"She's just as much a victim of this as her mother. She needs something to give her hope for the future. Maybe a college scholarship fund."

"That shouldn't be too difficult to set up. It could be done through a bank as trustee, with instructions that the donor not be identified."

"Find out how much would be needed for tuition to a good school. I'll have my financial guru, Mike Rich, figure out what investments would produce that amount by the time she's ready for college."

"I'll research it and get back to you," Urban said.

Taking steps to help someone else put her in a better frame of mind.

Until Forrest McGinnis called.

"I've been checking into the District Attorney's case," the attorney said, "and I found something you hadn't mentioned."

"What was it?"

"It seems that while questioning people in the area around Mrs. Ivey's home, the detectives discovered you had been seen there that morning."

Jaz couldn't believe what she had heard. "Somebody said I was around her home?"

"Not around it, but nearby. In a drugstore on Gallatin Road near a gap in the trees that led to the rear of her home."

Jaz felt her head spinning. It took a few moments before she could speak. "That hadn't entered my mind since the day it happened. When Detective Bart Masterson questioned me regarding my whereabouts, I mentioned stopping at a drugstore to get some headache pills for Marie Wallace, my housekeeper. She's, really more like an aunt, but...the point is I had no idea Earline Ivey lived in the area."

"The police and the prosecutor see it as further verification that you accidentally dropped the latex glove on her porch."

33

S ID WAS ABOUT READY to leave for the rendezvous at the florist shop when FBI Agent Baron Eggers returned his call.

"Have your people had any luck finding our hit man?" Sid asked.

"We got a good description from the car rental agent and tracked him onto a flight to Dallas. The Dallas Field Division got a positive ID. They're hard at work trying to pinpoint his location."

"Have you gotten anything out of Elena Ortiz?"

"She talked. It looks like Delgado was definitely a drug hit. He came here to avoid it but wasn't successful."

"If we need you to keep Djuan Burden away from a lethal injection, can you talk to the District Attorney?"

"We'd have to get clearance from Justice, but I'd think so."

Sid got off the phone with barely time to make his appointment in Green Hills. As he walked out and turned to check that the office door had locked, he heard steps approaching in the hallway. He looked around to see an elderly man walk haltingly toward him using a cane. The old fellow appeared to be around five-eight, though a bit stooped from osteoporosis. His black slacks and open-collared shirt reminded Sid of the World War II veteran he'd seen earlier in the elevator downtown. A plaid Scottish driving cap covered his head above gray sideburns, and he wore a pair of brown cloth gloves. Probably a skin condition. Sid hoped he'd never find himself in that shape.

"Is this where Doctor Knight's office is?" he asked in a shaky voice, stopping a few feet away.

Sid shook his head. "I know everybody in the building, and we don't have a Doctor Knight. I'm afraid you've got the wrong address."

The old codger reached a hand up to wipe a gloved finger under his nose. His sleeve rode up and Sid caught a glimpse of the man's watch. Black main dial and a couple of smaller dials. Expensive. The old guy must have been somebody in his day.

"Maybe you could let me use your office phone," the old man said. "I need to call my son."

Sid was torn between a desire to help the obviously confused man and the pressing need to get out to his car and head across town. He spoke with a concerned frown. "I'm really sorry, but I have to leave right now to make a meeting. There's a lady at the last door on the right who'll be happy to help. I can go with you as I head out to my car."

The man's eyes narrowed, and he shook his head. "Thanks, but go ahead. I don't want to hold you up."

Sid smiled at him. "No problem. Just be careful."

He checked his watch as he hurried out to the parking lot. He had no time to waste. Relaxing a bit after he swung onto Vietnam Veterans Boulevard and bore down on the accelerator, he wondered how the old guy had made out. He felt a twinge of guilt at not pausing to help, but he put it out of his mind as he navigated a glut of traffic near the I-440 turnoff.

Just as he pulled into the far end of the parking area outside the clothing store, he saw Victor Grimm climb out of a car and head into the florist shop. He recognized the two vehicles beside it as belonging to Bart and Wick.

He walked slowly to the shop entrance, giving them time

to move to the back room. The silver-haired florist smiled as he entered.

"They're waiting for you," she said.

"Thanks. I'll come after you when we're ready for your appearance."

He opened the door and stepped into the workroom, where Wick and Grimm sat at a table, with Bart standing beside it. Before anything was said, Grimm pushed his chair back.

"If this bastard is your source, I'm outa here." He started to get up.

"Come on, Grimm," Wick said, waving his hands in a downward motion. "Just sit down and listen to what he has to say. It's for your own good."

"I'm not listening to any pseudo-detective telling me how to run my investigations."

"For your information," Bart said, "Sid Chance put in more years in law enforcement than you've been on the police force. You should know he was responsible for catching that auto parts guy who committed three murders in Metro a few months ago." He looked across at Sid. "Let's hear what you have to say."

Looking chagrined, Grimm took his seat as Sid began.

"I'll start with the latest bit of news. I talked with FBI Agent Baron Eggers just before I left the office. The Feds have concluded that Omar Valdez, alias Estefan Perez Delgado, was the victim of a drug hit."

He told how he and Jaz had found the killer on bank surveillance camera footage, obtained photo enhancement from the FBI, and determined that the man had rented the car from TriStar Car Rental at the airport.

"With that information, the FBI tracked him to his home base in Dallas. They're currently trying to pin him down there."

Grimm could only stare in obvious confusion. "But everything pointed to that Burden boy," he said.

"Not everything." Sid leaned both hands on the table. "Mrs. Ransom assured you there was no way her grandson could have put that gun in her cedar chest after he got home. And when she stood outside the door where you found it, she heard you comment that the gun looked old and you wondered if it would still fire. She heard your partner say he could demonstrate that it would."

Sid stopped and the room was quiet for a moment. Bart broke the silence as he looked across at Grimm.

"I've always felt you were a decent, honest cop, Victor. You were a fine homicide detective until you got pissed at being passed over for sergeant, then you got too interested in closing cases at any cost. But I've never known you to stoop to tampering with evidence. Was it you or Kozlov who fired that gun before it was turned in?"

Grimm cast furtive glances around the room before speaking in a soft, hesitant voice. "If the FBI can prove...if they say the murder was committed by somebody else, what difference does it make if Ransom's gun was fired or not?"

"When the sergeants in the Office of Professional Accountability get onto it, you better believe it'll make a difference."

Though the director of the OPA was a civilian attorney, her investigators were a team of detective sergeants, one of whom rotated off every two months.

"But why would—"

"Mrs. Ransom strikes me as a lady who's going to demand some answers," Sid said.

Bart gave Grimm a cold stare. "Your only hope of keeping that badge is to come clean now."

Grimm breathed deeply and rubbed his hands together. "Kozlov said we'd be the laughingstock of the department if we turned that gun in and it wouldn't shoot. After we booked

Burden, he stopped at a wooded area out near the TBI, put on a glove, and fired one shot. Then we dropped it off at the lab."

"You told Kozlov about finding Jaz and me at the Prime Medical Equipment store last week, didn't you?" Sid asked.

"Yeah. The little punk thought it was hilarious."

Sid caught the "punk" reference and decided the relationship was not all rosy. "Did you tell him that we were using latex gloves to search for evidence?"

Grimm nodded.

"Did Kozlov tell you that he came by the store early that evening?"

"Why would he do that?"

"You'd expect him to tell you if he did, wouldn't you?"

"Of course."

"He didn't tell you what he did there?"

"I don't know that he was there," Grimm said, looking agitated. "What makes you think he was?"

Sid turned to the door and called in the florist. "Tell Detective Grimm what you saw out front the evening after I was here, the day after the shooting."

She described how she had looked around while locking up and saw a man park a black Dodge Avenger and enter the former medical supply store. Sid showed Grimm the photo of Kozlov she had identified as the man she saw.

"So what if he did?" Grimm asked.

Sid thanked the florist and let her return to the front. He turned back to Grimm. "We think he picked up one of the gloves Jaz LeMieux had worn and used it as a plant to incriminate her in Earline Ivey's murder."

The detective swung his head around his three interrogators. "I don't know anything about that. I only worked with him on this Burden case."

Sid hadn't intended to include Bart and Wick with his use

of "we" in the accusation, but it appeared to have influenced Grimm. He went into full defensive mode.

"There's a distinct possibility that the Ivey murder was committed by the same professional who killed Delgado," Sid said. He knew he was into area where he could offer no proof, but he could see no alternative. "If Kozlov provided the glove to leave at the murder scene, it would ally him with the drug traffickers who went after Delgado. Has he given you any indication of an interest in the drug scene?"

Grimm shifted his eyes about the room as he replied. "He talks about his buddies in narcotics, but I've never seen or heard anything...nothing that led me to believe he was involved in something illegal."

Sid wondered if the detective had suspected something but declined to admit it in fear of retribution by Deputy Chief Kozlov. There was no way to know. Bart and Wick counseled Grimm to contact the OPA about the firing of Mrs. Ransom's .22 pistol. If he didn't, they would report what they knew, leaving him at the mercy of the system. The grilling ended with Grimm practically running out of the shop, while Sid silently lamented his failure to shake anything loose that would help clear Jaz. His only hope was that an investigation by the Office of Professional Accountability would turn up evidence linking Kozlov to the murder.

Outside the florist shop, Sid thanked his friends for their help. "I knew it was a long shot, but I felt it was our best chance to help Jaz."

"Tell her we're a hundred percent behind her," Bart said. "We'll keep our antennas tuned for anything that looks promising."

Sid intended to call Jaz as soon as he returned to the office, but the phone was ringing when he walked in.

"This isn't an official call," said Agent Eggers. "I'd get into trouble for revealing some of this, but you've been a big help to me and I felt I owed it to you."

Sid listened with a growing sense of unease. After everything that had happened this afternoon, the agent's tone did not strike him as bearing welcome news.

"What going on?"

"They found your hit man in Dallas. He had fake driver's licenses, Social Security cards, passports, you name it, stashed in hidden compartments around his house. Guns, ammo, and suppressors."

"They have him in custody?"

"No. That's why I called. The neighbors last saw him early yesterday. We've had the place under surveillance, but he hasn't showed. The guess is that he's left on another job. We have no idea where."

Sid sat in his chair and leaned back. "Are you thinking he may be headed back here?"

"I have no way of knowing, but considering what else I learned today, I thought I should make you aware of the possibility."

"Okay," Sid said. "Give me the what else."

"Don't even think about breathing a word of this, Sid. Detective Ramsey Kozlov is the target of a current investigation involving the same drug outfit that hit Delgado. I don't know if your tip had anything to do with it. But based on what you told me, I'd say there's a possibility that Kozlov could've steered this guy onto you."

"So you do think he might be headed for Nashville."

"I think it's possible. He also could be headed for Peoria."

"I suppose I'd better summon the cavalry."

"I wish we could do something," Eggers said, sounding apologetic. "Without any hard evidence that he's headed here, we couldn't commit any assets to watching for him. But be careful. A guy like this researches his targets. With the Internet, he could know all about you."

And if I had a name, I'd know all about him, Sid thought. But he had no name. No description of what he'd look like away from home. Nothing.

34

SID PULLED THE SIG from its holster, ejected the magazine, checked the dozen .40 S&W cartridges, and shoved the magazine back into the gun. Eggers' warning had been clear. If Ramsey Kozlov had passed word along to Delgado's killer that PI Sid Chance had him as a target, the hired assassin could be looking to remove the threat. As he thought about the man's use of disguises, he recalled the old codger who had asked to use his telephone when he was leaving the office earlier. The gloves could have been used to hide smooth, younger hands. The voice would have been no problem for a skilled actor. And the chronograph would have been a natural for someone accustomed to split-second timing.

He walked down the hallway to the office where he had directed the man. The receptionist, an attractive Oriental with odd-looking glasses that turned up into points on the ends, smiled as he entered.

"How's the sleuthing business these days?" she asked.

"It's like turning over rocks to see what's underneath."

"When I do that I find black widow spiders."

Sid grimaced. "Unfortuntely, I sometimes turn up characters like that. Did an old gentleman with a cane come in here to use the phone a few hours ago?"

She raised her eyebrows. "Not while I was here."

"I just wondered. He stopped me on the way out and I suggested you'd let him use yours."

"Would've been happy to, but he didn't come in here."

Nothing positive, but strongly suspicious, he thought. He returned to his office and called Jaz. She told him about Forrest McGinnis' dropping another bombshell on her.

"Damn, Jaz," he said. "You hadn't mentioned the drugstore stop to me, either."

"I know. It never occurred to me to say anything about it. I just happened to mention it in passing when Bart was questioning me last Saturday. Now it's come back to haunt me."

"I have something even more haunting after a call from Agent Eggers."

He related the FBI agent's news about locating the hit man.

"He hasn't turned up at his house?"

"No. There's a good possibility that he could be in Nashville."

"Why here?"

"Eggers gave me some information that's highly confidential, and I swore not to mention it. The upshot of it is the guy could be after me."

"You?" She sounded incredulous.

He related his experience with the apparent old man who wanted to use his phone.

"Do you think he was trying to lure you inside your office?" Jaz asked.

"I considered that. If it's him, he's waiting for a better opportunity."

"Shouldn't you call Bart or Wick? See if the police can do something?"

"It would be the same as with the FBI. Without any clear threat, they'd take a dim view of allocating a lot of manpower to keep an eye on me."

"What about the old man?"

"It was certainly suspicious, but I couldn't swear he was anything but what he appeared to be."

"Maybe you'd better come over and stay at my place until they catch him."

"Get real, Jaz," he said, turning his chair toward the window to see cars leaving the mall. "I'm not going into hiding like some illegal running from an ICE agent. I can't hide forever. Besides, they may never find this guy. If he gets wind of his house being tossed, he'll never go back."

"So you're going to stand around and wait to be a target?"

"When I move around, I'll stay on alert, just like I did in Nam. But I don't look for any trouble on the streets. This guy's MO is up close indoors with a silenced twenty-two."

"So are you ready for a noctural visitor at home?"

"You know all the whizbang lights and cameras and alarms Jerry Jackson installed."

"Your electronic countermeasures buddy."

"Right."

"What if the shooter cuts the wires?"

"I have a warning beeper that goes off, plus some battery backup."

"Okay, Sid. I just hope your macho pride doesn't do you in. I don't want to see you laid out with a twenty-two caliber hole in your forehead."

After he put the phone back on its stand, he thought about what Jaz had said. Was he being stubborn and unrealistic? It would be nice to have someone watching his flanks, but that wasn't going to happen. The North Precinct, which covered Madison along with the entire northern half of the county, didn't have the manpower to keep a stakeout on his house. They concentrated their patrolling around Gallatin Road, where most of the businesses were located. It would likely be futile anyway. Sid lived in a quiet neighborhood, and this guy was smart. He would pick up on a car parked where it shouldn't be.

JAZ GOT UP FROM her desk and walked across to the door, then turned and circled the walls lined with shelves of books. She tended to be a pacer, often walking off anger or discontent. Glancing at the packed shelves, which had been mostly stocked by her father, one title caught her eye and eased the tension that had built during the call from Sid—*Men Are from Mars. Women Are from Venus.* It was easy to forget that, she realized. Instead of talking about problems with friends as she did, he would hole up in his cave and try to work things out on his own.

It didn't mean she had to act like a Martian. She called Wick Stanley and caught him at home.

"Our friend, Sid, has a problem," she said, and told him about their conversation.

"Sid mentioned Kozlov and the shooter, but I didn't realize it might come to this."

"You know Sid. He thinks he can handle things by himself, but that man is extremely dangerous. He might catch Sid at home asleep in the middle of the night."

"Sid's pretty crafty himself. He won't be easily surprised."

"Yes, but I don't like leaving things to chance."

"Is that an intentional pun?"

Jaz frowned. She hadn't thought of it that way. "No. I meant anything could go wrong. I hate to ask you to consider this when you probably need the sleep yourself, but is there any way you or Bart could ease by there during the night, see if anything appears out of order?"

"I guess I could cruise down his street a couple of times after midnight, maybe get Bart to do the same later. We'd have to do it in our personal cars."

"Good. It won't spook the guy if he sees you."

35

S ID PICKED UP A SUB sandwich on the way home. Before starting on it, he checked his surveillance system and found no indication that anyone had been around the place. He considered Agent Eggers' comment about the hired gun, that with the help of the Internet, the man would know all about his target. He recalled the newspaper stories that ran after the fracas at the Dixie Seals office a few months back, where he had unmasked a triple murderer. They had provided plenty of background.

After supper, he watched a rerun of the evening news, then one of the few cop shows realistic enough to hold his interest. He read a bit of the latest Lee Child novel, marveling at all the trouble Jack Reacher could get himself into and the deadly results of his efforts to come out on top. In contrast to the cop show, it was pure, and sometimes bizarre, fiction, but it provided a momentary escape from the stark reality of the day. He turned on the ten o'clock news and noted, happily, that nothing was said about the Earline Ivey slaying or its aftermath.

Not a fan of late night comedians and their talkathons, Sid turned off the TV and made a final check of his security setup. Windows and doors were locked. Using his computer, he switched around the views from his eaves-mounted cameras. The cloudy sky left little ambient light, but he detected nothing out of the ordinary. He looked over the settings in the alarm system. Everything appeared at the ready.

He angled the bedside clock so he could see it at a glance. He removed the Sig from its holster, jacked a round into the chamber, put the safety on, and set it on the table within easy reach. Satisfied that he had done everything possible to prepare for a visitor, he propped himself up, switched on the bedside lamp, and returned to Jack Reacher's latest caper. It was around midnight when he put the book aside and switched off the lamp. He soon drifted off to sleep.

THE BEEP-BEEP-BEEP of the alarm woke him instantly. He looked toward the red time display on the bedside clock and saw nothing. It had a battery backup, but he couldn't remember when he'd changed the battery. At the same time he realized the peculiar pattern of the beeps had signaled a power failure. He rolled out of bed in one swift motion. Reaching for the table, he found the phone on its charging stand. The light should have glowed. Without power, though, the phone wouldn't work. He grabbed the Sig off the table and crossed the room to the alarm console mounted beside the door. With the system operating on battery now, the display remained lit. Everything looked normal for the moment.

It had to be the unknown assassin. He debated the best way to handle the situation. The backup battery produced enough power to sound the high decibel alarm if a door or window were opened. That would likely scare off the intruder. But it wouldn't discourage him from coming back at a more opportune moment. No, Sid thought, it would be better to have a showdown now on his own terms. He reached out a finger and shut off the alarm. It would still give a short beep and indicate the location if a door or window should be opened.

He had difficulty seeing much more than shapes in the darkness. Turning back to the table, he felt for the small LED flashlight he kept there. Pressing the on switch, he searched the floor for his loafers and slipped them on. The rubber soles would make no sound, and they would prevent a muffled groan if a toe encountered a chair leg or a wall. He also grabbed a lightweight jacket off the chair and slipped it on over his pajamas. He needed pockets. Looking across at the bed, he had an idea. The assassin would likely try to catch him asleep. He puffed up the spare pillow and stuffed it under the covers, pulling the sheet well up to hide where his head should be.

With that done, he picked up his cell phone and flipped open the cover. A good cop always called for backup. Jaz was too far across town. He punched in Bart Masterson's number. Before his detective friend could answer, though, the alarm console beeped.

He had wasted too much time setting up his dummy.

He hit the button to cancel the call as he rushed across the room. The alarm display indicated the kitchen door had been opened. He checked the safety and slipped his gun into a jacket pocket. With a frenzy of punching, he set the phone's ring tone to zero so it wouldn't reveal his position if Bart returned the call. He stuffed the phone and the flashlight in his pockets, pulled out the Sig and moved into the hallway.

He crossed to his office door like a wraith in a darkened cemetery. Pausing, breathless, he listened.

Not a sound. Nothing.

Realizing the small red lights on his computer and a couple of other gadgets around his desk might be enough to pinpoint him, he moved across to a more obscure spot where he still had a view of the doorway to his bedroom. He reasoned that he would be able to detect movement going toward the door.

As he stood there willing his ears to pick up the slightest scrap of sound, he lowered himself to one knee. It made him a smaller target. He flipped off the safety and held the gun at the ready.

And waited.

The seconds ticked away in slow motion. The man was taking his time. Taking no chances.

Straining to catch a rustle of clothing or the squeak of a floorboard, he felt the tension build and his awareness heighten as adrenaline pumped through his body. For a moment he was transported back forty years to a night patrol in Vietnam. He could almost smell the rotting vegetation of the jungle, feel the oppressive heat and humidity.

Then a vague movement at the doorway snapped him back to the present.

After a moment of silence, a mocking voice broke the stillness.

"It's just like with that Ivey woman, Chance. I can see you, but you can't—"

Sid fired in the direction of the voice. He squeezed off five rounds, then lifted his finger from the trigger to save the rest. Deafened by the noise, he couldn't hear the return fire, but muzzle flashes revealed the assassin's position.

Sid fired two more rounds after a sharp pain sliced through his left arm. He'd been hit. The room reeked with the smell of gunpowder.

Something warm trickled down his arm, but his fingers still worked. With the shooting stopped, he pulled out the flashlight, switched in on, and pointed it toward the door. Seeing no one, he held out the Sig and rushed through the opening, turning his light and gun toward the kitchen. As he started to run, his toe caught on something, throwing him off balance, and he fell headlong in the hallway.

The flashlight clattered to the floor. The pistol came out of his hand and slid across the carpet.

That damned snag in the carpet he'd been intending to fix was all he could think of.

He scrambled to retrieve the Sig, grabbed the flashlight and shined it toward the kitchen, fearing the killer would be attracted by the sound of his fall.

When no one appeared, he directed the flashlight to the carpet. He saw the problem was more than just the snag. He had also tripped over a heavy set of goggles attached to a headgear. Night vision goggles. The intruder had seen him as clearly as if the lights had been on. Until he started firing.

A row of blood droplets stained the hall carpet. He knew he'd scored a hit. The guy had lost his goggles and probably couldn't find them in the confusion of trying to get away. Sid understood. His own head felt like he'd had his bell rung. Getting his thoughts together, he knew he needed to give chase but realized he had likely waited too long.

He sprinted to the back door and opened it. He could make out the shapes of objects in the sparse light, but he saw no one. Then he heard a car start out front.

Sid bolted for the front door and made it just in time to see a pair of taillights disappear down the street. A wave of fatigue swept over him, and he dropped the Sig to his side. He walked back to his bedroom and plopped down on the side of the bed, feeling the letdown that followed a high stress incident. His left arm throbbed now and sent out sharp pains when he moved it. But it still moved as before, which he took as a sign the bone was still intact. He laid the flashlight on the table beside his gun and stared at a hole in the jacket, where blood soaked through the sleeve. He wriggled out of the jacket and his pajama top. The bullet had pierced his upper arm and still oozed blood. He went into the bathroom, pulled a towel off the shelf, and wrapped it around his arm.

Back in the bedroom, he looked for his cell phone to report the shooting before his neighbors did. Hearing a sound louder than the ringing in his ears, he realized it came from the front of the house. He picked up the Sig and started toward the living room. On the way it came to him that someone was pounding on the door.

He unlocked the door and opened it to find a snarling Bart Masterson standing on the porch. Sid let him in.

"What the hell's going on?" he asked. "You called my phone and hung up. I've been trying to—"

His voice cut off when he saw the towel and the bloody arm.

"The bastard cut my electric and phone lines," Sid said. "He just high-tailed it out of here in a car about five minutes ago."

"Must have been the one I passed speeding down Neelys Bend Road. Looked like a black Ford." Bart pointed at the arm. "He did that?"

"Yeah. I got him with at least one shot. There's blood in the hallway."

Bart pulled out his phone and started making calls. Soon a patrol unit pulled up, then an ambulance, and a crime scene crew. Sgt. Wick Stanley added his car to the crowd in the street.

The next hour was mostly a blur for Sid. He told Bart and Wick what had happened and gritted his teeth while the paramedics patched up his arm. They insisted on taking him to the Emergency Room, but Sid refused to go until the initial investigation was finished. Bart agreed to take him later. The crime scene team brought in lights, helping them find two .22 caliber shells and the seven .40 caliber cartridge cases from Sid's gun. They took samples of the shooter's blood and bagged the infrared goggles. They took fingerprints from the back door, but Sid said they were probably his. The hit man had no doubt worn gloves.

Wick told Sid how Jaz had arranged for him and Bart to take turns checking out his house. The hired gun had picked a time between visits. Actually, while Bart was en route.

The detective grinned when Sid described what happened when he started firing as the intruder was talking. "It's a good thing you're trigger happy," Bart said. "I'll bet that's the last time he'll try that cutesy line."

"I'm glad he did on two counts," Sid said. "He gave me a chance to shoot first, and he admitted to killing Earline Ivey."

"Too bad he didn't tell you who hired him."

"Your guy Kozlov probably put him onto me."

"Ram Kozlov may be a cop, but he's not 'our guy,'" Wick said.

Bart had called in a description of the car he had seen, hoping that at three a.m. a patrol car might come across it. No such luck. The hospital ERs routinely notified the police when a gunshot wound appeared, but he arranged to have them all called to be on the lookout for a fresh victim. While Sid was being treated at the hospital, Bart called Jaz and told her what had happened.

JAZ PULLED INTO THE Emergency Room parking lot just after five. Inside she was directed toward Sid's cubicle. She found him on the bed with his shirt off, his left arm bandaged. Bart stood beside him.

"I'm glad it was your arm," Jaz said, "and not the middle of your forehead like I warned you."

Sid mustered a tired grin. "I'm touched."

Bart leaned against the wall. "I didn't tell you what the guy said to him."

She looked back at Sid, who was propped up in the bed. She spoke in a soft voice. "Say about what?"

"You'll have to speak a little louder," he said. "My hearing still isn't up to par."

"What did he say to you?"

"It was something like 'it's the same as with the Ivey woman, I can see you but you can't see me.' Only he didn't need night vision goggles with her. He shot her from behind in broad daylight."

Jaz felt a sudden wave of relief, like a yoke had been lifted from her shoulders. "Bless you," she said, striding over to the bed and leaning down to kiss him.

"Hey, don't I get one of those?" Bart asked. "I just missed him."

"When you catch the SOB, you'll get yours."

36

JAZ INSISTED THAT Sid go home with her. He didn't appear in a mood to argue and quickly agreed, but he said he needed to go by his house to get a few things. Bart followed the Lexus back to Neelys Bend and drew his weapon before leading the way inside. He used his big flashlight to illuminate the path as they followed.

"What a mess," Jaz said, gazing at the bullet holes in the wall and the blood on the carpet.

Sid shook his head. "I need to call Nashville Electric Service and the telephone company to get things restored."

"You'll need a repairman and maid service, too."

"I'll ask North Precinct to cruise around here a few times and be sure he doesn't come back," Bart said.

"I doubt he'll show his face around here again." Sid stuffed some clothes and his shaving kit into a small bag.

Jaz folded her arms. "Which leaves the question, where will he turn up next time?"

"We need to contact FBI Agent Eggers," Sid said. "They have a good description of him."

"If he's following his usual MO, he'll have a rental car," Bart said. "We'll check everybody at the airport and see if we can find what he's driving."

Jaz watched Sid as he picked up his bag and gave a deep sigh. "You look like you're about to drop," she said. "I'd better get you tucked in."

215

"With all that adrenaline gone, it's left me bushed. I didn't sleep much last night, either. Let's go."

The eastern sky had just begun to glow, showing a nebulous break in the clouds as Jaz steered toward I-65. She glanced at Sid slumped in the passenger seat but still a large presence in the semi-darkness.

"I nearly lost it when Bart called and said you'd been shot," she said. "I knew the guy had already killed two people with one shot to the head."

"It's funny, when I was there on my knee waiting for him, I had a sudden feeling that I was back on night patrol in Vietnam. I could even smell the jungle. The night sounds weren't there, but I think that got me keyed up to the point that I reacted instinctively to the threat."

"He wasn't hurt badly enough to slow him down on getting out of there. It would be nice to know what kind of wound he suffered."

"He's not going to a hospital. You can count on that."

"Unless it's superficial, and the amount of blood doesn't look like that, he'd have to get treatment before he could go through airport security."

Sid shifted his left arm, apparently to a more comfortable position. "He's got to be street smart. I'm sure he could find some sub rosa medical help."

"Do you think he's left town?"

"I would doubt it."

SID AWOKE IN A strange bed in a strange room. It took only a few moments to orient himself, though. He'd always been a light sleeper, a wake-up-and-jump-out-of-bed type. The pain in his arm brought things back into focus quickly. He sat up on the side of the bed and looked around. The walls were a pastel blue. Paintings with a Hawaiian flavor, lush greenery and tropical blossoms, hung about the room. He recalled hearing Jaz refer to her bedrooms as Hawaiian or Japanese or Alaskan. They were places her family had visited while she was growing up.

A clock on the bedside stand showed 3:08. He had slept a good eight hours. He felt much better, but he had things to do. He got up and padded to the door, opened it and looked into the hallway, saw no one. Closing the door, he crossed to the chair that held his bag and pulled out fresh underwear and a clean short sleeve shirt. After dressing, he walked into the bathroom and washed his face, then stared into the mirror.

That fuzzy bear doesn't look too threatening, he thought. He combed his hair and smoothed his beard and decided he didn't look too much the worse for wear. He checked around the room for his cell phone but didn't find it. Heading downstairs, he met Marie walking away from the kitchen.

"My, look at that arm, Mr. Sidney," she said, eyes widening. "Miss Jasmine said she hoped the other fella made out worse."

Sid grinned. "This bum wing just means I can't fly quite as fast as before."

Marie laughed. "Glad you still have your sense of humor. Can I get you something to eat?"

He glanced at his watch. "Looks like I missed breakfast and lunch. I could use a cup of coffee, but I'll hold off on the rest until dinnertime. Is Jaz in her office?"

"Yessir. I'll bring your coffee in there."

"Thanks, Marie."

He found Jaz at her desk, talking on the phone. He sat down until she finished a few moments later.

"That was Bart," she said. "The newsies have been looking for you."

"I guess they found my phone out of order."

"This, too." She handed him his cell phone. "I brought it

down here and turned it off so you wouldn't be disturbed."

He turned the phone on and saw a list of missed calls. "Anything new from Bart?"

"He thinks the guy bugged out. A rental car company called police when they discovered blood on the seat of a car turned in at the airport this morning. It matched the blood type on your carpet."

"Could they tell what part of the body it came from?"

"Bart said it was apparently from his back, on the right side. Probably the exit wound."

"That's why he didn't fire more than twice. I wonder if it hit him in the chest or if he was turned and it caught him in the side?"

"Either way, he's not a happy camper now. Bart said they're checking with the TSA folks at the airport to see if they noticed any passengers going through security with that sort of injury."

Sid opened his phone again. "I need to call Agent Eggers, and I've got to report my phone and electricity outages at home."

"The latter are taken care of," Jaz said. "Your phone and lights should be working by tonight."

"Thanks, you're a doll. Remind me to give you a raise."

Jaz tapped a finger against her chin. "Which brings to mind the business of what we are going to do about Djuan Burden?"

"I plan to bring that up with Baron Eggers." He punched in the FBI agent's number.

"This is Sid Chance," he said when Eggers answered.

"I've been trying to call you. I heard what happened last night. It sounds like our guy."

"Definitely," Sid said. He gave him a brief rundown on what had transpired around three o'clock this morning.

"He admitted to Ivey's murder?"

"Sure did. While he had me in his sights and knew I couldn't see him."

"He obviously considered you a special case. They aren't usually that talkative on the job."

"What do you know about him?" Sid asked.

"His name is Carlos Ruiz. He was born and grew up in Arizona. He joined the Army shortly before Nine-Eleven, and volunteered for the Rangers. While serving in Iraq, he was held on suspicion of murdering some civilians, but the charges were dropped for lack of credible evidence. However, the Army shrinks decided he should be separated. Sounds like they made the proper call."

"I served in Special Forces in Vietnam," Sid said. "I had an idea this guy could have been a military man gone bad."

"I hate to tell you, Sid, but your problems are just beginning."

"With Carlos Ruiz?"

"Right. The people who follow these cases at Quantico tell me that shootout will churn in his gut until he gets you or gets caught."

Sid reached over and took the coffee cup from Marie, who disappeared as quickly as she had come. "I sort of figured that," he said, a feeling of inevitability settling over him. He took a slow sip of coffee.

"I'll talk to Detective Masterson and see if we can help them on this," Eggers said.

"You can help Jaz and me by getting Metro off of Djuan Burden's case."

"I talked to my supervisor, but he doesn't want to do anything that might jeopardize the investigation of Ramsey Kozlov. That's also why he wants to leave Ruiz to Metro for the moment."

"Kozlov is about to be on the hot seat with the Office of Professional Accountability over the gun firing."

He told Eggers about the confrontation with Detective

Victor Grimm he had engineered with the help of two Metro officers.

"Tell your supervisor if he doesn't want to talk to the Davidson County District Attorney and get Djuan out of jail, I'm going downtown to see the U.S. Attorney."

Eggers hesitated for a moment. "Look, Sid, you've established a good relationship with the office here. I'd suggest you forget about my supervisor. Just go ahead and talk to the U.S. Attorney, explain what happened and get him to intervene. It'll take us both off the hook."

When he shut off the phone, Jaz asked, "Will he talk to his supervisor?"

He told her what Eggers had suggested.

"Good," she said. "We need to call Mrs. Ransom and the lawyers at Arnie Bailey's office. What was this about the shooter? His name is Carlos Ruiz?"

"Right. And Eggers confirmed what I suspected."

"What's that?"

He detailed Ruiz's background and the Quantico analysts' prediction that the ex-soldier would not rest until he had arranged a final encounter with Sid or was caught.

"What are the chances he'll be caught?" Jaz asked.

"Right now I'd have to say not too good. Eggers said the FBI was leaving it up to Metro for the moment. He said he'd talk to Bart and offer their help."

Jaz tapped her fingertips together and eyed him with a somber look. "So what do we do?"

Sid considered the possibilities. While he still doubted that Ruiz would come after him again at home, there was the office to consider and countless other places he might go during an investigation.

"If this has become a personal vendetta, he'll want to catch me somewhere alone," Sid said.

"Why don't you move in here with me for the present? I can bring in a table for you to use and have your office phone temporarily re-routed here. You can access your computer through your laptop."

He squinched his eyes and looked around. "I hate to crowd you like that."

"No problem. So long as you don't boss me too much."

He smiled. "I've never known you to accept much bossing."

"Is it a deal?"

He shrugged. "I guess I don't have much choice. I'll have to go back to Madison and get what I need, including my car."

"I'll take you after dinner. Marie will be overjoyed. She's always said I should have a man in the house besides John."

37

JAZ CALLED RACHEl Ransom to give her the good news while Sid got on the phone with Hardy Vandenberg and Brainerd Hersholt. He told them he planned to visit the U.S. Attorney in the morning. When they had finished their phone calls, Sid turned to Jaz.

"I've been thinking about what Agent Eggers said to me earlier, that this contract killer could find out a lot about me on the Internet. I haven't Googled my name in a long time. How about putting it in and see what comes up."

"I'll try it both ways, as Sid and Sidney." She punched in the names and a list of links and their descriptions flashed on the screen. "Come around here where you can see."

Sid moved beside her at the desk. He saw links to various news articles about him, most dealing with the toxic chemical dumping case he had worked a few months ago, his first job with Arnie Bailey. It had resulted in the conviction of a former prison inmate who had gone straight until he started murdering people to cover up a past crime. There were also several old newspaper accounts of his arrest and subsequent exoneration after the drug scam in Lewisville. Then he spotted a feature story one of the local tabloids had done on him following the pollution case last fall.

"That one probably gave him all he needed," Sid said, pointing to the feature link.

Jaz clicked on it and brought up the article. It had Sid's

picture at his desk and the story of how he had opened Sidney Chance Investigations after exonerating an employee of Jaz's company who had been framed by a crooked manager. It gave the background of the false bribery charges that had disgusted him so thoroughly that he holed up in a hillside sanctuary about fifty miles east of Nashville. Working alone, he had built a one-room cabin, hauling materials up a steep incline. He had lived there in the backwoods for three years, almost completely shut off from the outside world, except for occasional forays into a nearby town for food and other provisions. He worked out daily and built a firing range to maintain his firearms proficiency. The article mentioned that he had called it his Mountain Hideaway.

Jaz looked up with a grin. "I'll never forget the day I followed a deputy sheriff up that overgrown hillside and knocked on your door."

"I'd made friends with that deputy. Otherwise I might not have opened the door."

"I'm thankful I talked you into giving up that monkish lifestyle and coming back here."

"Oh? If I hadn't gotten you involved in this case, you wouldn't have suffered all the agony you've been through the last few days."

She cocked her head to the side. "You forget I was the one who insisted you take the case."

"Well, I'm glad it's over, for all intents and purposes."

Marie called them to dinner shortly and led them into the dining room, where she had the table set with Sid's place at the head.

"You shouldn't have gone to all this trouble," he said, knowing they usually ate at the kitchen table.

"You two deserve a little pampering after what you've been through," Marie said.

Sid saw there were only two places set. "Aren't you and John going to join us?"

"I knew you needed to eat early since you hadn't had any food all day. We had a big lunch. We're not hungry yet."

Sid and Jaz talked about the Djuan Burden case as they ate. She speculated that Carlos Ruiz had access to the Mexican drug gang by virtue of being Hispanic.

"He's probably one of their top enforcers," Sid said. "Eggers told me that Valdez-Delgado had set up the Medicare scam with money he skimmed off the drug profits."

"Just to be safe, we'd better get on over to your place before dark and pick up what you need."

SID FOUND THE LIGHTS and phone back in working order when they arrived. He checked out the bullet holes in the walls and spots in the carpet that had been cut out by the crime scene crew. He needed to replace it anyway. Jaz worked on his computer so he could remotely check the surveillance cameras from his laptop.

When he had everything he needed from home, he drove over to RiverGate with Jaz following. There were only a couple of cars parked at the building. Sid checked the office carefully and saw no evidence of tampering. He needed to call the girl down the hall tomorrow and ask her to keep an eye on the place.

He told Jaz to go ahead and followed her out to Franklin Road. The waiting game would continue.

38

U P AT HIS USUAL TIME on Friday, Sid donned his sweats and quietly made his way downstairs. He was surprised to encounter John Wallace near the front door.

"I'm off for my morning run," he said. "What are you doing up this early?"

"I'm an early riser," John said. "In recent years I've also been early to bed. Marie won't be up for another hour, at least. You gonna run with that bum arm?"

"It'll hurt, I'm sure, but I need the exercise. I don't think I'll get out on Franklin Road, though. Maybe just run around the perimeter of Jaz's property."

"Good idea. Lots of crazy drivers on that road."

"If Jaz gets up, tell her where I am."

"Yessir," John said. "I will."

The cool morning air felt refreshing on his face. The jarring run over uneven ground left his arm feeling somewhat less than pleased, but it was a far cry from his last gunshot wounds. Those had brought an end to his National Park ranger career. It had come on a day not unlike this one. He had been patrolling a remote area on the lookout for wildlife poachers when he spotted fresh tire tracks going into an old service road no longer in use. He drove in a short distance, then set out on foot.

Like now, it had been early morning. Evidently the

intruders hadn't expected a ranger to be out this time of day. He soon came upon a pickup truck and heard voices back in the trees. He drew his weapon and moved stealthily in their direction. When he reached a cleared area, he froze. Two men were cutting marijuana plants right there in the middle of a national park.

Sid stepped out and ordered them to put up their hands and turn around. As he approached them, a third man who had been hidden by nearby trees opened fire. Sid got off a shot, but he took two bullets in the chest, one of which would have been fatal a fraction of an inch to one side. The only reason he survived was the ability to call for help on his radio. His attackers were caught while trying to push his car out of the narrow road to get their truck free.

Those wounds resulted in nearly a year's convalescence. The Park Service higher ups decided he was no longer fit for duty. He had fought bitterly to stay on but lost. He was sure it stemmed from his unorthodox habit of doing things his own way. Something of a loner from an early age, he had nevertheless considered himself a team player, except when the team wasn't playing by the rules as he interpreted them.

Reliving that unfortunate chapter of his life kept him from dwelling on the sore left arm. When he decided he'd had enough, he headed back to the mansion and walked toward the kitchen to rehydrate. He smelled bacon frying and found Marie stirring eggs in a bowl.

"Are you ready for some breakfast?" she asked.

"Right now I need water," he said. "Then I'll need a quick shower."

After he drank a tall glass of water, he started out the door and Marie called after him. "Knock on Miss Jasmine's door and tell her breakfast will be ready in a few minutes."

The master suite was at the opposite end of the hall from

the Hawaiian Room. Sid stopped at the door and knocked. He heard a rustle inside and then the door opened. Jaz stood there barefoot in her pink nightgown staring through wide blue eyes.

"Oh, God, I look a fright," she said, running fingers through her short blonde hair. "I thought you were Marie."

Sid smiled. "Sorry, but I disagree. You look fabulous. I like to see women in their natural state, without all the adornments."

"Thank you, I think." She looked down at the rumpled nightie. "At least this covers up most of the natural part."

"I've seen more in the swimming pool."

Jaz laughed. "We'll have to have a pool party when it gets a little warmer."

"You may not like it when you see my bullet hole scars."

"I saw those when you were on the gurney at the Emergency Room."

"Oh, the reason I knocked, Marie said to tell you breakfast will be ready in a few minutes. I need a shower after my run."

She shook her head. "You're way ahead of me. Better be careful with that arm in the shower."

He thought about adding a quip that he might need her to scrub his back, but he knew she'd endured more than her share of sexual innuendo during her days as a cop.

Sid bathed and dressed, then joined Jaz and the Wallaces in the kitchen. A large plate of bacon and eggs, plus homemade biscuits and strawberry preserves, washed down with hot coffee, left him ready to face the day's hurdles.

"What are you going to do about that arm?" Jaz asked. "They told you in the Emergency Room to follow up with your regular doctor."

"I'll give it a chance to start healing before I undergo that ordeal. Right now I'm interested in getting some action out of the U.S. Attorney."

HE FOUND THE OFFICE in a large building behind the U.S. Courthouse on Ninth Avenue South. After navigating all the security, Sid explained his problem to a receptionist and was directed to the number two man, who held the title of first assistant U.S. Attorney. After telling his story for the second time, he was escorted in to meet the boss. A pleasant looking man with bushy dark hair, the top federal lawyer for the Middle District of Tennessee gave him a firm handshake and directed him to a chair.

"It sounds like you have an intriguing story to tell," he said. "An innocent man is being held for murder?"

"You may be familiar with the Djuan Burden case," Sid said.

The attorney nodded.

"My firm was hired by Burden's grandmother to look into the case. We found evidence of Medicare fraud at the store where the owner was shot and turned it over to the FBI. We also discovered evidence indicating that a hired killer was probably responsible for the murder. The FBI followed up and confirmed that it was a hit man from Dallas."

"The FBI told you this?" he asked.

"I've been working closely with Agent Baron Eggers. He tells me his supervisor is reluctant to go to the District Attorney because it's still an active case. Djuan Burden spent half of his life in prison for a mistake he made at age twelve. He's tried to make amends since being released, but he's been jailed the past week and a half for a crime he didn't commit. It's an injustice I hope you can do something to correct."

"This is a serious matter, Mr. Chance. I appreciate your bringing it to my attention. There are a couple of investigations under way that might be involved, but I'll certainly look into it and see what can be done to rectify the situation as far as Burden is concerned."

Sid thanked him and left. Back in his car, he called Rachel Ransom and told her to relax, that mountains were being moved. She thanked him tearfully. Next he called Bart Masterson, to see if the police had uncovered anything new regarding the intruder from Wednesday night.

"I know you've talked to your FBI friend," Bart said. "He gave us the info on Carlos Ruiz, which saved us waiting for DNA results. The check with TSA agents at the airport didn't produce any sign of him, though. I still think he's gone. If he got treated, it wasn't by any legitimate clinic."

"I figured as much. But considering what Eggers heard from the folks at Quantico, I doubt that he's left. They think he'll want another showdown with me."

"You don't need that, Sid. It could be true, though. I heard something this morning I discounted at the time. Maybe I should have paid more attention."

"What was it?"

"A passenger returning on a flight from Atlanta reported his car stolen from the airport garage. It could have been Ruiz after he turned in the rental car. Nobody's reported seeing the license number yet."

"They won't," Sid said. "He likely used a plate he'd stolen somewhere else. What kind of car was it?"

"Black twenty-eleven Focus."

"He likes Fords. Probably used the same tag that was on the rental car when he came to my house."

"Sounds like you're dealing with a smart bastard, Sid. Staying at Jaz's house is probably a good move."

"Yeah, but I can't stay there for long. I hope he makes a move you guys can tune in on."

"We'll keep looking. By the way, Wick called. Grimm told him he'd been by the Office of Professional Accountability. So the shit's headed for the fan."

BACK AT JAZ'S PLACE, Sid set up his table in her office and worked on the missing heir case. He had narrowed down the woman's location to New Orleans but found records lost or misplaced after Katrina. Jaz had gone downtown for another meeting with K.C. Urban about the upcoming hearing at the Tennessee Human Rights Commission. She called to say it would be after noon before she got home.

After lunch, Sid linked to his computer at home and checked his alarm system. The log was clear. Nothing had been triggered. He called his next-door neighbor, a Dupont retiree from the nearby Old Hickory plant, to find out if he had seen anything unusual.

"Hi, Ralph," he said. "This is Sid. How's everything around there?"

"Fine. What about you? Haven't had any more trouble, I hope."

Ralph had wandered out that morning to see what all the lights and sirens were about.

"No, no more problems. I'm staying with a friend for a few days, but my alarm system at the house is up and running. I'd appreciate your giving me a call on the cell phone if you see anything out of the ordinary."

"I was just about to go check my mailbox. Want me to see if you have anything?"

"Sure. You can let me know if you find something that looks important."

"Just hold on, Sid. I'll carry my phone and you won't have to wait."

Ralph chattered away about neighborhood gossip as he walked out to the street. Sid could hear him shuffling papers when he got to the mailbox.

"Looks like junk and a bill or two," Ralph said. "Hmm, you got an invitation to a party. Card says something about a

Mountain Party. Don't see a date. Want me to take your mail in and hold it for you?"

A Mountain Party? That sounded like something he needed to look into. "Just leave everything in the box, Ralph. I'll come by and pick it up."

He told John that he needed to go by home to check his mail, that he would be back shortly. Mid-afternoon traffic on the interstates moved through town with no delays, and he soon pulled into his driveway. At the mailbox he found a few inconsequential flyers, bills for garbage pickup, water and sewer, and a post card with what appeared to be a hand-lettered message. He climbed into the car and looked at the card.

YOU ARE INVITED TO A MOUNTAIN PARTY.
COME AS YOU ARE.
YOUR HIDEAWAY PARTNER

He checked the postmark. Yesterday afternoon at the central mail facility on Royal Parkway, near the Donelson Pike exit to I-40. That's why it got such quick delivery. He read the message again. Two key words stood out—Mountain and Hideaway. He thought back to that newspaper article Jaz had pulled up on her computer yesterday. It mentioned that he had referred to his secluded cabin as a Mountain Hideaway. To get there you needed to travel some fifty or so miles east on I-40.

The message came through loud and clear. Carlos Ruiz had invaded his property and challenged Sid to come after him.

39

URING THE DRIVE back to Franklin Road, Sid pondered that cryptic message and what he should do about it. He had gone into his house and retrieved a small scale map of the area showing details of his property. The hired killer's apparent decision to take over his cabin galled him beyond words. He had worked his butt off building that structure, and it had served as his home for three long years. Sending the invitation was a brazen move. His first reaction was an urge to head for the hinterlands and flush out Carlos Ruiz. After a little more prudent consideration, he realized that rushing off without careful planning was exactly what Ruiz hoped for. It would be an invitation to disaster.

He found Jaz in her office when he arrived at the mansion.

"John told me you had to make a trip to your house," she said. "What's up?"

Sid dropped the card on her desk. "Look at the signature line. That ring a bell?"

She stared at the message. "Your Hideaway Partner...your hideaway. The cabin?"

"Bingo. My *Partner* is a sick joke by a sick character who would like to complete a trio of murders."

Her eyes narrowed. "And he's betting you'll be motivated by a challenge to your machismo."

Sid grinned. "I thought about it."

"Bart and Wick won't be any help up there."

"Bart, maybe, if we can convince Metro that it's a chance to get a suspect who's likely committed two murders, as well as an attempt on my life."

"What about the county sheriff up there? As owner of a rather large hillside, or mountain if you prefer, you're a taxpayer."

"It's a small county. I'm sure he wouldn't be willing to allocate the manpower without a request from another police agency. We have no evidence of a crime in his jurisdiction."

"Could Agent Eggers get involved?"

"As he told me, the FBI has chosen to leave the murder case to Metro for the present. Eggers' main interest in Ruiz is to find out if his employer is involved in Medicare fraud."

Jaz got up from her desk and strode across to the nearest bookshelf, running a fingernail along the spines as she moved around the room. She stopped and looked back at Sid.

"It's the old rock and hard place, isn't it? If we don't follow up quickly, he'll think you aren't coming and check out. Next time you may not get a warning."

"And the chances of getting law enforcement to move that fast on anything are pretty slim. I did pick up something favorable from my visit with the U.S. Attorney."

"Is he willing to step in and give Djuan a break?"

"He sounded definitely interested in the case. He promised he'd follow up to see what could be done. Again, it's a question of how fast the Feds might move."

"Did Bart pass along what Ruiz said to you about the Earline Ivey murder?" Jaz asked.

"Yeah, but I don't know if his superiors have bought it, particularly with Chief Kozlov involved."

Sid opened the envelope containing the map he had brought from home and spread it out on the table. "I'd better start working out a plan to go up there tomorrow."

"We'd better work out a plan," she said. "You're not going up there without me. You got mired in this mess in an effort to get me out of it. We're in this together, Sid."

He didn't like the idea of putting her at risk, but he knew there would be no changing her mind. He had to admit another gun would double their odds.

"Okay," he said. "I have a map that shows details of the area. I know every inch of that property on foot, but I need to refresh my mind on the big picture."

"I have a suggestion. I'll call Agee, the company helicopter pilot—you remember him."

"Yeah. He flew us down to Centerville during the pollution case."

"If the chopper is available tomorrow, he can fly us up there and make a low level pass over the cabin. We might even spot Ruiz."

Sid looked up at her. "Are you planning to rappel down?"

"No, dummy. I'll have Cassie, my admin assistant, drive the car up. Pick us a place where he can land and let us out near the car. She can fly back here with Agee."

"Call him and see what he can do. I'll go over this map and get to work on devising a plan of attack. "

After getting the flight arranged, Jaz called her assistant and asked her to come by and pick up the Lexus. She also called her lawyer to inform the court she would be making a short business trip in the morning.

While they watched a TV news show in the rec room after dinner, Bart called Sid's cell phone.

"They've done it to me again," he said in a voice that dripped with disgust.

"Done what?" Sid asked.

"I've been pulled off everything in the precinct and

assigned to a special unit investigating the murder of that bank president in Belle Meade."

Sid had read about the case, which took place in the small satellite city on the west side of town, Nashville's posh old-wealth residential area.

"Who's taking over the Carlos Ruiz case?"

"I don't know who they'll assign it to...or when."

"If Jaz and I are successful, Ruiz won't be on the loose after tomorrow anyway."

"What are you talking about?"

Sid told him about the postcard with the Mountain Party invitation and what it meant. He explained their belief that it they didn't make a move now, Ruiz would be gone.

"You two are going up there after him like a couple of vigilantes?" Bart asked.

"Do you know of any cops who want to go with us?"

Bart grunted. "Right now it would probably take an act of Congress to get things moving here."

"I don't think this guy's going to wait around before making some kind of move," Sid said.

"He's a sharp cookie, Sid."

"I know."

"He's not going to be holed up in that cabin waiting for you to jump him."

"We have a plan of attack."

"Don't you have a contact in the sheriff's office up there?"

"Yeah. I plan to call him in the morning before we go."

"I wish I could go with you and make everything legal, but there's no way, not with this new assignment they've stuck me on. I've been at it most of the day. Just got home a few minutes ago."

After he shut off the phone, Sid thought about the new assignment. Had it come from the CJC, like the order to take

Bart off the Ivey case? Chief Kozlov in action again, keeping the pressure off of Ramsey.

"I heard you mention the Ruiz case," Jaz said. "What happened to Bart?"

Sid told her about the Belle Meade murder assignment. "Frankly, it smells a little fishy to me."

"Do you think Ramsey had a hand in it?"

"If he's into this business as deeply as we think, I'm sure he's figured out that Ruiz is his man."

"I don't know much about hired guns, but I'd think they would keep their clients at arms length."

"True. Kozlov would likely have dealt with him through a third party, maybe his drug contact."

Jaz twisted around in her chair to face him. "Tomorrow had better be this guy's final day of contacting people with murder on his mind."

Sid agreed, but he knew they were headed for a real fight. Carlos Ruiz would not give up easily. This was not just another assignment. He had the strongest of motivations—survival.

40

SID SKIPPED HIS RUN Saturday morning. Battling the difficult terrain on his property would provide more than enough exercise for the day. The years he'd spent there hauling materials up the hill, including forty-pound bags of concrete mix, sheets of plywood, and large four-by-four posts, had honed his body into the best shape he'd been in since rehab from those gunshot wounds. Before leaving Jaz's house, he called the deputy he'd befriended while living at the cabin. He was the only one familiar with the rugged path up the steep incline.

"Hi, Cliff, this is Sid Chance. I trust you're keeping the county safe these days?"

"Trying to. You back at your cabin?"

"I'm coming up in a little while. Thought I'd give you a heads up."

He told the deputy he had reason to believe a suspect in a Nashville murder could be hiding out on his property.

"What makes you think that?"

"I got something anonymous in the mail. It's sort of complicated, and I could be all wet, of course, but that's my take on it. Jaz LeMieux and I are coming up to check it out."

"Does the Metro PD know about it?"

"I told a detective friend, but they're not currently looking in that direction."

"You're a former cop. I don't need to tell you to be careful.

If you see any evidence that the guy could be around, give us a call."

SID AND JAZ SHOWED up at John C. Tune Airport dressed in green and brown camouflage outfits and hiking shoes. The rest of their equipment had been stashed in the trunk of Jaz's Lexus. Agee, a short, broad-shouldered man, met them on the ramp of Nashville's general aviation airport beside the Bell Jetranger III. He had learned his trade with the 101st Airborne Division at Fort Campbell. He wore a green military style flight suit.

"Good to see you again, Mr. Chance," he said, shaking Sid's hand. "So we're flying up to the Cordell Hull Dam area."

Sid took out his map, handed it to the pilot and pointed. "There's my property. The location of the cabin is marked. We think there's a guy in the area who has no business being there. We need to fly by at fairly low level and low speed to get a good look at what's going on. We don't want to be too obvious, though, and tip him off."

"No problem." Agee looked around at Jaz. "You resemble a couple of special ops types."

"That's what I was in Nam," Sid said. "Army Special Forces."

"I remember now." He glanced at the map. "And I'm supposed to land you where?"

Sid pointed to an intersection. "Right here."

"Okay. Let's get on board and crank up this critter."

He climbed into the pilot's seat. Jaz and Sid followed, taking the rear bench. Agee began flipping switches. The whine rose in pitch and the engine slowly came to life. Sid could feel the rotor turning overhead as the pilot checked his instruments. He had a sudden feeling of déjà vu, but the plush burgundy interior was a far cry from what the Army had flown in Vietnam.

Agee studied Sid's map and made some marks on his navigation chart as the chopper warmed up. The noise made conversation difficult, and the passengers lapped into silence as the aircraft lifted off and headed east across the city. A few thousand feet above them, the clouds thickened. Sid remembered other chopper flights when he had carried a rifle and a bulky rucksack. A few of them had proven near disasters. Not wanting a repeat of that scenario, he mentally reviewed the plans for this mission, looking for any holes that might cause a problem.

The time passed quickly as a patchwork of fields, a web of country roads, and occasional blocks of buildings marking small towns passed beneath. The overcast remained a uniform dark gray. Soon Agee turned and shouted. "We're only a few minutes out. I'll pass with the cabin on your side, Mr. Chance."

Sid saw his wooded hillside ahead as Agee steered a course that would put them only a few hundred feet above the terrain. Though most of the trees had leafed out, many still lacked their full foliage. He spotted the cabin nestled among the greenery, facing west, its front windows looking out on the valley below. The chopper headed just to the right of the rustic log structure. He felt a twinge of nostalgia as the wooded panorama unfolded before him as colorful as a multi-page spread in *National Geographic*.

"Here we go!" Sid yelled.

Agee had slowed their airspeed, allowing Sid a clear view of the area around the cabin. He looked for signs that anything had been moved or altered. A few logs lay haphazardly beside a stack out back that he'd cut for the fireplace. No smoke appeared around the chimney. He thought a strong wind might have blown them off the stack. All of Middle Tennessee had been plagued by strong winds lately. Checking the main trail that squirmed up from an access road to the north, he saw a clump of brush that appeared to have been pushed to the side.

Agee looked around after they had cleared the area.

"Want to make another pass?"

Sid shook his head. "Let's go find the LZ."

"Roger," the pilot said.

Sid turned to Jaz. "Did you see anything?"

"Maybe. Is that pond on the back side part of your property?"

"Right."

"I thought I saw something moving around it, but I'm not sure."

Agee dropped just above the treetops beyond the next hill. It took them out of sight of anyone on Sid's property. He turned toward the Landing Zone, the rendezvous site Sid had picked to meet up with Jaz's administrative assistant. They soon descended to a cleared area beside the road where the red Lexus was parked. Cassie stood beside it, waving.

When they were on the ground, Agee left the chopper idling, its rotor turning slowly. Sid climbed down and helped Jaz out. They ducked their heads as they moved away toward the car.

"Don't you two look cool," Cassie said with a grin.

"Let's hope we stay cool," Sid said.

Jaz reached out to take her keys. "Thanks for bringing the car, Cass. Go hop in the helicopter and let Agee get you back home."

When the chopper lifted off, they retrieved their weapons and other equipment from the trunk. They climbed into the car, and Sid directed Jaz to the road on the north edge of his property, where a cleared area well off the pavement provided his usual parking spot. Less than a hundred yards down the road stood a large red barn where a neighbor had stored tobacco. It was no longer in use. Lots of room to hide, he thought, but he had been in it before and knew doors on both ends were secured from outside.

"Let's go check out that barn first," he said.

"You think he's hiding in there?"

"It's possible. But more likely his car could be."

He had donned his old cop belt from Lewisville, and he checked his equipment as he started toward the barn. Besides a gun holster, the belt held a spare magazine, handcuffs, a flashlight, a small pair of binoculars, and a civilian model of the Taser. Called the C2 Electronic Control Device, it would fire a pair of fishhook-like probes up to fifteen feet and penetrate two inches of clothing. Like all police officers who used them, Sid had taken a shot from one, experiencing the total loss of muscular control the electrical charge produced. He considered it the best non-lethal weapon around. He didn't think he'd have a use for it on this mission, but he had brought it along anyway.

They found the barn secured as before by two-by-fours slotted into handles on the doors. Although there appeared no way somebody could have locked themselves inside, they drew their guns before Sid removed the barrier and opened one of the doors. A shiny black Ford Focus with a Nashville license plate sat inside.

"Apparently he has brand loyalty," Jaz said.

"Erases any doubt, if we'd had any." Wide cracks in the structure let in plenty of light, but Sid shined his flashlight into dark corners. "Now we need to find out what he has in mind for us."

"Where do we start?"

"You said you saw movement around the pond. Are you sure it wasn't an animal?"

"It definitely wasn't a deer. Looked like a two-legged animal, and not a turkey."

"Okay, let's get started. Remember, this two-legged animal could bury us in an instant."

"How well I know." She rumpled her brow. "We need to keep our eyes moving."

"I did a lot of animal tracking in my ranger days. Those clouds mean plenty of moisture in the air, so sounds will carry far and relatively fast. We're in no hurry, so walk carefully. Try not to step on anything that will make a loud noise. If you hear natural sounds, like a bird's call or the rustle of a squirrel, use it to help cover your movement. We need to maintain silence as much as possible. We'll communicate by hand signal."

He showed her a few basic signals they might use, such as stop, come, freeze, hurry.

"Looks like it'll be hard to move stealthily with all the underbrush around," Jaz said.

Sid shrugged. "Animals have the same problem, and there are plenty of them around. This'll be a stroll down Broadway compared to what it'll be like when the growing season gets under way. Just be careful and try not to snap any large twigs as you go along. There are tons of dead limbs around."

Jaz followed behind him as he took a roundabout path through the woods. He found it slow going stepping over trees that had fallen during the winter. It was almost impossible to move along without making any noise. An occasional deer or rabbit crossing their path up ahead provided sounds that had a natural similitude. He knew they caused no more disturbance than the wildlife.

But was somebody watching and listening?

After nearly thirty minutes, they stopped in a thickly wooded area. Trunks of towering red oak and white ash trees provided good cover as they looked down on the pond Jaz had seen from the air. Spotting no one among the nearby trees or the banks of the pond, Sid motioned Jaz to follow him down to the waterside. He pointed to a few footprints in the soft dirt and whispered next to her ear.

"He was here, but he's moved on."

"What now?" she asked.

"He may have been spooked by the chopper, but we didn't make a second pass. Let's move up to the north side of the cabin. There's a good observation point there. And a nice little surprise."

The clouds continued to thicken and lower until they seemed to form a dark, lumpy canopy you could almost reach up and touch. The air had cooled and smelled of rain. Sid wished he had brought a waterproof jacket, but that would have spoiled the camouflage effect.

The thick underbrush slowed them at one point when Jaz's pants leg got snared by the thorny tentacles of a briar bush. Sid used his gloves to help free her. They kept a few feet of separation most of the time to provide a less-inviting target. A careful survey of the area showed no further sign of Carlos Ruiz.

But where was he?

41

THE CABIN RESTED ON a flat area at the crest of the hill, sitting at the edge of a precipitous drop to the west. A six-foot deck extended toward the wide valley below, supported by tall posts Sid had dragged up from the access road. The east side of the cabin provided the only ground access, with a small wooden porch and a sturdy wood door with double locks. Sid knew they were no match for a dedicated criminal, such as the one they faced now. When they reached a point in full view of the home he'd visited only once since leaving about a year ago, he signaled Jaz to stop and stay down. He kneeled behind a tree, pulled out his binoculars, and focused on the porch.

The first thing to catch his attention was a chair. A chair he had fashioned by hand, like everything else about the cabin. It should have been locked away. It meant Carlos Ruiz had been inside.

And could be now.

Sid scanned the area from the fire pit at one side to the outdoor shower he'd rigged on the other side. Nothing moved. Then he spotted something odd. Several tin cans had been strung together, probably with the ball of twine he kept in the cabin. As he looked about, he spotted barely visible evidence of string winding through the trees several yards out. It was the shooter's early warning system.

If Ruiz was inside, they had a problem, even if they avoided the makeshift alarm. A frontal assault was out of the question unless they had something like a flashbang grenade. They could wait until after dark to make an attack, but Ruiz might have an additional warning scheme they couldn't see. Sid had chosen to come in the daytime, figuring he would be less likely to expect them then.

While he weighed the alternatives, gazing through the binoculars, the cabin door opened. A man stepped out onto the porch, gazed slowly from left to right, pulled a lighter from his pocket and lit a cigarette. Sid tightened the focus and saw a pleasant looking young man with short black hair. He wore a blue shirt and jeans, a pistol stuck under his belt. It was no small .22 but a full-sized semiautomatic.

Ruiz let himself down gently onto the chair, as if bending his upper body would be painful. No doubt a result of the gunshot, Sid thought. But it apparently hadn't nicked a lung as he puffed deeply on the cigarette. Sid shoved the binoculars back into their pouch and moved toward Jaz in a low crouch. He signaled her to remain silent and follow him.

In a near crawl, he crossed to where the ground began its drop-off to the west. Just below the crest of the hill, which put them out of sight of the porch, he began to pull small limbs and brush away from several large rocks. As he moved the rocks, gray roofing shingles appeared, and beneath them a piece of blackened plywood about four feet square. Jaz reached him as he lifted the plywood to reveal a large hole in the ground. She grinned. It was the entrance to the cave he had told her about.

They crawled in and Sid pulled the plywood back over the opening. He switched on his flashlight.

"It's a little snug," he said, squirming around her while making a sniffing sound. "Your perfume makes a cave almost pleasant."

"I'll take that as a compliment."

"Please do."

He shined the light down the tunnel, which went fairly straight with a slight downgrade. Nothing had changed since his last visit. He had stumbled upon the cave a year after arriving at the property. It varied in height from three to four feet, requiring a crawl to negotiate.

"This comes out under the deck?" Jaz asked.

"Right. I have no idea who or what tunneled it out, but it apparently follows a fracture in the rock. Keep your head down, so you don't bang it on a jagged piece." He directed the beam along the ceiling. "We need to move quickly so we can catch him on the porch. It looked like he might stay there for awhile."

"It's times like this that it pays to be small," she said.

"Okay, little partner, let's get with it."

He crawled along, keeping as much pressure as possible off his left arm, holding the flashlight, shoving an occasional rock aside. On his first trip in here, he had been wary of animals, but with both ends sealed, he expected no visitors.

He could see Jaz's flashlight beam over his shoulder occasionally. After a few minutes, he paused and called to her. "Everything okay?"

"Peachy. How's that arm doing?"

"It isn't too happy, but it's still working."

He should have brought knee pads, he realized, as his knees kept colliding with the hard surface of a rock. But he pushed ahead relentlessly and soon saw a slight turn that meant they were near the end.

"We're almost there," he said. "When we get out, you go around the left side of the cabin, I'll take the right. Have your weapon ready and watch out for him. He may have left the porch. If he draws on you, fire."

"Okay, boss."

The exit beneath the deck was smaller and covered with a

thin slice of Crab Orchard stone, a popular building material quarried about eighty miles up I-40. When he reached it, he told Jaz to shine her light while he pushed the stone aside. He needed a maximum effort with his good arm to dislodge the growth of weeds that covered it. When he got space for a good handhold, he eased the slab aside.

Looking up at the deck, he saw no one. He took out his Sig and swung his head around as he crawled to the ground.

All clear.

He signaled Jaz to come ahead. Taking her hand, he pulled her out, then glanced at their clothing and shook his head. They looked like dirt-smudged derelicts. Then he noticed it had started to rain. The deck above protected them, though water dripped through the cracks.

The cabin sat a few feet above them. The rock ledge at each side was like steps. Sid climbed carefully. He stopped and looked across to be sure Jaz was ready. Then he gave the signal to move out.

With no windows on the sides of the building, he had no fear of being seen if Ruiz had gone back inside the cabin. The rain began to pelt down harder as he looked about the area. He saw no movement. As he walked toward the front, he holstered his gun and pulled out the Taser. Ruiz alive was more valuable than Ruiz dead. At the edge of the porch, he squatted, swiped a sleeve across his forehead, and peeked around.

He froze as a muffled cry sounded from across the porch.

Had Jaz slipped and fallen?

As he watched, his heart pounding, Ruiz turned in that direction and reached for his gun.

42

S ID AIMED AT THE center of his adversary's back and pressed the trigger. The twin probes streaked across the porch and lodged in their target before Ruiz could fire. He collapsed as his muscles lost all control. His gun fell to the floor.

Sid pulled the handcuffs from his belt as he ran toward the fallen man, breathing hard. He rolled him onto his stomach, pulled his arms together, and snapped on the cuffs. There on his left arm was the chronograph the old man had worn outside Sid's office. He picked up Ruiz's gun, ejected the magazine, and stuck it in his pocket. He quickly patted down the disabled man, finding a thin-blade knife strapped to his leg.

Jaz struggled to her feet beside the porch, brushing herself off. Her face looked ashen.

"What happened?" Sid asked.

"I tripped over a root just as I spotted him," she said, the color returning as she shook her head. "And I was trying to be so careful. Did you Taser him?"

"Yeah. I figured we needed him to answer for what he's done." Sid reached out a hand to pull her onto the porch.

There was a sudden flurry of Spanish and a floundering around behind them. The Taser's thirty-second charge had shut off, and Ruiz was doing his wet hornet impression. Sid stepped up and pulled the probes out of his back, then helped him to his feet.

"Carlos Ruiz, you're under arrest for breaking and entering," Sid said. "And that's just a start."

The hired killer looked confused, his face registering pain. "They didn't tell me you were a cop."

"I used to be. Right now this is a citizens arrest, but I'll have a cop here shortly." He turned to Jaz. "Is your ankle all right?"

"It's fine."

"Then keep your gun on him while I call my buddy."

He took out his cell phone and called his deputy friend at the sheriff's office. "I've got a guy named Carlos Ruiz in handcuffs, Cliff. He broke into my cabin and looks like he planned to steal everything. That should be good enough for a burglary charge."

"Everybody okay?"

"Yes. I used my Taser on him. I'd appreciate it if you could come get him and hold him until Metro can pick him up. They should have at least one murder charge against him."

"Okay, Sid. We'll be there shortly."

Sid put Ruiz in the chair and tied him up. The only thing they got out of him was a brief taunt.

"As soon as I get in touch with my lawyer, I'll be out of here."

When the two deputies arrived to get him, they said there would be no phone calls until Metro came to take him over.

Sid's phone rang while Jaz was driving down I-40 toward Nashville.

"When you get out of town, buddy, things start to move around here," Bart said.

"Like what?"

"This afternoon the District Attorney announced that new evidence had come to light proving Djuan Burden innocent.

Charges against him are being dropped."

"Did they say who was being charged instead?"

"The police department will have an announcement shortly."

Sid laughed. "If you'd like to make the announcement, I'll give it to you."

"Did you find him?"

"Carlos Ruiz is now in the county jail up there."

"On what charge?"

Sid told him what had happened.

"Have you called anybody in Nashville?" Bart asked.

"I wasn't sure who I should call. Here's the rest of the story. I went to the U.S. Attorney yesterday morning and told him the FBI had evidence showing the Valdez-Delgado murder was done by a hit man."

"And you asked him to contact the DA."

"Yeah. He must have moved faster than I expected. Has the department assigned anybody to my assault case?"

"I have no idea, but I think you should call the chief directly. I'm sure he knows where the DA's information came from."

Sid saw the Metropolitan Nashville and Davidson County highway sign. They were almost home. "I wonder if Deputy Chief Kozlov is involved?"

"That's another item. It hasn't been announced yet, but I got wind of it a little while ago at the CJC. DEA agents pulled a major raid today on a gang affiliated with the Mexicans. A Metro detective was included. Deputy Chief Kozlov was closeted with the chief."

"Agent Eggers told me Ramsey Kozlov was a target of the investigation. It must have been a lot further along than I anticipated."

"Sounds like the deputy chief has a problem."

When he got off the phone, Sid painted the picture for Jaz as they breezed past the airport.

"You going to call the chief?" she asked.

He began punching numbers on his cell phone. "Done."

When he finally got through to the chief's office, he explained who he was and that he had important information for the chief on the Delgado and Ivey murders. Although it was late on a Saturday afternoon, the MNPD head man remained in his office. He finally came on the phone.

"What information do you have for me, Mr. Chance?" he asked.

Sid explained briefly that they had captured Carlos Ruiz at his cabin and turned him over to the local sheriff.

"I was aware that you've been investigating the Delgado and Ivey cases," the chief said. "I'd like to talk with you about it. Could you possibly come by my office now?"

Sid was a little shocked but quickly agreed. "I'm riding with Jasmine LeMieux, who has been helping me with the cases."

"Bring her along," the chief said.

A CAREER NASHVILLE policeman, Galen Thorne had served the department for more than thirty years. Starting as a patrolman, he had worked in all of the bureaus, including Field Operations, Investigative Services, and Administrative Services. Along the way, he had picked up a degree in criminal justice. Sid knew the chief's reputation as a cop's cop. And seeing the expression on his face across the desk told him it had been a most trying day.

"I'm familiar with your background, Mr. Chance," Chief Thorne said. "District Attorney Sam Grizzard in Franklin is an old friend. He told me about the raw deal you got in Lewisville. He's quite fond of you."

Sid nodded. "That's nice to know."

"It's my understanding that you got involved in the Delgado murder case at the request of young Burden's grandmother."

"That's correct."

"What led you to this hired killer, Carlos Ruiz?"

"It's a long story, Chief. Basically, Mrs. Ransom told us her grandson went to Prime Medical Equipment to inquire about a Medicare EOB showing she owed money on a power chair she knew nothing about. When we searched the place, we found evidence indicating it was involved in Medicare fraud. We turned it over to the FBI and got their help when we found a witness who saw a man leaving the rear of the store about the time of the murder."

"Was this information shared with the detectives on the case?"

Sid glanced at Jaz and back at the chief. "At our first meeting, we were told it was obvious Burden was guilty as sin, that we'd better quit tinkering with a Metro homicide case and get back to chasing scumbag husbands."

Chief Thorne twisted his face into a dark frown. "That was unfortunate. I understand you've reported a new development in the case against Miss LeMieux."

"Yes, sir. When Carlos Ruiz tried to kill me in my house early Thursday, he wore night vision goggles. He said, 'It's just like with that Ivey woman, Chance. I can see you, but you can't see me.' Of course, he shot her in the back of the head."

The chief pointed to a stack of papers on his desk, which appeared to include a couple of "murder books," binders that contained evidence gathered in homicide investigations. "I've done a lot of reviewing on these cases this afternoon. If Ruiz murdered Mrs. Ivey, and I'm not doubting your word, how do you explain the gloves with Miss LeMieux's fingerprints?"

"Detective Grimm confronted us during our search of the

medical equipment store. He saw Miss LeMieux pull off her gloves and drop them in the chair where Delgado was shot. One of them was the glove found on Mrs. Ivey's porch."

"You're accusing Detective Grimm of creating false evidence?"

"No, sir. Detective Grimm mentioned the gloves to his partner, Detective Kozlov. A witness saw Kozlov enter the closed store late that afternoon. When I questioned Grimm, he admitted telling his partner about the gloves and acknowledged that Kozlov said nothing about going back to the store."

The chief tapped his fingertips on the desk. "So you believe Detective Kozlov provided the glove to drop at the murder scene?"

"I have no direct evidence. It's purely circumstantial, but the circumstances fit. And there's one more thing."

"What's that?"

He told the chief about his encounter with Ramsey Kozlov outside the Ram's Horn Bar Monday night. "I believe that led to Carlos Ruiz's decision to come after me."

"This is terribly disturbing," Chief Thorne said, shaking his head. "It's the most distressing situation I can recall during my tenure with the department. What you've just told me fills a lot of holes in the picture I've received from the DEA, the FBI, and these files. Detective Kozlov has been arrested by DEA agents for providing protection to a drug gang in the Nashville area. It makes sense that his handling of the Delgado homicide was an effort to cover Ruiz's complicity."

"And the Ivey murder looks like an effort to take us out of the picture," Sid said.

Chief Thorne stood and leaned his hands on the desk. "It's sad what one or two bad apples can do to foul the air. This department is filled with dedicated, hard-working officers who put their lives on the line every day for our citizens. They deserve everyone's trust. I'm committed to preserving that trust, and it starts with freeing Djuan Burden and removing the blot that has been placed on your reputation, Miss LeMieux."

43

S

UNDAY MORNING'S NEWSPAPER devoted most of the front
page to the aftermath of a Texas hit man's murderous
rampage through Nashville, and the parallel drug bust
that netted a gang of traffickers and one Metro detective. Carlos
Ruiz maintained his silence, admitting nothing. He was held
without bail. Ramsey Kozlov was still undergoing
interrogation. His father, the deputy police chief, announced
his retirement after a long career with the department.

With Bart reassigned to the attempted murder at Sid's
home, he continued the investigation and soon got a ballistics
report on the .22 shells found in the hallway. They had been
fired from a pistol recovered with Ruiz's belongings left in the
rental car stashed in the barn beside Sid's property.

Working in cooperation with the FBI, the Office of
Professional Accountability investigators put together two
conspiracy to commit murder charges against Ramsey Kozlov,
who had been decommissioned as a police officer. One involved
the Ivey murder, the other Ruiz's attempt on Sid's life. He also
faced other charges, including tampering with evidence.

Later in the week, following news stories exonerating Jaz
of any complicity in the murder of Earline Ivey, Sid got together
with Jaz in her office to go over final details of their
investigation. She planned to talk with the local Welcome
Home Stores manager about finding Djuan Burden a job. As
Sid made a final check of the report, the gate warning sounded.

Jaz turned to the monitor and saw a woman who appeared to be late thirties or early forties, long black hair, large cross earrings dangling down her neck.

"Can I help you?" she asked into the microphone.

"I'm Francine Thomas, Earline Ivey's sister. Vanita and I would like to talk to Miss LeMieux."

Jaz stared at the screen in astonishment. She got a glimpse of the girl in the seat beside her aunt.

Recovering quickly, she pressed the button to open the gate. "Please come on up," she said.

Jaz and Sid walked out to the front porch, where they watched a brown Toyota Carolla pull up to the parking area. The woman and the girl got out and walked toward them. Vanita was a small, thin girl, her hair tied in pigtails, one on either side of her head.

Jaz smiled as they approached. "I'm Jaz LeMieux. This is my colleague, Sid Chance. I'm pleased that you've come to visit me." She looked down at the girl. "I wanted to come to your mother's funeral, but with everything that had happened, we didn't think it would be appropriate."

Vanita stopped a few feet away and held a hand up to her face, her large eyes moving to Sid and back to Jaz.

"I understand," Francine Thomas said. "It was a bad time for all of us."

"Won't you come in?" Jaz asked, motioning toward the door.

"I don't think that's necessary. I brought Vanita because she wanted to say something to you."

Jaz stooped down to the girl's level. "What is it, honey?"

Vanita gripped her hands in front of her. "I wanted you to know my mom wasn't a bad person. If she hadn't said those things about you, she wouldn't have died."

Jaz felt like Vanita's small hand had clutched her heart. "I know she wasn't a bad person. She was caught in a terrible situation, faced with the prospect of losing your home. She had to make a choice about how to save it."

"Earline made the wrong choice," her sister said, a contrite look on her face. "She had lost her savings in a scam that was supposed to've made her a lot of money. She got behind on her mortgage, and those people approached her with a way to keep her and Vanita in their house. She didn't want to do it at first, but then she got the final foreclosure notice. It tore her apart."

"I wish I'd known," Jaz said. "I might have been able to help her."

"After all the publicity came out, and the newspaper and TV folks hounded her, she told me she was sorry she'd gone along with it. But it was too late then. I'm sorry for all the trouble it caused you."

Jaz reached out and hugged the girl. "I'm sorry for all the heartache it's caused everyone, especially you, Vanita."

She felt the small arms encircle her and looked down to see tears coursing down Vanita's cheeks.

Jaz turned back to Francine. "Please let me know if I can help out in any way."

"I think you already have." The woman gave Jaz a tight-lipped smile.

Jaz kept her composure until Vanita waved as they drove away. She turned to Sid as the tears poured out. He put his arms around her and held on until she stopped crying.

It was finally over.